DOUBLE DOG DARE

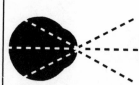

This Large Print Book carries the
Seal of Approval of N.A.V.H.

DOUBLE DOG DARE

LINDA O. JOHNSTON

WHEELER PUBLISHING
A part of Gale, Cengage Learning

Detroit • New York • San Francisco • New Haven, Conn • Waterville, Maine • London

GALE
CENGAGE Learning™

Copyright © 2008 by Linda O. Johnston.
A Kendra Ballantyne, Pet-Sitter Mystery.
Wheeler Publishing, a part of Gale, Cengage Learning.

Wheeler Publishing Large Print Cozy Mystery.
The text of this Large Print edition is unabridged.
Other aspects of the book may vary from the original edition.
Set in 16 pt. Plantin.
Printed on permanent paper.

LIBRARY OF CONGRESS CATALOGING-IN-PUBLICATION DATA

Johnston, Linda O.
    Double dog dare / by Linda O. Johnston.
       p. cm.
    ISBN-13: 978-1-59722-865-7 (softcover : alk. paper)
    ISBN-10: 1-59722-865-6 (softcover : alk. paper)
    1. Ballantyne, Kendra (Fictitious character)—Fiction.
2. Missing persons—Fiction. 3. Cloning—Fiction. 4. Large type
books. I. Title.
PS3610.O387D68 2008
813'.6—dc22
                                                    2008035527

Published in 2008 by arrangement with The Berkley Publishing Group, a member of Penguin Group (USA) Inc.

Printed in the United States of America
1 2 3 4 5 6 7 12 11 10 09 08

Linda wants to express ongoing appreciation to those writers and critiquers who give her great suggestions, as well as an occasional hard time, when she attempts to describe Kendra's stories on the computer: Janie Emaus, Heidi Shannon, Marilyn Dennis, and Ann Finnin. And special thanks to Marcy Rothman, who lends additional moral support.

Then there's Linda's husband, Fred, who claims he occasionally reads a paragraph or two of Kendra's adventures. Kendra doubts it. Linda, too. But at least Fred's a great help on outings when Linda's Lexie is invited along.

— Kendra Ballantyne/Linda O. Johnston

CHAPTER ONE

Where was he?

For the past nine days, that enigma had bombarded my brain nearly every conscious instant: Where was Jeff Hubbard?

After all the angst I'd gone through to determine whether or not to move in with the hunky P.I. and security expert, I'd finally made the huge decision to go for it.

Mistake? Maybe, since that was when he'd disappeared.

I sighed, as I'd been doing a whole lot lately. At the moment, I sat in my law office, staring at the same file I'd been blinking at for at least half an hour. A couple of weeks ago, I'd have absorbed the plaintiff's pleading immediately — a complaint in a new lawsuit involving one of my boss's senior citizen clients. Not now, though. Instead, I was thinking about Jeff. Again. Still.

And . . .

My desk phone rang. Excellent. A diversion.

I lifted the receiver and held it to my ear. "Kendra Ballantyne."

"Hello, Ms. Ballantyne," said a familiar, smooth voice.

"Ned?" Why was the cop sounding so formal? It wasn't like we hadn't solved several murders together. Okay, maybe I'd been the one to solve them and shove that in his face — which happened to be an especially nice-looking African American one. But —

"Yes, Ms. Ballantyne, this is Detective Ned Noralles."

Again with the formality.

"I know," I asserted, then stopped. And started shivering. I suddenly had a good idea why this guy might stoop to formality with someone he was so well acquainted with. "Wh-what is it?" I managed to stutter softly.

"There's some news about Jeff," he responded, sounding nearly as hoarse as I did.

Obviously not good news, or Ned would be his usual brash self.

I wasn't sure I wanted to hear.

"Have you found him at last?" I asked airily. "Put him on the phone." I figured I could either act flippant or start sobbing

8

before I had any answers.

"He hasn't been found, Kendra, but his car has — submerged in one of the California Aqueduct canals west of Palmdale."

Palmdale is a town north of L.A., in the Antelope Valley, in an area sometimes called the high desert. It's —

Okay, so my mind dashed off defensively in a geography lesson instead of focusing on the awful thing it had heard. Well, potentially awful. "That's a partly good thing," I finally responded, realizing that I was stabbing the palm of the hand that didn't hold the phone with my not-so-long nails. I relaxed my fist a little. "If he wasn't found there, then he got out of the car. So, he's okay. We just need to —"

"There's blood in the car, Kendra. Not a lot, but some undoubtedly washed away. The authorities up there have sent it to a lab for DNA testing."

I paused for a hugely long moment as I tried to speak around the lump that suddenly inflated inside my throat. Or maybe it was the tears I felt streaming down my cheeks that drowned my ability to talk.

Drowned? *What an awful word choice,* I chastised myself. I wasn't drowning.

But Jeff . . .

"Spit it out, Ned," I finally said as force-

9

fully as I could, muster. "Are you trying to tell me Jeff's . . ." *Dead.* My mind spit out the word. Shrieked it inside my brain. But I couldn't say it.

Saying it aloud might make Ned think it was so. And if he did, then where did that leave me?

"We still don't know anything for certain," Ned said gently. "We've only found his car with evidence that something may have happened inside it. The window was broken, apparently from the impact."

"You're sure of that? I mean, could Jeff have broken it himself to escape?" Okay, I could have been grasping at straws —

"It's possible, but —"

"See! Jeff could have swum out the opening. He's probably fine. Wherever he is."

"I hope so. I really do."

I purposely tuned out the doubt in his tone. I didn't bother to remind Ned that the two of them had been nearly arch-enemies for years, from the time that Jeff, too, had been a cop and they'd gotten into a fistfight. Jeff had supposedly won, although the unapologized-for fiasco had ultimately cost him his job with the LAPD. In the ensuing years, they hadn't exactly become best friends.

But I wanted to believe Ned. Maybe he

did hope that Jeff was alive and thriving . . . somewhere. So they could argue again, if nothing else. Trade barbs and insults and one-upsmanships.

"Now, then." I attempted to sound all business as I leaned forward and rested my arms on my desk. "How are the authorities up north conducting their search? Now that they have a vicinity to look for Jeff, it's time to call out whatever resources they have, right?"

"That's what I understand they're doing."

"Search and rescue teams? Including K-9s? And —"

"Oh, right, since you're a part-time pet-sitter, I'll bet you trust dogs even more than people."

"Could be. So . . . ?"

"I'll head up there tomorrow to talk to the guys in charge. I'll let you know how they're looking. But, Kendra, after all this time, the possibility that Jeff's — er, Jeff floated out that window and downstream rather than swimming out . . . The authorities in the area may be conducting a cadaver search."

"Then you have to convince them otherwise. No cadaver search, unless the evidence is clear and convincing that there really is a cadaver instead of a living, breathing,

11

injured human being. Right?"

"We'll see." Which of course meant no.

"Well, thanks for the update, Ned." I attempted to sound grateful and upbeat. But inside, I was shredding apart.

One thing I knew, though.

Ned and I were likely to be in the same neighborhood up north tomorrow.

I couldn't concentrate on that complaint I'd been reading at all now. And I had a client meeting on another matter to prepare for, starting in half an hour. So, after I hung up, I leaned back in the ergonomically ideal chair my boss, Borden Yurick, had gotten for me that was upholstered in the same brilliant blue as my visitors' chairs, and thumbed through that client's file.

Until I realized I couldn't see a damned thing through the mist that covered my eyes. Nor could I still my heavy breathing that would, with even a small loss of control, turn into an onslaught of sobs.

"Damn it, Jeff," I whispered, my eyes closed and my body a trembling mess as I curled into a small ball on my big chair.

He'd been out of town on business when he disappeared. How had he gotten back to the L.A. area without letting me know? *Why* had he done such a thing?

Had he done such a thing?

I'd met Jeff during the most miserable time in my life, when my license to practice law had been temporarily toast. I'd lost my job and nearly everything else important in my life — except, thank heavens, my adored Cavalier King Charles spaniel, Lexie. And my big, beautiful Hollywood Hills home — although I'd been forced to lease it out and move into the maid's quarters over the garage. I'd taken on pet-sitting so Lexie and I could eat. Jeff had been my first pet-sitting client — he and his adorable Akita, Odin.

We'd been through a lot together. He'd advised me in the many murders I'd somehow wound up solving since becoming a murder magnet, despite my strong preferences to the contrary. He'd also become my lover.

And now . . .

Well, one person would know about Jeff's return to L.A. I straightened, picked up the phone receiver again, and pressed in the numbers that had become extremely familiar over the last bunch of months.

"Hubbard Security," answered that very person I'd expected to hear, although I had to concentrate for a second to ensure I'd recognized her hoarse, quivery voice.

She knew.

"Althea, it's Kendra," I began, hating the huskiness in my own tone. I wanted to be strong for Jeff's ultimate computer geek and my good friend.

Jeff had described her as middle-aged before I'd met her. Which she was — in her fifties. And a mother of five, and a grandma to one or two. A techie whiz who could circumvent nearly any computer boundary, legal or not, although we seldom talked about that aspect of her acumen. But none of those descriptions had led to a picture in my mind of the genuine Althea, a slender blond who dressed like someone my age — midthirties — or younger, and looked really good in jeans and cropped Ts.

Only at the moment, I pictured her green eyes being as bloodshot as my blue ones.

"Oh, Kendra," she said much too softly. "Have you heard from Ned Noralles?"

"Yes, he just called. I . . . have you had a chance to look into what he said? I mean, did you confirm that Jeff was even back in the L.A. area? And if so, why up north, in the Antelope Valley? And have the authorities confirmed it was really Jeff's car they found in that ditch? And —"

"Slow down, Kendra." I heard an almost-laugh in her raspy voice. "We're the investigation and security experts, remember?"

14

"Of course. And I'm sure Buzz is already doing the legwork, and you're looking into everything you can on the computer. But I want to make sure you don't miss anything. After all, Jeff's the head of the company, and you're all emotionally involved if he's really . . . If he's really . . ." I couldn't say it, let alone allow myself to think it.

As if I could actually stop my thoughts from twisting along that damned awful road.

"No matter what Ned thinks, we're not going to go there until and unless it's proven," Althea said fiercely, her usual feistiness back in her voice.

Which gave me heart, too. "My sentiments exactly," I said. "Tomorrow, I intend to go up to northern L.A. County to see the slim evidence Ned described and get my own take on it."

"Buzz, too." Buzz Dulear, another employee of Hubbard Security, LLC, was more an expert on the installation of security systems than private investigation, but he'd been known to follow up on a lead or two. And with Jeff out of pocket, I wasn't surprised that Buzz had leaped in to do the company's professional snooping.

Jeff out of pocket? Hell, what we needed was to find out what pocket of the Antelope Valley he'd crept into and dig him out.

Alive. And absolutely kicking.

Like Althea, I wouldn't assume anything else was the case unless we had evidence that Jeff truly had been there, done that, and left only his lifeless body behind. . . .

I choked at that thought, then thrust it away. "Okay, then, have Buzz call me in the morning. Maybe we can go up there together and share the gas." As always, California gas prices these days were among the priciest in the nation.

"Will do. Oh, and Kendra?"

"Yes?"

"We'll get Jeff back. We have to. He's too ornery to just up and die on us, especially without even a hint about something strange going on. . . . Right?"

"Right," I agreed unequivocally, said goodbye, and hung up.

And hung my head for an instant as I prayed that what Althea and I had professed was the absolute truth.

"You okay, Kendra?" asked Borden Yurick in his high-pitched voice when I appeared in the hallway outside my office a few minutes later. I'd received a call from our chirpy receptionist, Mignon, informing me that the clients I was scheduled to see this afternoon had arrived and were ensconced in our conference room.

"Okay enough, considering," I told my boss, whose long form was, as always, decked out in a Hawaiian shirt — with bright green and yellow flowers on this day.

Silver-haired Borden had been a partner in the high-profile law firm I'd worked for when my troubles had tugged my professional legs out from under me a while ago. The other partners had considered Borden a nutcase, simply because he'd taken a round-the-world excursion to escape the awful burdens of his law career. When he returned, he had opened the doors of Yurick & Associates, a modest-size firm headquartered in a former restaurant in Encino, in the San Fernando Valley. He'd taken a lot of our old firm's lucrative clients along with him, but particularly specialized in representing senior citizens.

He'd adopted a really great attitude about practicing law. Great for me, at least. He made me a junior partner, and as long as I worked on his many cases, he allowed me lots of leeway as to the time I spent lawyering — which permitted me to keep on pet-sitting, the career I'd taken on while my law license was on hold. I'd enjoyed it enough to keep it up, even now.

Plus, I'd gotten involved in a lot of legal

dispute resolution that involved — what else? — animals, since I met all sorts of pet-lovers in my second vocation. Many of the clients I brought to this firm had pet-related issues that I helped to resolve.

Like the clients now awaiting me in our conference room.

"Okay, I'm waiting," Borden said. "Considering what? And before you fib and tell me 'nothing,' I can see that you've been crying, Kendra. Spill it. What's up?"

I gave him a stripped-down description of what Ned had said, ending with the same upbeat assumptions that I'd discussed with Althea. "There isn't enough evidence to draw any ugly conclusions right now," I told him. "As far as I'm concerned, Jeff's still out there, somewhere, and he's okay."

Borden's big eyes grew sad beneath his bifocals. "Of course," he said, obviously humoring me. "And with your background lately of getting involved in investigating criminal cases, I'm sure you'll find out the truth. Take whatever time you need to work on it. I'll get one of the other lawyers to help out on my cases."

The "other lawyers" included some senior attorneys Borden had hired after they'd been booted from their previous firms. One of the crankier ones had been murdered right here in the office a while back. I did indeed figure out whodunit, and the victim's big, beautiful Blue and Gold Macaw, Gigi, came to the office often with her current owner, Elaine Aames.

"Thanks, Borden," I said, and headed for the reception area.

Our effervescent receptionist Mignon gave me one of her big, bright smiles. "The Hayhursts are here," she announced in her habitually cheerful voice.

"Great," I said. "In the conference room?"

She nodded, and her auburn curls did their usual bob. And then she frowned, not something I was used to seeing on Mignon's perky face. "You okay, Kendra? You look awful."

Oops. "I'm fine," I lied, then took a quick detour to the restroom to fix my face a bit before meeting with my clients.

Okay, so my blue eyes were a bit bloodshot. Otherwise, my face seemed its ordinary self. My brown hair was blunt cut, a tad shorter than its usual shoulder length. I'd grown used to its natural shade; although I'd originally stopped highlighting for lack of funds. Jeff seemed to like it this way. . . . *Stop it!*

I was still slender, thank heavens, in my business casual sky blue suit. But enough

— it was time to stop primping and start attorneying.

The clients were ensconced in the large room that had once been the restaurant's bar. The big, wooden bar part was still there along the inside wall and booths remained by the windows, but the center area was now the setting for a large conference table.

Sitting at that table were a couple I guessed to be about a decade my senior, and although they both had the polished brightness of Hollywood sorts, the years had taken a toll. The guy looked somewhat soft and untoned in his tight jeans and partly unbuttoned beige shirt. Lots of wrinkles lined his face, and gullies had already begun to form beside his lips. His dark hair was thick, though, and well styled about his pudgy face.

The woman, a blond with bright blue eyes, was somewhat trimmer and better groomed, yet her face, too, showed wear beneath her too-thick makeup.

"Mr. and Mrs. Hayhurst?" I inquired.

The man nodded. "I'm Corbin, and this is Shareen."

We shook hands all around.

"Please sit down," I said, and after inquiring if they wanted any coffee, stepped out to ask Mignon to get us some. I used the occasion to glance at my watch. My intent was to keep this meeting short. And not to think at all about Jeff.

That command to myself made me think of him, of course. I felt tears well up in my eyes and blinked them back.

"So tell me why you need legal representation," I said to the couple over our foam coffee cups, once I got my emotions back where they needed to be. Or at least hid them well enough. I hoped.

I knew some of the Hayhursts' dilemma since they'd been referred to me by my dear friend Darryl Nestler, owner of the Doggy Indulgence Day Resort.

"Some of our customers are threatening to sue us," Shareen said tearfully.

"Let's back up a bit." Corbin pursed his narrow lips before speaking again. "I'm sure Darryl told you we own a company called Show Biz Beasts. We train people's pets, mostly dogs, so they have the skills and tricks needed to get jobs in Hollywood. We also have an agency where we use our contacts to try to get them roles. And we have everyone sign agreements where they acknowledge we don't make any promises."

"But a number of our customers say we lie," Shareen asserted dramatically. I got the impression that her usual demeanor leaned toward the dramatic. "They say we never, ever place any of our training clients in films or TV."

"And do you?"

Corbin shrugged a pudgy shoulder. "Not always, but occasionally. And our own trained dogs often get roles in commercials."

"Can you help us, Kendra?" Shareen pleaded. "It would ruin us to be the subject of a lawsuit. Who would ever take one of our training classes again?"

"I'll need some more information before I can tell you for sure," I said. "If you can get me a copy of the contract you have your human customers sign, along with a list of the kinds of pets that have been trained over the last couple of years and the roles that any of them, and your own dogs, have secured, I'll let you know what kind of advice I can provide. Do you know if any of the disgruntled customers have hired lawyers?"

"They've said they have," Corbin said with a frown, "but so far we haven't heard from any."

"Well, it does sound like the kind of situation I'd be interested in handling," I said. But not at this moment, although I didn't tell them that.

Not while my mind kept ducking out of

the room to consider my other, life-affecting situation.

Even so, I described how the Yurick firm worked and what they'd be charged for my time. "If you get me the information I've asked for, we can meet again in a week or so and decide where we go from here. Assuming, of course, you want to hire me then, and I'm ready to take on the case."

"That's wonderful," Shareen said, standing as smoothly as a starlet might. "We appreciate your time now, and really hope you can help us, Kendra."

"I happen to have some of the paperwork you asked for with me," Corbin said. He showed me a file that he'd lifted from the floor. "Would you like to look it over now?"

"Just leave it, please," I said. "And I'll call you once I've had a chance to read it." Like Shareen, I was now standing, although I doubted I'd stood with nearly as much grace as she had.

I ushered them cordially yet quickly out the door. The case sounded interesting.

But at the moment, I had a missing, and possibly presumed dead, P.I. to find.

CHAPTER TWO

Darryl was waiting at the door of Doggy Indulgence. My tall, lanky, sympathetic friend would have stood there with a glass of wine had I asked him to. Or even something stronger.

I'd called him, of course, to say I was on my way, and what awful occurrence was on my mind — that phone call from Noralles.

And then I'd driven east to Studio City in the compact and uncomfortable car I'd rented after the accident that had probably totaled my beloved Beamer. The insurance company was still deciding whether it was repairable or a total loss, and was paying for the rental in the interim.

"You okay, Kendra?" Darryl asked as we strolled inside the single-story building on Ventura Boulevard. As usual, he wore a Henley-style green knit shirt that hugged his skinny shoulders, with the Doggy Indulgence Day Resort logo over his heart. His long, thin legs were clad in tightish jeans. Though I'd been clothed quite appropriately for my law firm and client meeting, I felt a smidgen overdressed.

It was a bustling place, as always, and smelled of disinfectant overlying the scent of doggy accidents. Some of his employees stood by the big front desk, checking pups out to their owners. Those dogs not yet checked out were all over the place, occupying each of the areas designed for their ongoing delight. One contained doggy toys for unending games. Lexie's favorite area, over in the corner, was filled with human furniture and dogs lolling on sofas, chairs, and area rugs on the pinelook linoleum floor. I noticed the light-and-dark furry spot that was Lexie at the same time she saw me and started dashing toward the door.

"I'm doing okay," I assured Darryl, albeit fibbingly. "And I'm a lot better now that I'm with you. And Lexie," I added as that special pup all but leaped from the floor and into my arms. I bent to gather her up and let her wag her whole body, especially her tail, as she proceeded to cover my chin with wet doggy kisses. No matter what else was on my mind, I couldn't help laughing. Who could, with a loving and cheering Cavalier hugged close?

"Come on into my office, and we'll talk," Darryl said.

"Okay, but where's Odin?" I asked — but didn't need to, since Jeff's middle-size, fuzzy Akita emerged from behind some toys in the play area and strolled toward us, his tail curled over his back. I bent to put Lexie down and give Odin a big hug. As I stood again, I looked toward Darryl. "This is one of those times I'm glad they don't understand English and I can't speak Barklish. How could I tell Odin about what —" I hadn't anticipated it, but my voice broke and I felt the tears start again. "Damn," I whispered.

Darryl took my arm and led me into his office. The dogs stayed outside, where there were more things for them to get into.

I sat on a chair facing Darryl's cluttered desk. He sat down in his own plush seat and stared solemnly at me through his wire-rimmed glasses. "You want to talk more about it?" he asked.

"Not. Really." The words came out slowly and soggily, and I inhaled to catch some control. "Okay, yes. I can't figure out how Jeff even got back here without telling me — assuming it really is his Escalade they found, and with the license and vehicle ID numbers, I have to assume the cops got at least that right. I thought . . . I thought we were an item now. And if it is him, and he had a good reason not to tell me . . . where is he?"

Darryl shook his head so sadly that I almost didn't want to hear what he had to say. "I have no idea. And what reason could he have not to tell you? Or if not you, his employees?" He peered at me over his eyeglass rims. "You're sure you can trust them to be straight with you?"

"Yes," I stated emphatically, then dropped my head. "I think. If Jeff told them to keep something from me, they would. Under most circumstances. But now . . . Well, surely they'd say something, at least hint they were aware of a secret. But Althea seems as baffled and upset as I am. I haven't talked to any of the others, but I'll probably be with Buzz tomorrow when we check out the site where the Escalade was located."

"So you're not just hanging around waiting for the cops to figure everything out? What a surprise. And just think of all the situations you've resolved lately, Kendra. You're getting to be a master at solving puzzles. You'll work this one out, too."

"Right," I responded brightly. "I have cleared a lot of wrongly accused people lately, haven't I? Unlocked what actually occurred. Determined who . . . killed . . . someone else." I sagged in my seat. "Does that mean Jeff has to be dead before I can discover what happened to him?" I looked at Darryl beseechingly, begging him to reassure me that my investigation prowess didn't perpetually have to involve a body.

"Of course not," he said, his brightness clearly feigned. Which made me sag all the more.

"Maybe this time I'd better just leave it to the authorities to figure out so I don't jinx Jeff," I said morosely.

Darryl's brief laugh was genuine this time. "That'll be the day — when Kendra Ballantyne sits back and lets someone else solve a mystery that's important to her."

I took the dogs and drove the car to my home-sweet-garage-top apartment for a few minutes, to collect my clothing for the next couple of days. There, behind the wrought iron gate, I ran into the daughter of the tenant of my big, beautiful, pseudo chateau, who also happened to be my pet-sitting assistant, Rachel Preesinger. Nineteen years old and a sassy aspiring actress, Rachel had followed her father, Russ, to L.A. when he had become a location scout for a major studio. With her was her beautiful Irish set-

28

ter, Beggar — short for Begorra — who immediately led Lexie and Odin off to romp on the house's sprawling, lush green front yard.

"Hi, Kendra, hope you don't mind, but I was waiting for a check from that production company I worked for last month, so I sorted our mail and stuck yours in that pile where I usually . . . What's wrong?" she demanded, her hands on slender hips covered by her usual uniform of jeans and film studio T-shirt — Sony this time. We stood on the driveway near the carport where I parked my car. Her huge brown eyes appraised me, and the cocking of her head knocked her short, dark curls askew. "You look *awful.*" I'd been hearing that assessment an awful lot that day, and didn't particularly appreciate it.

I nevertheless filled her in.

"Oh, Kendra, not Jeff." She looked almost as stricken as I felt. "I knew he was missing, but I just figured he was off on some super-secret case. He's too young and hunky to die."

I wanted to boot her in the butt for even suggesting he was dead, but heck, I was considering the possibility much too much myself. "Yeah," I agreed instead.

She gave me a rundown on the clients of

Critter TLC, LLC, my pet-sitting company, that she was caring for, as well as her upcoming schedule. She was always heading off to casting calls and occasionally wound up with a small movie walk-on here and there. Commercials, too. At this moment, though, all she had was a few roles behind her, a lot of hope, and zero pending productions.

I promised to keep her informed about Jeff, she promised to keep me informed about our pet-sitting customers, and I hurried off to collect clothes, then dogs.

I had decided we would spend our night at Jeff's.

I didn't say we would sleep at Jeff's. At least the dogs would get their nighttime snoozes. Judging by the way they hovered around me before bedtime, I guessed that they sensed something was wrong. But I might not have explained it to these sensitive canine kids even if I'd believed they could understand. Which they couldn't. And so, they slept.

I didn't. At least not much.

I hadn't decided to stay at Jeff's house simply because I felt closer to him here. Sure, that was part of it, but I also figured it would give me more ability to snoop in his stuff.

Even though I'd had the opportunity to do so, I had not dived into his belongings before to try to figure out where he was. At least not much. I had checked the desktop computer in his office to look at the last websites he had accessed before he left. I'd also asked Althea to hack into his business e-mail to see if she could learn anything there; but if she had, she hadn't spilled it to me. Nor had she enlightened me about his most recent office and cell phone calls, although I knew she was fully capable of hacking into the phone companies' most secure systems.

Not that I'd ever blab on her, of course. She's a friend. And very handy that way when I'm ensconsed in an investigation.

I sent Althea an e-mail asking her to send me copies of any pertinent credit card charges — another thing she could get with ease. Better yet, I asked her to give me instructions about how I could access all Jeff's personal stuff myself.

I wouldn't have invaded his space this way — at least not this deeply — under normal circumstances. For one thing, I wasn't a licensed investigator, although I'd professed now and then to be a junior sleuth working under Jeff's company's license when that seemed appropriate, always with his prior okay.

Before.

But these weren't normal circumstances. And if I could have asked Jeff about doing things this way, I would have. Of course, if I could do that, I wouldn't need to pry at all.

Was I acting unethically as a lawyer? Well, Jeff wasn't a client, at least not officially. And I wasn't about to trumpet to the world any helpful information I unearthed — unless it helped to find, and to save, the real P.I. in this situation. Stealing information I wasn't entitled to probably wasn't the most principled thing to do, but I was doing it for the best of reasons.

Would that save me from another ethics inquiry by the California State Bar?

I hoped I'd never find out.

To get the earliest start possible the next day, I decided to leave the dogs at Jeff's. I walked them first in his nice neighborhood in the flats of Sherman Oaks, north of Ventura Boulevard. Jeff's place was a charming pseudo-Mexican single-story home that resembled many of the others surrounding it.

I'd been here often enough that I'd gotten to know a few of the neighbors by sight, if not by name. I waved at the small woman who always walked a mellow Great Dane on the opposite sidewalk, and she waved back. Lexie and Odin acted as though they'd like to trade butt sniffs with the other dog, but there wasn't time today.

Despite the early hour, a couple of dilapidated trucks indicated some gardeners were ready to start clipping, weeding, and mowing. One, a guy in a big straw hat, seemed to be instructing others who also were clad in work clothes. Another familiar neighbor, a habitual jogger, loped by and gasped a hello. Across the street, in a fully fenced yard where three mixed-breed dogs who appeared to have been rescued from shelters usually bounded about, another guy in grungy clothes had already begun his yard work. As we passed, someone I didn't recognize loped by with a little Lhasa Apso trotting alongside, and I had to keep Lexie and Odin from lunging in that direction, both barking eagerly.

This was a typical May day in the San Fernando Valley. Spring, with jacaranda trees losing their pretty purple flowers. Warmish, without threatening stifling heat later in the day. A cloud-free, brilliant blue sky.

A cheerful day. Or it should have been.

I was often alone here walking the dogs, since I frequently stayed at Jeff's to care for

Odin while Jeff was out of town. It usually felt comfortable to be strolling his neighborhood with my two canine charges.

Today, it just reminded me more poignantly that I had no idea when Jeff would return. Or *if* he'd —

Nope, I'd promised myself not to let my mind go in that dire direction.

"Okay, gang," I finally said after stooping to do poop patrol after Odin produced. Lexie had been the winner in that contest today. I'd picked up after her earlier. "Time to go back."

I gave them each an extra treat before heading off to tend my morning's pet-sitting clients: Piglet, Fran Korwald's pug; Abra and Cadabra, Harold Reddingham's cats; Widget, a terrier mix; and Stromboli, a shepherd mix; plus a wave at his human and canine next-door neighbors, Maribelle Openheim and her terrier mix, Mephistopheles. Not long ago, Maribelle had neglected Meph. Now they were best buds, and she and I kept in close touch.

And when I was done with my pet-tending — feeding, walking, cleaning, grooming, and a whole lot of hugging — I arranged to meet Buzz Dulear at a fast-food joint's parking lot for our journey to the Antelope Valley.

Buzz Dulear was a guy with a long, long body and short, short hair, plus a receding hairline. He was more a security expert than an investigator, and I gathered that was because he was more technologically oriented than ingenious in extracting information from people.

I'd met him the first time I visited the offices of Hubbard Security. My initial impression was of a guy who was talking on the phone to someone he wasn't overly fond of. In fact, he swore profusely at whoever was on the other end.

I hadn't gotten to know Buzz well after that, although I was certain there was more to him than a prolifically censorable mouth. I still didn't know him well. He seemed extremely reticent as he drove his hybrid SUV north toward Lancaster. Or maybe his vocabulary was mostly limited to swear words and he had nothing particularly nasty to say to me.

"How long have you worked for Jeff?" I asked.

"Coupla years." He looked into the rearview mirror.

"Do you enjoy it?"

"Pretty much." He put on the turn signal and stayed slow until a few cars passed.

"How many security systems have you installed?"

"A bunch."

No way was this going to get my mind off where we were going and why, so after he'd merged onto the 5 Freeway heading north, I asked, "So, do you think Jeff's okay?"

No answer. I looked at him.

Buzz had an oval face except for a boxy jaw. That jaw was even tighter than usual now. His lower lip — was it trembling?

Damn! That told me even more than if he'd expressed it in words.

"We'll find him, Buzz," I said fiercely. "And he's got to be okay, or I'll wring his neck."

Which finally got a grin from the guy.

He turned a news station on, and we listened to traffic reports and some food news for the next half hour or so. Then there were national news highlights at the top of the hour.

Nothing about the Escalade found in the aqueduct canal. And, thank heavens, nothing about a body found floating anywhere.

Eventually, we got onto the 14 Freeway north, and around Palmdale we exited and started cruising narrow avenues outside the

36

town, heading west. Buzz had apparently printed some maps off the Internet, and referred to them now and then to see where we were heading.

The land was arid around here, and sparsely populated once we were out of town. The roadside businesses tended to be car shops and small restaurants. Then there was what appeared to be farmland. Here? Where it was so dry?

Oh, yeah. The aqueduct brought water to this locale.

We reached the part of a canal where lots of officially marked vehicles hung about. A narrow bridge overhung a long, straight canal with visible concrete sides. The water moved, but it didn't seem too strong a current.

If Jeff had fallen in with his Escalade, could he have been washed away?

Buzz found a spot to park on the shoulder of the road and we got out. A bunch of people milled busily about. Some were in uniform. Judging from their cars, they were mostly from the Los Angeles County Sheriff's Department, and others were from the Palmdale and Lancaster police departments.

Some staved off hordes of newshounds who shot photos and called out for quotes.

Was that Corina Carey? Why would the media type I'd come to know best, a stellar staff member of the TV show *National News-Shakers,* be here? More to the point, why not? This was, undoubtedly, breaking news. She saw me at the same time and shouted, "Kendra! Hi. Is that the car of your friend private investigator Jeff Hubbard?"

"No comment," I called, and turned my stiffened back.

In the middle of the officials was a member of the LAPD, Detective Ned Noralles.

This was way out of his jurisdiction — not only because it wasn't L.A. proper, but also because he was a homicide detective. And despite what anyone's opinion as to Jeff's fate might be, it seemed way premature for a homicide investigation.

Nope, Ned had to be here for reasons similar to mine: curiosity. And caring.

Well, okay, the latter was a stretch. Maybe he wanted to make sure his former nemesis actually existed no more.

In any event, he looked up from the people he'd been chatting with as Buzz and I approached. "Ms. Ballantyne," he said. "Mr. Dulear. What brings you here?"

"You called yesterday, Ned," I reminded him. "We're here to see whatever evidence there may be that Jeff Hubbard passed

38

through here."

"Come on, then." Ned led us away from the group and the canal, and toward a parking area filled with police cars.

And a large flatbed truck I hadn't noticed at first. On its flat bed crouched a highly damaged vehicle. A black one. One that had once been a gleaming, gorgeous Cadillac Escalade.

Like Jeff's.

Trying not to flinch or shriek, I approached it calmly. From the back, I could see the license plate. With Jeff's combo of letters and numbers.

Okay, then, it probably was his. The body was scraped and dented — a real shame, considering how well Jeff cared for his pride and joy.

And, yes, the driver's side window was smashed out.

"It's his," Buzz confirmed grimly, as if I needed his acknowledgment.

"I think the crime scene technicians are about done," Ned said. "The guys here said they'd keep me informed as a professional courtesy. And I've said I'll provide whatever additional expertise they might need if this turns into a homicide investigation."

I felt myself blanch even as I aimed a belligerent glare at Ned. "You're exaggerating the importance of this," I insisted. "I'd imagine Jeff parked his car at Ontario — that's the local airport he prefers flying from — and someone stole it, took a joy ride, panicked, and dumped it up here where it wasn't likely to be found fast."

"I'll say," Buzz interjected morosely.

"Any indication of where Jeff might have gone?" I asked Ned. "I mean, you mentioned possible blood evidence, but even if it was Jeff's, that's not enough to be sure of anything except that he was hurt. Any skid marks on the road? Any search and rescue K-9s hunting for him?" I wouldn't inquire about cadaver dogs. "Anything in the water that suggests he washed away — alive or not?" I nearly choked on the last, but it had to be said. And considered.

And hated.

"Far as I've been told, there's nothing clear one way or another. The K-9s haven't found anything. But like the crime scene folks here promised me, I'll keep you informed about anything that tells us something. Or at least anything that's permissible to release to the public."

"I'm not the normal public, Ned," I countered.

"No." He looked down at me with dark brows raised in almost-amusement. "You're

40

a meddling civilian, and you've got more of an axe to grind in this investigation than in most of those where you interfere. Look, Kendra, I know you're close to Jeff, and even though you're not his family, I'll treat you as if you are, and request that the authorities who really have jurisdiction treat you the same. It's the best I can do."

"Thanks, Ned," I said. And I would of course inform Althea and Buzz, Jeff's employees.

It was far from being good enough, but it was something.

And, besides, I had no intention of relying on Ned or any of the authorities to find Jeff. If they did, so much the better — or so I hoped.

But in the meantime, I had snooping to do.

CHAPTER THREE

On the drive back to L.A. with Buzz, I actually got him talking about his technical background installing security systems. His growing up in Long Beach. His enjoyment of investigations he'd been involved in. And his pessimism over the fate of his really cool boss.

That part I didn't really want to hear.

I ignored several calls from Corina Carey. I wanted to talk to the nosy reporter as much as I wanted to be back watching Jeff's car extracted from the aqueduct.

Since it was still a workday, I eventually headed back to my law office, intending to do just that: work. Better to concentrate on arcane legal issues than to let my mind wander about that fractured Escalade and its missing driver.

Of course I nearly regretted my decision to go there the moment I stepped into the building and Mignon's usual smile became even perkier — an obvious attempt not to show the sympathy she undoubtedly felt on my behalf. "Hi, Kendra," she chirped. "I wasn't expecting you to come in today."

"Just think of all the fun you'd miss if I didn't," I retorted, and hurried down the hall toward my office. I closed the door. Too many friendly and sympathetic faces would drive me batty. Not to mention the possibility they'd make me break down. I needed time to turn my mind in a different direction.

And so, I picked up the breach-of-contract complaint against some of Borden's senior citizen clients that I'd started to read yesterday. A response was due within the next few days, and I turned to the computer on my desk to start composing an answer. Soon, I was engrossed in it, a good sign that I was performing at an expert level.

I was nearly done with a credible first swipe when my cell phone rang. Or sang. I'd had it programmed for a long time to play Bon Jovi's "It's My Life," but was considering tossing this aging phone against the wall. Or settling for some bland, canned ring that had come with it. I didn't exactly feel like I was really tackling life head-on these days.

I checked the caller ID. And swallowed

hard. It was Jeff's office.

Had Buzz or Althea gotten more bad news?

I answered anyway, cringing as I awaited whatever.

"Hi, Kendra, it's me." Althea sounded slightly more exasperated than depressed, which allowed me to straighten my shoulders.

"What's the good word?" I asked.

"Mothers!" she exclaimed.

Now, in my background, "mother" wasn't a word I'd consider good. My parents had divorced ages ago. My mother remained a happily divorced attorney in the Washington, D.C., area. My father had remarried and had a second family, and I didn't exactly consider his wife a relative. In fact, of my immediate family, I felt somewhat close only to my brother, Sean, a motel magnate in Dallas. Of course, we only talked about once a month unless something mandated a more immediate conversation.

Then again, Althea's tone hadn't suggested sweetness and apple pie, either.

"Whose mother?" I asked.

"Jeff's. She's been hounding me with questions."

I swallowed. "Does she know . . . I mean,

is she aware we haven't seen him for a while?"

"Yes, and the cops have called his dad and her about finding his car at the bottom of the canal. She says she knows Jeff and figures it's part of one of his cases to pretend he's missing, but she's insisting that I put her in touch with him anyway."

I'd never met Mrs. Hubbard, but I envisioned a gorgeous middle-aged woman in a G-string each time I thought of her. As I did now. Jeff had told me his mom had supported their family by exotic dancing when he was a child, without telling his dad. Jeff had found out by investigation, which had ultimately led him first into law enforcement, and then into becoming a P.I.

Resourceful lady is how I thought of her. I'd no idea what she did these days, whether dancing exotically or another occupation. For all I knew, she could have gained eighty pounds and become more of a sumo wrestler. Did she and Jeff's dad still live in the Chicago suburb where he had grown up?

"What did you tell her?" I asked. Like, did you hint that she should potentially prepare for the worst?

Well, hell, I wasn't about to do that, so why should Jeff's mom?

"I tried to be tactful, but let her know that

45

if Jeff's on some kind of secret case, we didn't know about it — and that we're really worried about him. That's when she said I should put her in touch with you."

I sat up straighter in my suddenly uncomfortable seat. "Me?"

"Yes. She said Jeff has told her about the really great woman he's dating — versatile enough to practice law, take care of people's pets, and solve mysteries — all at once. She indicated she wants to talk to you about something."

Uh-oh. If Jeff told her I solve mysteries, he'd exaggerated. Well . . . maybe. But if she thought I'd be able to solve the mystery of his disappearance, she surely could figure I'd already been trying.

Still, I put myself in her shoes. Nice, sexy stiletto heels, I was sure, if she was still an exotic dancer. She'd be worried about her son. Grasp at straws to learn where he was.

I might not have answers, but maybe we could help each other get through this time of uncertainty.

As long as she wasn't the kind of demanding demon my mother was.

"Did she give you her phone number?" I asked Althea.

"Then you'll call her?" She sounded extremely relieved. "That's so nice of you,

46

Kendra."

I only hoped I wasn't compounding an already unnerving situation.

First, though, I returned Corina Carey's ever-mounting mound of phone messages. "Yes, it was Jeff's car, as you know," I told her. "But I still don't know where he is, and neither does anyone else."

"Interesting mystery," she oozed. "I'll see if there's anything on the media side that will help, if you'll keep me informed on your end."

"Sure," I lied. Exactly what I needed. More media prying into my private life. Although if she did learn something useful about Jeff . . . Well, if that happened, I'd consider cooperating with her.

Meantime, I got down to my next call . . . sort of.

Okay, call me a coward. Better yet, call me a dedicated attorney. I finished the answer to the complaint for our clients before I looked at the number I'd jotted down during my conversation with Althea.

A number with the 708 area code. Still the Chicago area, wasn't it? I wasn't sure till I checked it out on the Internet.

And then I looked at my e-mail. Nothing new.

And then I organized a couple of files on my habitually cluttered desk.

And then . . . then, I finally stopped procrastinating.

I reached into the bottom desk drawer where I kept my purse and extracted my cell phone. The call would be long-distance, and I didn't need a record of it on the office system. We generally attributed our calls to a client or to a general administrative number. Personal calls were okay as long as they were limited, but of course they showed up on our monthly accounting statement.

And so, I closed my eyes for an instant, then opened them and resolutely pressed in the number that would connect me to Jeff's mother.

"Hello?" said a husky yet sexily feminine voice. Just as I'd anticipated.

"Mrs. Hubbard? This is Kendra Ballantyne, calling from California. I'm a . . . friend of Jeff's."

"More than that, aren't you?" She sounded somewhat amused. "According to my son, you're pretty special."

Good thing we weren't videoconferencing. Otherwise, the woman would see the flush I felt creeping up my cheeks. "He's a good guy, but he exaggerates." I didn't give her time to comment before continuing.

48

"Anyway, Althea, from his office, said you wanted to talk with me. Mrs. Hubbard, I just want you to understand that —"

"Irene."

"Pardon?"

"My name's Irene, not Mrs. Hubbard. Otherwise, I sound like that old nursery rhyme, 'Old Mother Hubbard.' Ugh!"

I grinned despite my inner turmoil. "Got it. Okay, Irene, I need for you to understand that none of us who . . . care about Jeff really knows where he is."

A pause. Then, "Unfortunately, I've figured that out, my dear. I've even spoken with Jeff's Aunt Lois."

"Aunt Lois?" We didn't frequently discuss our families, and I doubted I'd heard of her.

"Not really his aunt, but a dear friend of mine who's acted like a kind of mother to Jeff since he moved to California. She lives near Ontario Airport and they don't get together often. But she's much more the maternal type than I've ever been, so they're close. Or at least they used to be."

I wasn't sure why he hadn't mentioned her. Or maybe he had, and I hadn't focused on her possible importance in his life.

"Anyway, I needed to tell someone I thought I could trust about what Jeff was working on when he went back to California. I gathered from Althea that no one from his office even knew he was in the state when he . . . when they lost track of him. He'd gone back earlier than he'd anticipated because Lois called and asked for his help. And his discretion."

My heart had speeded up to a phenomenal rate. At last! A clue about why Jeff had come back to California without a word even to anyone at his office, let alone me. "Do you know what she asked him to do?"

"Why, investigate, of course. That's what he does these days — that and install security systems."

I beat down my internal frustration. "Right. And the investigation — any idea what it involved?"

"Not really. Only Lois knows. Although she did tell me she thought you'd be interested in it, once she gave Jeff the go-ahead to let you know."

"Me?"

"She knows about you, too, of course. Anyway, she's as frantic as I am to find out what's happened to him. That's why we're both willing to talk to you. Not the police, and not any of Jeff's employees, in case they're involved. We don't know you, but he does, and we understand that he trusts you. So, you call Lois now, and she'll fill you in

— as long as you promise your discretion. And as long as you keep us both informed about what you find out. Okay?"

"I'll need to know more about it first," I equivocated. "I mean, if it's against the law, or if I need to inform the authorities to protect Jeff, or —"

Middle-aged Mother Hubbard laughed. "Jeff did say you were a lawyer, Kendra, and now I can tell that's true."

And you? I wanted to ask. *What do you do for a living now?* But the moment passed before I thought of a tactful way to inquire.

"Just promise you'll keep things as discreet as you ethically and legally can, will you? And keep me in the loop?"

"I'll do what I'm able, Irene. Now, can you give me Lois's phone number?"

That evening, Lexie, Odin, and I were piled in my rental car, heading east on the 10 Freeway.

I'd gotten my assistant Rachel's promise to care for the pet-sitting clients I needed to visit that night, and dropped off all the keys, instructions, and my general gratitude with her.

We were on our way to see Lois Terrone. She lived in Ontario — California, not Canada — which might have explained why

51

Jeff sometimes flew on business trips from the alternate L.A. airport there, rather than Burbank or LAX. I'd assumed it was economics or convenience or both. Now, I realized he had a different reason.

Why hadn't he talked more about Lois? Or had my attention been focused elsewhere when he had?

When I'd called Lois, she'd sounded urgently upset, yet eager to talk to me. I didn't need to mention my pet situation, since she knew about Lexie and assumed I had possession of Odin, too.

Obviously, Jeff and she had been in communication before his disappearance. So why was she such a mystery to me?

Of course there was probably a lot about the guy I'd nervously agreed to move in with that I didn't know.

Might never know. . . . No, I wasn't going to do that to myself. Not now. Hopefully, not ever.

I'd done a MapQuest computer search for Lois's address before departing from Jeff's. She was located north and west of the Ontario Airport, south of the freeway. Due to these directions, I had no trouble locating her home. Its appearance amazed me. It resembled a fairy-tale cottage, with several pointy parts and a roof that looked thatched, even though the shingles were clearly of the fire-retardant kind, compulsory for Southern California. Its chimney was tall, and its façade a charming golden stucco. The yard was fenced — white pickets, naturally.

I leashed the pups and walked through the front gate of this quaint and cozy setting. And was met by some loud barking from inside.

"Uh-oh," I said to my charges. "Maybe we'll leave you in the car for a little while." But before I could take care of that, the front door opened and a lady several inches shorter than my five-five, wearing dark slacks, a corn-colored shirt, and a long, flowing scarf, was towed outside by the sizable Akita whose collar she held.

Intelligent Lexie cringed. Odin looked ready to attack his larger and belligerent breedmate, whose coat was darker and fuzzier than his. Not a comforting situation.

But then the woman barked, "Ezekiel, sit!" and damned if the territorial and confrontational canine didn't obey. "Welcome, Kendra," she continued, "and Lexie. And especially Odin." She all but crooned the last as she proffered her palm. Odin obediently approached, and although Ezekiel eyed him suspiciously, neither male made as if he was about to attack. Instead,

Odin sniffed the human's hand and started wagging all over, like one big puppy. Which, despite his Akita assertiveness, he was.

The lady knelt and grinned and hugged Odin, then looked up at me. "I'm Lois," she said. "Let's all go inside, shall we?"

She seemed to have a slight limp as I followed her, as if one leg might be slightly shorter than the other. She walked fast nevertheless, the length of her scarf trailing after her. Ezekiel, ignoring us, stayed by her side.

From behind, seeing only her long, blond curls, I'd have assumed she was a whole lot younger than she looked head-on.

I'd gotten only a glimpse of her face, but I had a hint of a once-lovely woman with shining green eyes. But age hadn't been amiable to her, resulting in skin folds and pouches beneath beautifully high cheekbones. If she'd resorted to Botox, surgery, or other artifice, they'd been ineffective.

Her front door led directly into a quaint living room with an overstuffed sofa in an orange print and matching, disorganized chairs on a paler orange braided rag rug resting on a gleaming wood floor. The large chimney I'd noted outside backed an enormous hearth piled high with apparently fake logs. The walls were covered with doggy photos. All appeared to be Akitas, though not every one was Ezekiel. Some had lighter fur and were smaller. Others were darker and larger. One looked like mostly Akita with a blunter face and floppy ears instead of the usual erect and alert ones.

"Please have a seat," she said. "You can let Lexie's and Odin's leashes go. They can roam. Ezekiel's a good host, I promise."

Feeling a bit uneasy, I nevertheless obeyed. Akitas often tend to be territorial, although Odin had accepted perky little Lexie as a friend first thing. Maybe it was because she was clearly no threat to his bigger and more assertive alphaness. But could I count on that here, on Ezekiel's turf?

Amazingly, Ezekiel immediately sat down beside a chair, probably Lois's favorite, since that was where she lit. But only for a second.

"Now you get comfortable," she said, standing again. "I've got home-baked cookies in the kitchen. Do you prefer coffee, tea, soda, water — ?"

"Coffee sounds great," I said. "If you already have it made, that is. Don't go to any trouble."

She grinned, lifting some skin folds and displaying large, white teeth. "Jeff said you were one polite lady, most of the time. And

55

a handful if you got peeved, which he claimed happens a lot. So, I'll try not to peeve you. I anticipated coffee, and that's what I want, too. It's already made." With that, she exited into the kitchen.

Not Ezekiel, though. He stayed where he was, keeping an eye on Odin, who stood by me as I sat on the sofa, Lexie on my lap. The host Akita might be polite, but he still hounded us like . . . well, a male dog on his home turf.

I studied the other Akita photos. They were cute and soulful and entrancing.

"Do you breed Akitas?" I asked when Lois returned to the room. She put our cups of coffee on the low, rough-wood — what else? — coffee table. She'd also juggled a plate of cookies, but after letting me choose one, she set it on the mantel, beyond the reach of the dogs.

Her pouchy face sagged into additional wrinkles as she again took her seat. "I used to," she said sadly. "But it's a lot of work, and it was always so hard to sell the pups when I wanted to keep them all. Now I have only one or two at a time. And that's part of the problem. About Jeff, I mean."

"Jeff?" My ears felt as if they perked up like a pup's. "I don't understand."

"No, I'm sure you don't. Not till I explain

it to you. But I know what Jeff was up to when he disappeared. And I can't help suspecting it has a connection with what I asked him to do."

"What's that?" I demanded, edging so far forward in my seat that Lexie started wriggling.

"Can you keep a secret?" she asked. "Because if I tell you, and you blab about it . . ."

Her green eyes suddenly grew fierce, and I sensed what she wasn't saying.

Her small laugh sounded anything but humorous. "I used to say something like 'I'd have to kill you.' But that's not funny. Not now. Not when I don't know whether my request for help killed Jeff." And she started to cry.

CHAPTER FOUR

I attempted to remain calm while everything inside me churned and reeled. And screamed, *What are you talking about?*

I gently placed Lexie on the floor and approached Lois. I knelt beside her chair and slipped an arm around her shoulders.

And waited until she regained enough control to explain.

For only an instant, she leaned her head toward mine until they touched, then sat up straighter. "I'm okay now," she said. "Thanks, Kendra. Sit down and enjoy your coffee."

I complied with the sitting and sipping, but I wasn't quite ready to enjoy the brew. Sure, it was strong, but I could have gone for something stronger. Harder. Alcoholic.

Even so, I was better off this way with a drink that could help to clear my head with its caffeine, instead of muzzying it.

Obviously understanding that his mistress

was upset, Ezekiel took my place near her and laid his head on her lap. She hugged him, then started stroking him as she looked at me with my two canine charges poised protectively on the floor at my sides.

"Sorry for coming apart like that," she said soggily. Now her face wasn't only pouchy, it was splotchy as well. Good thing she didn't have a mirror on her picture-laden living room walls. "Do you know much about my relationship with Jeff and his family?"

I shook my head. "No, sorry to say I don't."

"Well, I go back a long way with Irene, his mom. Years ago, we danced in the same clubs together. Not the most refined of establishments, you understand."

"Jeff did tell me a little about how Irene helped their family when he was a kid," I admitted. Lois wasn't exactly my image of an exotic dancer, not even one who'd reached middle age. She was still somewhat slim, but I couldn't visualize her in skimpy clothing and sexy poses.

Had Jeff's mom aged as ungracefully? Now I was really curious to meet her in person.

"I know what you're thinking." This time, her laugh reflected some humor. "You can't quite imagine me back then, can you? Well, I can, every time I look in the mirror, believe it or not. Anyway, Irene's now a dance instructor. Did you know that?"

Aha! I shook my head, glad for this update and insight.

"Me, when I started getting a touch of arthritis, I went back to school. Became a paralegal. I can see that surprises and maybe even impresses you. I know you're a lawyer, so I'm sure you've your own opinion of paralegals. A little different from exotic dancers, eh?"

"Sure are," I agreed.

"Way back then, when Jeff figured out what his mom really did for a living, she called and cried on my shoulder. But she was damned proud of his ingenuity. And his discretion. He promised never to tell his dad, who thought Irene was a waitress at an upscale restaurant in downtown Chicago." She waved a curved finger at me when I started to suggest he could have known the truth. At least Jeff had told me his dad had wondered about it. "He never mentioned it to her if he suspected otherwise. Anyway, I was already living in the L.A. area when Jeff got out of the army, received a degree in criminal justice, and joined the LAPD. I liked the area out here better than L.A.

proper, so we didn't see each other as much as I'd have liked, but I was still sort of his second mom. I knew when he got into a fight and wound up leaving the force in shame. I also knew he'd be a great P.I. on his own — lots of spunk and creativity in that one. And the security system angle — well, that just added to how special he is."

Though I enjoyed hearing about Jeff and their relationship, this conversation wasn't getting me where I wanted to go.

"So you recently requested that he do something for you?" I prompted.

"Patience, my dear. I'll get to that." For a moment, Lois stared into space. Or maybe she was regarding one of the photos on her wall. "The thing was, I fell in love."

"Tell me about him," I said. Had her lover disappeared, so she'd sent Jeff after him?

"Not him. Her."

I must have appeared surprised. Not that I've anything against same-sex relationships, but I hadn't anticipated it with this former exotic dancer.

She laughed. "Not a person. A dog — mostly Akita."

"Oh," I said, as if I suddenly understood. But I didn't. Not really.

She sipped her coffee, then rose to retrieve the plate of cookies. I'd eaten the first but hadn't exactly tasted it. A sugar cookie, I thought. I accepted a second. This time, I savored a bite. Yep, definitely sugar. A great-tasting cookie. I watched as all three dogs stared and started to beg. "Mine," I informed them.

"Just a sec." Lois disappeared toward her kitchen and returned with dog biscuits in her hand. "Okay if I give them a treat?"

"Sure." But I was feeling more than a little impatient. Where was her story heading? She'd fallen for a dog. That involved Jeff how?

She soon sat down and explained. Sorta. "So I became a paralegal. And when I moved here, I also got religion. I joined a local church and became really active. A pillar of the community. On the board and many committees. Lots of good friends, and people I could talk to. But that wasn't all. Like I said, I used to breed Akitas, but it got to be a bit much. And then, one of my bitches got loose while in season and was knocked up by a neighbor's dog. I wasn't exactly excited — until the litter was born. They all were adorable — and the cutest and smartest of all was Flisa." She gestured toward the picture on the wall of the pup with the floppy ears. "I found the others good homes, but why wouldn't I keep the best for myself?"

An obviously rhetorical question, so I didn't attempt a response.

"But as dogs and people do, she started to get old. And then I heard of the most wonderful organization . . . or so I thought. What if I could have not just another Akita, or even an Akita mix, but another Flisa?"

I suddenly suspected that I knew what she meant. "Did you go to —"

"That's right. The Clone Arranger. My first mistake."

She started to explain how she'd intended to keep quiet about it. Cloning was quite controversial, especially in many religious environments — at least the possibility of human cloning, but sometimes animal cloning as well. Even so, she adored Flisa and decided to see about getting a pup with her exact genetic makeup.

"I understood heredity isn't the only factor in getting another perfect dog. Environment plays a role in determining personality. But if I got a baby Flisa and brought her up like her mom, I figured they'd be close enough."

But she was dead set on her church friends, her surrogate family here, not knowing about it.

"Flisa was getting older and less limber. I

brought her in for the cloning and paid a fortune, but figured it would be worth it. Only . . . no puppy resulted. And then . . . and then . . ."

I was afraid I knew what she was about to say. "Oh, Lois," I began in premature commiseration.

"She died." Lois's head sagged and her hair flowed about her face. "It was awful. I didn't know whether The Clone Arranger did something to her or not. In any event, they apparently can't create a clone from dead DNA. So it was over. No Flisa." She swallowed a sob. "But they kept my money, since they claimed they'd charged me a bargain price. Hah! They said it was part of their contract that they made no guarantees. I was crushed. But even more, I was suspicious of something foul and needed answers. That's when I called Jeff."

I kind of got it now. She had asked him to investigate this organization. And I suspected it merited investigation. Hadn't I heard how hard it was to clone cats — and that dogs were worse?

Even so . . . "You wanted Jeff to figure out if they'd hurt Flisa?"

She nodded slowly. "But he had to be discreet. I didn't want them to get the slightest inkling that they were under investigation. And I absolutely didn't want anyone from my church to find out I'd even considered buying a clone. They'd be horrified. I'd lose all of their respect — although in my estimation, if God allowed man to figure out how to clone, He must have thought it a good idea."

I wasn't about to enter into a theological discussion, so I just nodded. "Could be. But, Lois, are you saying —"

"I'm saying I asked Jeff to return to Southern California without telling a soul. Not even you. Maybe that was too much silence, but I begged him, and he agreed. And then . . . well, I couldn't reach him, not even on his cell phone. I figured at first that he'd just gone deep undercover on my behalf. But then the police contacted Irene, and she called me. And I started feeling so guilty . . . and I remembered what Jeff told me about you, that you conduct your own investigations. I don't believe he's dead, Kendra, but we all need to know what happened to him. And I suspect I . . . I could have sent him into an awful situation that caused all this."

"Then you think —"

"I think something about the investigation into The Clone Arranger caused Jeff's disappearance."

That was all the arm-twisting it took. Lois had intrigued me. Given me at least a nugget of new information to investigate.

So here I was, the very next day, pulling into the parking lot of The Clone Arranger.

My initial reaction on seeing the large, single-story gray building behind a big but open fence was to wonder who had stuck a movie studio here in the middle of the middle-class, ethnically transitional small city of Glendale.

My second was to admire the ingenuity of the owners of The Clone Arranger. They'd hidden this potentially controversial business in plain sight — at least for Los Angeles. There were movie studios nearly everywhere around here — like right next door, in Burbank. And if inside this particular soundstage setting there happened to be scientific laboratories instead, who would know?

Except, of course, those doing business with The Clone Arranger.

Like me. Or, rather, like Kenni Ballan, my persona today. I'd used it before while attempting to go undercover and was outed almost immediately, but that was a different situation, months ago, when I was attempting to solve murders of which I personally was under suspicion. I could have made up another name, of course, but why bother?

With me, in my rental car, was Meph — short for Mephistopheles, a wiry terrier mix. I'd borrowed him from his owner, Maribelle Openheim, whom I'd visited yesterday while pet-sitting for Stromboli, her neighbor's pup. A while back, I'd believed Meph to be neglected and had introduced myself to Maribelle. I'd also wound up introducing Maribelle to a sort-of old friend of mine, Judge Baird Roehmann, he of the roamin' hands. They'd been an item for a while, until Maribelle had wised up about men and depression and dog care. Now, Maribelle seemed quite content on her own. I pet-sat for her, now and then, and visited when I could.

For this particular outing, I'd needed a canine companion other than Lexie or Odin. Since Maribelle and I were friends, I had spewed my confusion and sorrow to her over Jeff's disappearance. Having extracted herself from her own depression, she'd made it her mission to comfort others.

She happened to call last evening when I returned from visiting Lois, which was when

I was hatching this day's plot. And she'd volunteered Meph, no questions asked, when I'd asked to borrow him for a confidential reason having to do with finding Jeff. Of course, I'd intended to return Meph to her safe and sound, while being superbly grateful for his assistance in this distressing matter.

Now, Meph climbed eagerly on my lap as I slowed to pull into the parking lot. It contained half a dozen cars. As I maneuvered my little rental car into a spot, I spotted the entry door immediately — maybe because it was the only door visible. There were no windows in the stucco sides of the building, again like a movie studio. Maybe that's what this structure had actually been in an earlier incarnation.

I grabbed Meph's bright lime leash and walked up to the door. It opened easily. Right inside was a large lounge, brightly illuminated and furnished with myriad metal chairs upholstered in yellow. The beige linoleum floor gleamed. The only other furniture consisted of several small tables piled high with what appeared to be photo albums. And then there was a sign on the room's only other door: PLEASE WAIT. SOMEONE WILL SOON BE HERE TO GREET YOU. Not exactly an invitation to go farther inside, but I tried the knob anyway. Unsurprisingly, the door was locked.

"Hi," said the room's only other human occupant, a pretty lady perhaps a decade my senior who looked vaguely familiar. At her side was a beautiful chocolate Labrador retriever, who rose at our entry and issued a warning growl, causing Meph to stand at attention and yap. The lady laughed as I stooped to pick up my pup of the day.

"Hush, Meph," I cautioned him.

"Melville won't hurt anyone," the lady said. "Will you, sweetheart?" She rose from her chair and knelt, her mid-length red skirt tickling the floor, to hug the medium-size dog, who wriggled and licked her slightly sagging chin.

My turn to laugh. But I wasn't here to observe a canine admiration society. I had research to engage in. "Are you here to get Melville cloned?"

"Sure am." She stood and nodded as if extremely proud of her intent, while Melville remained standing at attention and staring attentively at Meph and me. The woman noticed it and said, "Friends, Melville. Sit." He obeyed, and seemed to take her at her word about our amity, relaxing considerably. A little hyper for a Lab, I thought. Or maybe just overly protective of his mom. Which mom continued to me, "The Clone Arranger did a marvelous job cloning my other Lab, Churchill."

"Really?" I hoped I didn't sound as skeptical as I felt. When I'd gotten home last night, I'd spent hours on the Internet researching not only this outfit but cloning in general.

I'd soon understood why Lois Terrone had hoped to keep her interest in such a situation secret since she was so involved in her church. It was indeed highly controversial, especially in religious circles.

But beyond that, the ability to clone pets and livestock to any respectable degree had initially seemed somewhat iffy. Sure, Dolly the sheep had been cloned. And the livestock aspect appeared to be thriving, as was research into genetic makeup of pets, such as whether actual backgrounds matched supposed pedigrees and if certain genes presaged particular personalities.

At least one outfit had managed to clone cats for owners willing to pay dearly for a duplicate of their dear pets, but apparently had been unsuccessful with dogs and ultimately went out of business.

And even where the possibility of pet duplication was discussed, all descriptions contained a caution that creating another being with the same DNA didn't mean one could count on an identical twin of its parent. Things could get modified in the process. Even more compelling, no one could guarantee a similar personality, let alone the same one, possibly the result of environment versus heredity swirling into the mix.

But my intent wasn't to analyze the realities of cloning. It was to investigate whether Jeff had leaped in to look at this company on behalf of his mother's good friend Lois — and, if so, whether it had somehow led to his disappearance.

I listened intently as this pretty, brown-haired lady, speaking with arms in motion, described how she had brought her aging yellow Lab, Churchill, here several months ago and got him cloned. "I now have the most adorable golden Lab puppy at home. He's so very much like Churchill was at that age. I've named him Cartwright. That's a town in Labrador. So are Churchill and Lake Melville."

"How fun!" I exclaimed. "This is Meph. He isn't very old, but I adore him and would love for him to have a little brother just like him for company."

The woman held out her arms and hugged Meph briefly, though Melville, back at at-

71

tention, appeared less than pleased by the idea. "I'm Beryl Leeds, by the way," she said.

Beryl Leeds. The name sounded as familiar as her face looked. . . . Oh, right. "You were in the TV series *Simi Valley Sins,* weren't you?" I hoped I sounded suitably impressed, although it hadn't been one of my favorite shows. "I'm Kenni Ballan."

The room's inner door opened just then and a couple of men emerged.

Again Melville stood and bared his teeth and yanked on his leash, but Beryl used her earlier strategy to assure him these were friends. Even so, he sniffed their hands before he appeared satisfied.

"Hi, Mason and Earl," Beryl said. She then introduced them to me.

Mason Payne was the company's CEO, according to their website. He looked like a CEO: moderate height, middle-aged, and all silver hair and silver tongue as he greeted us. His white-on-white shirt and dark trousers managed to appear both dressy and casual at the same time. "Delighted to see you again, Beryl. And to meet you, Ms. Ballan. And — this is Melville? Hi, Melville," he crooned, stooping to give the now relaxed Lab a big hug. "Do you want a baby brother?"

Melville, though obviously eager for the attention, didn't assert his opinion.

Earl Knox was, I supposed, another executive. He seemed more my age, midthirties, tall and grinning and as short-haired as Melville the Lab. Holding a few file folders in one hand, he greeted me. "Hi, Ms. Ballan." But he didn't seem as excited to see Meph as his boss was to see Melville. "And this is who you want to have cloned? Hi, guy." He, too, nearly knelt without putting his khaki-clad knees on the floor. "What's his name?" he asked me, standing again quite quickly.

"Meph," I responded. "Short for Mephistopheles, and he really is a cute little devil, don't you think?"

"Absolutely. And definitely worthy of cloning, aren't you, Meph?" He crooned a bit, which raised him more in my estimation.

Meanwhile, Beryl and Mason headed for the inner door with Melville. "Wait," I called. "I'm a little nervous about this cloning stuff, and since you've been through it before, Beryl, could I contact you later to discuss your experience?"

I actually was a tad uneasy about the digging I was about to do here, but I mostly wanted to ensure I had a way to contact

Beryl if I needed additional info from her.

"Sure." She reached into the big handbag over her shoulder — red to match her skirt. "I'll give you my card."

"Of course we'll answer all your questions," Earl said smoothly at my side. "But it always helps to get recommendations from our pleased customers." Mason beamed at him, then swept Beryl through the door.

I glanced down at the card she'd handed me. It identified her as an actress and contained contact info including website, phone number, e-mail address, and a P.O. box in Beverly Hills.

"Okay, then," said Earl to me. "Let's talk a little about our cloning procedures and your expectations." His voice was on the tenor side, but he kept it soft and soothing as we went over the legal disclaimers The Clone Arranger's attorneys undoubtedly advised them to assert — all apparently included in the lengthy contract Earl extracted from one of the folders he'd been toting.

They'd attempt to extract a suitable sample of Meph's DNA, then do their magic that Earl couldn't quite describe because of its proprietary nature, then, abracadabra, presto-change-o, Meph might have a new baby brother who looked a lot like him.

Or not. No guarantees.

"Is there any danger involved?" I asked anxiously, although of course I wasn't about to do anything. Certainly not pay the exorbitant charges.

"Not really, although I do have to disclose to you that occasionally one of our clients has overreacted and had to seek veterinary care."

"Overreacted how?"

"Fear of needles, perhaps? I don't exactly know. Anyway, if you'd like to look all this over and decide what to do, that will be fine."

"Could I see your lab facilities?" I asked. "To assure myself of their safety?"

"I'm afraid that's against our policy, unless you actually become one of our clients."

Drat! Well, I wasn't exactly sure what I was looking for, anyway. Some telltale sign that Jeff had been here on his quest to help Lois, sure, but what would that be? Some big placard proclaiming JEFF HUBBARD WAS HERE? Not hardly.

"Okay, I'll think about it," I said. "Er — Ms. Leeds appeared happy about the cloning you did for her. Could you tell me if there are people who are dissatisfied? And if so, why?"

He seemed to stiffen. In fact, he quite suddenly became very remote. I'd apparently struck a nerve, but surely genuine clients must sometimes ask such probing questions. Didn't they?

"As with any business, there are always people who find fault, Ms. Ballan. Mostly people who assume that the clones of their pets will be identical to the parent animal, but personalities, and even features, can often differ. And in those rare instances where the parent does not react ideally to the DNA extraction procedure — well, owners can get very upset about such things. That's why we insist that our clients — the human ones — sign such a detailed contract, to ensure they understand." *And waive all their rights to argue, undoubtedly.* "Read it, talk it over with Meph, then let us know if you're still interested. Although I have to tell you that smaller, mixed breeds like Meph — well, our scientists will need to look him over before we can take him on, even if you're sure you want to go forward. I hope we hear back from you soon."

Was that true? I somehow found myself being accompanied to the door. Odd.

Well, until I'd read the contract and decided how else to approach this strange and secretive organization to get the information I was determined to extract, I was okay with leaving. For now.

I took Meph home to Maribelle, walked and fed his neighbor, the shepherd mix Stromboli, then checked in with Rachel. She was handling some of my pet-sitting for me this evening.

I couldn't have been happier to get to Jeff's and be greeted by my adoring canine children, Lexie and Odin.

Well . . . yes, I could have been happier. If Jeff was there, too.

But the pups and I still had a pleasant evening, eating, walking, then snuggling up in front of the TV on Jeff's furniture.

I phoned Lois, telling her what I'd found out about The Clone Arranger: nothing especially untoward, though certainly some suspicious behavior.

I even managed to get some sleep that night. Good thing I didn't know what awaited me the next day.

My morning routine ran like proverbial, precise clockwork. Lexie and Odin stayed happily home at Jeff's, and all pet charges were pampered as always. Then I slipped into my fashionable lawyer's shoes and dug into work in Encino.

Around two in the afternoon, I was sitting in my office, minding my own attorney's business, sorting a stack of legal papers, when my cell phone rang.

Okay, call it foolish, but my heart raced in its usual eager anticipation of hopefully hearing from Jeff at long last as I lifted my phone out of my purse to answer.

Only . . . although the caller ID was familiar, it wasn't Jeff.

"Kendra? Oh, thank God I reached you." Lois's voice sounded strained and strange. "This is Lois. I need your help."

"Is something wrong with Ezekiel?" I asked immediately. Why, besides her Akita, would she be calling me . . . unless it had something to do with Jeff?

"No. He's fine, but someone's going to need to look in on him tomorrow. Kendra, I'm under arrest. In Glendale. I'm accused of murdering Earl Knox, the guy at The Clone Arranger who killed my poor Flisa."

CHAPTER FIVE

A little while later, Lois and I sat in the food court in the Glendale Galleria, a gigantic shopping mall. We glared grimly at the disposable coffee cups before us on the table.

I'd noticed before that age hadn't treated Lois well. Now, she seemed to have added a decade or two. Her chosen clothes, a loose knit top over baggy blue jeans, didn't help her appearance. Her beautiful blond curls appeared to be a futile attempt at an attractive hairdo.

She said she'd come here straight from the local police department, where she in fact hadn't been arrested, though she still feared it. They had neither read her her rights nor kept her in custody. She nevertheless assumed it might be a matter of time till that situation was reversed. And although Lois had a neighbor who watched her Akita, Ezekiel, when she wasn't around, she was extremely worried about how the neighbor would care for him if Lois were incarcerated.

I had no idea where the Glendale police headquarters was, but Lois certainly did . . . now.

"It's only a few blocks from here," she informed me after my initial inquiry, "in the Civic Center, which is pretty close to the commercial area. The library's not far, and . . . But that's not really what you came to talk about."

"No," I agreed. "Let's discuss Earl."

I'd already heard a little while listening to one of the news radio stations as I sped here along the freeway from Encino. There had been an incident at a business in Glendale, an apparent homicide, and local authorities were investigating.

Since Glendale is its own small city, it has its own municipal police department, which meant there would be detectives other than Ned Noralles on this case.

That didn't necessarily mean he'd keep his nose out of it. Any more than I would. He could call it professional courtesy. I could call it unprofessional but absolutely interested snooping. On behalf of a friend — Lois. Perhaps on behalf of two friends, including Jeff, although so far I had only

Lois's suggestion to tie him to The Clone Arranger via an investigation he'd been involved with prior to his disappearance.

Several people with food on trays strolled by, seeking the perfect table, I supposed, since the food court wasn't especially busy and there were plenty of places to sit. I inhaled the scent of something delicious from one of the stands surrounding this cluster of tables — grilled meat, I guessed. Instead of succumbing to the hunger that suddenly spread through my half-empty stomach — I'd nibbled some nuts earlier — I took a sip of the strong but cooling brew in front of me.

"Okay," I said, "I'll ask some obvious questions. What were you doing at The Clone Arranger this morning? I mean, if the cops took you in for interrogation after an apparent murder there, I'd imagine you were at least nearby, right?" Her presence in Glendale supported this presumption.

She sighed so deeply that the wattle beneath her chin wiggled. "Yes, I was. After you and I talked last night, I couldn't sleep. So much was going on that involved those awful people. I'd asked Jeff to look into what had happened, how they'd caused Flisa's death instead of cloning her, and Jeff vanished. You, at least, were still around —

although I'd held my breath after sending you there — but they seemed to be pulling the wool over your eyes."

Suddenly feeling defensive, I opened my mouth to protest. Okay, I hadn't learned anything useful, except that the cloning company appeared to disclaim even more than I might if I was their lawyer . . . maybe. So what had I derived from my visit? A whole lot of additional questions.

"I wasn't there long enough to form an informed opinion," I began, but Lois held up her hand.

"Well, there's definitely something wrong with the place. Jeff knew it, too, which is why we can't find him."

"So you think — what? That Earl Knox did something to make Jeff disappear, and now Earl's dead, too?" I nearly bit my tongue at the faux pas I'd just committed in saying that terrible word "too."

"What do you know that I don't, Kendra?" Lois frowned fiercely. "Have you got something about Jeff?"

"No," I asserted. "I misspoke. And even though there's an apparent connection in our viewpoints, that doesn't mean the authorities will agree. So far, there's nothing to connect Jeff to The Clone Arranger except your request that he look into the place, and you've made it clear you don't want anyone to know about that. Only now . . ."

"Now I did tell the policeman who interrogated me," she said with a sigh. "He got such a gleam in his eye that I was sure he thought I'd delivered a confession, complete with motive."

"What, because you asked a friend to look into the place, and the friend seems to have floated off in a California Aqueduct canal, you decided to kill one of the employees?"

She buried her face in her deeply wrinkled hands. "Oh, Kendra, if you put it like that, they're sure to arrest me. And I haven't even told them yet that I think Earl somehow killed my poor Flisa."

"How?" I inquired, trying not to either shake my head or form an anti-Lois opinion. I knew what it was like to have a whole lot of evidence against me in a murder investigation. *Two* investigations. And I'd been innocent.

Hopefully, Lois was, too.

"Why would you think Earl Knox had anything to do with your pup's death?" I repeated. "I mean, even assuming her death had something to do with her visit there, why not blame one of the other people at The Clone Arranger? Besides Earl, I met only the owner, Mason Payne. Why not him, or someone else?"

"Honestly? I don't know. But Mason seems to personally handle the people he thinks can give the most publicity — and investment funds — to the organization. His sister, Debby, is a quiet soul, but jumps in to take care of the animals there for cloning, so I guess it could have been her. And Earl? Well, he struck me as a loose cannon, though I can't tell you why. He sold their services, took charge of cloning procedures, and generally managed nearly everything. That's why I assumed he was there when the DNA sample was taken from Flisa. I can't swear she was mishandled, but they told me soon afterward that the sample wasn't effective and they'd try again, but weren't optimistic. But before I could get her there, she . . . she . . ." Lois suddenly started to sob.

I filled in the final word. "She died," I suggested softly, and Lois nodded while stuffing a napkin in front of her soggy face. "How old was she?"

"Eleven. And she had some physical problems, so I knew she wouldn't be with me much longer. That's why I wanted her baby this way. One that would be as close to being *her* as possible. Only . . . only . . . it didn't work out."

Which didn't necessarily mean that anyone there had mishandled the ailing and aging pup. Yet Lois obviously assumed so. Were her accusations of their misdeeds spoken only in grief and not in threat?

"Why do the police think you might have harmed Earl? Did you go there today with some reason in mind?" My coffee was now definitely tepid, but I didn't want to go purchase a refill in the middle of what I'd been hoping to learn for the last twenty minutes.

"I went because I wasn't happy with how things went with you yesterday. No new information. I just figured I'd go there and say I had another Akita, a purebred, I was considering cloning, although I absolutely had no intention of bringing Ezekiel along and risking his life. And when I got to talk to some of the people again about what went wrong with Flisa — they'd seemed sort of willing to discuss it before — I figured I could offhandedly ask if they'd had anyone asking too many questions lately who didn't seem interested in their services. Reporters, maybe. And, gee, any investigators?"

I wondered why she hadn't done that before, instead of getting me involved. But I didn't think now was the best time to ask. "And did anyone answer?"

"No one spoke with me, although there were other people in the waiting room. Earl came in and gave me one of his awful grins. I shouted at him when he started to shut the inner door in my face."

"So you gave up?"

"No. I sat there for a while, thinking. A few people leaving the facility stared at me, but no one was around to see when I actually left."

"And somewhere around that time —"

"Supposedly, not long after that, Earl was killed."

"How?" I asked.

"They didn't say." And neither had the news. "The cops said they're just looking at all possible suspects. Why they may have singled me out over, say, Mason, I can't tell you. But —"

"But you think they have."

She nodded. "Kendra, there's some stuff I'd like to tell you, as an attorney. You see —"

"I'm not your attorney," I interrupted immediately. "I'm not an expert in criminal matters, and if I don't represent you, I might have to testify to stuff you tell me. But I happen to know of a really good criminal attorney. Would you like me to put you in touch with her?"

Lois nodded yet again. "Is she expensive?"

"She's reasonable. Just talk to her about what you can afford." And I gave her the contact info for Esther Ickes, the attorney who'd helped me through some awful times.

I would warn Esther, of course.

And I wondered when in the world — if ever — I'd stop being a murder magnet.

By the time we finished our coffee and conversation, it was late enough in the day that I decided not to return to my law firm. Sitting in the parking garage in my rental car, I called Mignon on my cell. Our receptionist assured me that no emergencies had occurred. Not that day at the office, at least. I promised I'd see her tomorrow, then hung up.

Next call, as I ignored a glaring guy who seemed eager to grab my space, was to Jeff's office. I reached Althea immediately. "Hi, Kendra," she said eagerly. "Any news?"

"That's what I was going to ask you." I paused. "Actually, there is something I'm looking into. I have a lead on what Jeff was working on when he vanished, but the person who hired him wanted strict confidentiality." Did I have an obligation to Lois not to tell the person who just might have the best resources in the world to look deeply into The Clone Arranger and its reputation? Sure, Jeff might have been sworn to secrecy. Lois had asked me to step in and help find him. Did that mean I had to keep her secret, too, presumably to protect her with her church friends?

I supposed I'd better check with her. Or not. Turned out that astute Althea gave me the answer herself. "You mean about that murder at The Clone Arranger? Was Jeff investigating that outfit?"

"How did you know . . . ? I mean, I have to check with someone before I can say anything, but —"

"Lois Terrone? You know I can't give you any particulars, Kendra, but I used my usual resources and found out she was inter-rogated by the Glendale P.D. for that homi-cide. I've never met her, but know she's a good friend of Jeff's family. His cell phone records suggested they spoke recently. And I followed up on his credit card records and learned he flew back to Ontario Airport. I put two and two together — did I add it up correctly? You don't have to say yes, but if you don't say no, you won't have revealed anything that might be confidential, right?"

I'd been the beneficiary of several of Althea's adept online hackings — er, investigations.

"Four," I said.

"For what . . . ? Oh, you mean my two and two is on target. Good!"

I heard a honk behind me. A different car sat there, apparently awaiting my departure. Well, I actually did have better things to do with my time than spend much more of it sitting in the Glendale Galleria parking garage. But I didn't want to humor the ill-willed motorist in his attempt to move me prematurely. So, before I pulled out, I said into the phone, "I'm not saying anything affirmative, Althea. But if you happen to learn anything interesting about The Clone Arranger or any of its employees, it wouldn't be out of line for you to pass it along to me. I can't say that it might help locate Jeff, but I won't say that it won't, either."

"Got it. Thanks, Kendra."

"Thank *you*," I said, then turned the key in the ignition, ignoring the line of cars that had formed behind the bozo waiting for my space. Hey, that was *his* bad.

I didn't even get to the 134 Freeway heading west before my phone rang. I glanced down at the caller ID, inevitably hoping for Jeff's number. Nope, not his, but another familiar name appeared on my cell phone screen.

"Hi, Kendra," said a sweet, senior female voice. I'd learned well that Esther Ickes might be a mite beyond middle age, but she was one heck of an attorney.

She'd helped me through a bankruptcy a while back, and then had been my choice for criminal defense when I was accused of a couple of murders.

After I caught the real killer, I wound up referring a number of friends and acquaintances to Esther during their dark hours as murder suspects.

And I'd just done the same with Lois Terrone.

"I owe you another dinner," she said after I greeted her effusively.

"Lois called you?" Oops. I'd intended to warn Esther.

"She did. She's another friend of yours?"

"Actually of Jeff's."

"Oh, yes, honey." Her tone turned suddenly sad. "How are you getting along?"

I was fortunately — or unfortunately — making a merge onto the freeway, so I didn't have time to sigh or sob or react in any other way to her obvious assumption of the worst about Jeff.

"I'm fine. Hold on just a second. . . .

There. I'm in a lane. Anyway, I'd love to get together with you for lunch or dinner or whatever one of these days." I kept my voice so perky I could puke, but I wasn't about to go all maudlin. Not now. Hopefully, not ever — since I refused to assume there was a reason to mourn.

"Great," she said, and we made tentative plans. And then, always-supportive Esther added, "And, Kendra, you know I'm always available if you need to talk."

Good thing I didn't anticipate another lane change for a couple of miles, since suddenly my vision blurred with tears.

It was time to take back more of my own pet-sitting duties, so I hurried home to meet up with my assistant, Rachel, and retrieve a bunch of keys and instructions I'd left with her.

Idling briefly on the street, I pushed the control I'd put inside the rental car to open the wrought iron gate, then drove up the short driveway to my carport. That's when I saw a stranger working in the yard. I parked, exited my vehicle, and headed up the front walk toward my rented-out mansion.

I'd called Rachel to alert her, and she immediately opened the front door. As she exited, so did an excited Beggar, who ran to me as if expecting my usual dog accompaniment, but I hadn't yet retrieved Lexie and Odin from Jeff's house. Obviously disappointed, the gorgeous Irish setter commenced loping around the yard. She stopped beside the stranger, who didn't appear to be gardening. Nor had I noticed the usual gardener's beat-up truck along the street.

"Who's that?" I inquired.

The guy didn't look much older than Rachel, late teens or early twenties. He wore a white muscle shirt and frayed jeans, and his bronze skin, black hair, and jutting cheekbones suggested a Hispanic background. And it wasn't weeds he appeared to be pulling up with a big basket on a stick, but doggy do-do.

"He's with our new poop-scooping service," Rachel said, regarding the eye-candy guy with appreciation. "I'd heard some of the neighbors talking about it. It's called What's the Scoop, and when I was walking Beggar, I saw the guy who appears to be the owner talking to Phil Ashler."

My silver-haired senior citizen neighbor had recently adopted a medium-size mutt named Middlin from one of the animal shelters. I'd worked with them a little to help ensure Middlin was potty trained properly. He was a sweet-natured rescue dog, and I adored Phil for taking him in.

"Phil told me what a great job the new scooper was doing for Middlin and him. He recommended the new outfit, so I said I'd give them a try. The owner sent his helper here this afternoon." She gestured toward the young guy now scouring the yard for errant piles of poop. "I've been keeping an eye on him."

"I'll bet," I interjected dryly.

Rachel's gaze was irritated as she added, "I mean, since I've let him onto the property. I think he's doing a good job."

"We'll see how many piles he misses," I retorted. But I felt too distracted to perform any poop patrol and figured I'd let Rachel do any feces reconnaissance. I had pet-sitting to complete this evening, my own canine and Jeff's to go home to hug — and that same man to stew about. Again. Still.

I'd call Althea again to see if she'd gotten any additional leads for me to follow regarding some connection among Jeff, Lois Terrone, The Clone Arranger, and the death of Earl Knox.

What if Jeff was still alive and he'd staged his own vanishing to hide that he'd been about to off Knox for reasons of his own?

I considered that absurd allegation as I

headed my car back toward his home an hour later, after my evening pet-sitting visits to Abra, Cadabra, and Stromboli, and a quick visit to Meph, Stromboli's neighbor and my clone cohort, and his human mama, Maribelle, just for fun.

I'd decided to spend some time the next morning taking Stromboli and Meph, along with Lexie and Odin, to a dog park. They deserved some extra exercise and attention.

And I deserved some additional distraction. Assuming it would get my mind off Jeff.

But for now, my brain kept brimming over with questions and ideas that led . . . nowhere.

Where could I go next in my investigation into Jeff's disappearance?

Chapter Six

I'm a confirmed listophile. A listaholic. That was how I handled all of my litigation. My pet-sitting. My life. But I had no idea how to list a plan of attack to locate Jeff.

That night before bed, I sat on Jeff's white sectional sofa, in his sunken living room, surrounded by sympathetic dogs. Lexie's head was on my lap, and Odin's butt abutted my leg on the other side. I held a pad of paper and a pen in my hands, and the news on Jeff's big-screen TV near the huge stone fireplace was on mute. I'd turned it on in case there was something more about the murder at The Clone Arranger.

So what did I have to jot down? Not a lot, yet much too much.

A missing lover whose Escalade was located at the bottom of an aqueduct canal. A missing lover whom I really missed. . . .

No, Kendra, concentrate on your list, not your possible loss.

Okay. Next was a friend of that lover, Lois, who'd been put in touch with me by that lover's mother, Irene. Irene belonged on the list only peripherally. Lois, on the other hand, seemed of central significance. She claimed to have set Jeff on a supersecret investigation of The Clone Arranger.

I'd visited there to commence my own look-see into the secretive place. Met a quasi-famous lady there, Beryl Leeds, star of a long-ago TV show, who'd brought her Lab to be cloned. She'd had a prior good experience with The Clone Arranger.

I also met two Arrangers — CEO Mason Payne and Earl Knox. The latter was subsequently and swiftly murdered. Because of me? Unlikely. But didn't his death smack of some too-incredible coincidence?

Well, hell. As much as I despised giving credibility to such stuff, my whole life had shifted into a series of incredible coincidences. Once again, I'd become a murder magnet. Too many people I knew became victims or suspects.

Like Lois Terrone, now an apparent suspect. I didn't really know her any better than I'd been acquainted with Earl, but she had the advantage of Irene Hubbard to vouch for her. And, presumably, Jeff — once he was found.

Unless . . . could Lois have killed Jeff, then gone after Earl? But though she had an apparent motive for killing the guy at The Clone Arranger who'd failed to clone her elderly dog before its demise, why dispose of Jeff?

Okay, this list was way incomplete. Assuming Jeff's disappearance had even a slight relationship to his investigation into The Clone Arranger, I needed to know more about that organization and its personnel, and people with grudges against them — especially against Earl.

I swiftly woke the dogs and displaced them as I stood and headed for Jeff's home office, where I got on his computer. I checked my e-mail. Nothing from Althea, so I sent her an inquiry: Anything new to report? Her immediate response? Negative.

Shaking my head, I headed for bed.

And didn't sleep much, not even after taking a relaxing, warm shower.

I got up early, groggily and grumpily, but I wouldn't take it out on Lexie and Odin. "Let's take a quick walk," I said to them. "Then I'll let you come pet-sitting with me. And romping in a dog park. I owe that to some of our slightly neglected clients."

Lexie cocked her cute head until one of

her long ears nearly swept the rug. Odin simply stood and wagged the tail curled over his back, his tongue hanging out as if suggesting starvation. I couldn't help laughing and giving them both big hugs. At least I wasn't alone on this disconcerting morning.

My cell phone rang before I loaded canines into the car. It was Tracy Owens, my friend and fellow member of the Pet-Sitters Club of Southern California. In fact, she was the PSCSC pres.

"Good morning, Kendra," she said. "Are you still up for that dog park visit you mentioned yesterday?"

"I'm on my way there now. Care to come?"

"Wouldn't miss it. I'll only have Phoebe with me, so I can help if you have some extra dogs along."

We agreed to meet in forty-five minutes. Our choice for our canine outing was a dog park nestled high in the hills above Lake Hollywood, midmountain beneath slopes including the one that houses the famed Hollywood sign. It was a relatively central meeting place between Tracy's abode in Beachwood Canyon and Jeff's home in the San Fernando Valley.

I parked at the curb on the steep street and sat for a few seconds, attempting to calm the extremely excited dogs. Since Lexie and Odin had been here before, they knew where they were. And I'd picked up Stromboli, whom I was sitting, and his next-door neighbor Meph.

Four pups to exercise? Was I nuts?

Maybe, but I had Tracy's promise of assistance. Plus, the more stuff I had to keep my mind on, the less I'd think about things I didn't want my brain wrapped around.

It was Friday — still a weekday, and therefore a workday. I had to get to my law office later. Sometime.

I saw Tracy at the edge of the park almost immediately. She had the adorable puggle Phoebe on a leash. She must have noticed me at the same time, since she started toward us.

"Kendra!" She sounded extremely happy, but why shouldn't she be, with only one well-behaved baby in her charge? She looked almost chic, wearing slim khaki slacks and a short matching jacket over a white knit top.

Me? Well, I had to head to work later, so I'd worn nice slacks, too, but they were charcoal and not extremely new, and my pink print blouse had seen some significant wear.

I'd noticed often, since meeting her, that Tracy stayed slender yet managed to appear somewhat chubby thanks to full cheeks. But their fullness seemed to be a result of her frequent smiles.

And why not, when she was no longer a murder suspect? All the other problems in her life seemed behind her, too.

She threw her arms around me in a big bear hug, no mean feat considering I was attempting not to let four separate leashes get tangled despite the fancy footwork of the dogs to which they were attached.

"I'm so glad to see you." She stepped back, examined me with intense brown eyes, then reached for a leash. I complied, giving her Meph's. Despite the sudden pressure on her arm she remained still except for shaking her head. "You don't look so good. Still no word about Jeff?"

This time I was the one to shake my head. "Only his car." I filled her in on the wet Escalade escapade in the aqueduct canal as we walked toward the busy, grassy area.

Though this was usually used as an off-leash park, we kept our exuberant pups under the best kind of control. We left their leashes clipped on, despite many a glum doggy stare when they noticed they were in the distinct minority here, where canines mostly ran wild. We watched our steps as we proceeded, past picnic benches and children's play equipment, to traverse the large lawn area.

Which reminded me of Rachel's new poop-scooping group. Not wanting to keep our conversation maudlin, I asked Tracy, "Have you ever heard of a company called What's the Scoop? I guess it's the latest poop pickup service provider in the Valley and Hollywood Hills."

"No, but if you get me information on it, maybe I could use it. Although my favorite Valley customer won't be hiring me for a while. He lost his dog recently — an older Lab. Very sweet. When he's ready, I'll try to find him a rescue to help ease the pain." She stared at me sideways, sadly. "Speaking of people's pain, what about yours? Do you think Jeff . . . I mean, after finding his car that way —"

My attention wavered from Odin, Lexie, and Stromboli for only an instant as I considered how to tell this good friend, who undoubtedly meant well, to stay off that preferably taboo subject. Which was exactly when a huge off-leash Rottweiler decided to assert his dominance.

That led to a brief altercation with Odin, who despite being a neutered male sometimes had dominance issues of his own.

By the time Tracy, the Rottweiler's angry

male owner, and I separated and disciplined the dogs, Odin had a bloody wound on one shoulder.

"Damn," I said, feeling suddenly despondent. Not only couldn't I find Jeff, but I wasn't taking perfect care of his abandoned baby. I got the owner's ID info and assurances his dog was up-to-date on rabies shots.

Tracy had Phoebe under one arm, and Meph obediently sat on the ground beside her. She knelt and took a close look at Odin's injury. "It doesn't look too bad, but you should have it examined by a vet. Do you want me to —"

"Thanks, but I'll take Stromboli and Meph home, then go get Odin his medical care. Unless you think it's an emergency."

Her thoughts would be important to me, since my own sorrowful mind was clearly mush.

"No, he'll be okay. But tell you what. Give me instructions, and I'll be glad to get Stromboli and Meph back where they belong."

"Are you sure?" I asked, feeling relieved. I wanted to get Odin to a vet immediately, emergency or not.

"What are fellow pet-sitters for?"

I handed her the keys to Stromboli's

house and described where to go. "Meph's owner Maribelle is at home, and she can keep watch over Stromboli's house when he's there, till I arrive for his evening visit. You can also leave the keys to Stromboli's with Maribelle for me to pick up later."

I loaded Lexie and an obviously aching Odin into my rental car. Fortunately, its seats were flimsy vinyl, so if they collected a little blood despite the clean paper towels I put on Odin's wound, I figured I'd be able to scrub it off.

I was, however, worried about Odin. So I didn't head for the closest vet.

Instead, I got on the Ventura Freeway heading west toward the office of the best vet I knew, Dr. Tom Venson. I'd sort of dated him while wondering where my relationship with Jeff wasn't going.

Despite his assurance that he wanted to stay friends after I'd informed him I was about to see Jeff exclusively, this would be the first time I'd seen him since then.

He wouldn't take the situation out on Odin. He was too nice a guy for that.

But how uncomfortable would this visit be for him?

Or me?

I'd expected awkward. Instead, I received

open arms.

"Kendra, it's good to see you," Tom said. We were in one of his disinfectant-scented examining rooms, Lexie on a chair behind me and Odin uneasily up on the shining metal table, thanks to a big boost from me.

Edith, Tom's young receptionist with the older name, had welcomed me and found me a room immediately, emergency or not. She'd promised to get Dr. V's attention fast, and she had.

I used the term "open arms" figuratively, though. He'd shaken my hand — warmly — but no hugs. Which was only appropriate, considering that he assumed I was in a committed relationship.

Unless he'd seen it on the news, he had no way of knowing that the other person in that relationship, committed or not, had apparently evaporated into some unknown ether. Although it was just as well that Tom refrained from embracing me, I needed a huge number of supportive hugs these days. But as a former potential romantic interest, he could misconstrue it.

I could misconstrue it.

"Good to see you, too, Tom." At least I was truthful about that, since he was a very good vet when I needed one. However, observing him across the examining table, I noticed lots of lines at the edges of his eyes.

I'd enjoyed Tom's looks because they were nice but not extraordinary. He was nearly six feet tall with regular features, and his dark hair formed an adorable widow's peak right in the middle of his forehead. His brown eyes always looked sincere, especially when they filled with fondness for me.

But right now, those eyes appeared squinty, strained, and somewhat bloodshot.

I didn't have time to ask how he was before he started tending to Odin's injury. He made shaving around it, cleansing it, treating it with antibiotics, and bandaging it appear simple.

"He should be fine," Tom soon said. "If he starts biting at the bandage, we may have to fit him with a plastic collar, but see how he does for now."

Odin appeared more bored than bitey. He lay down on the table, regarding me almost affably for having brought him here. That had to be good. He didn't seem to be hurting.

Tom, on the other hand, looked haunted. "And you?" I inquired softly. "How are you doing, Tom?"

Could he be mourning the loss of me and what we might have had? The possibility made me go all gooey inside, even though our separation had been entirely my choice.

"I've been better," he admitted, and I braced myself for him to declare how he wanted me back. "A friend of mine just . . ." He seemed to perk up a little as he stared at me.

A friend? Clearly this wasn't about me, which was entirely right. Wasn't it?

"Kendra, maybe you can help." His tone sounded stronger. "You told me when we went out to dinner and all that you jokingly considered yourself a murder magnet."

I opened my mouth to protest that I hadn't been joking, as much as I wanted to be. But I stayed silent.

This was about a murder? A *friend's* murder?

How many murders were there every day in L.A.? Probably lots. And who said Tom's friend was even a local?

But The Clone Arranger, where Earl Knox had worked, was all about animals. Tom, a veterinarian, was also all about animals. Still . . . That would be one heck of a huge coincidence — both of us interested in the same murder.

Like I said, I'd been the victim of incredible and innumerable coincidences. How else would a sweet and innocent person like me become a murder magnet?

Keeping my voice light, as if I actually was joking, I said, "Of course I'm a murder magnet, Tom. I've become quite skilled at solving them, too. You have one you want me to look into for you?" I made myself laugh. "Or are you intending to commit one?"

"Not hardly," he said, running his hand gently over Odin's back as the Akita started to stir impatiently. "But — well, I didn't know the guy that well, but his death hit me hard because he worked for a company that I do a lot of veterinary work for."

"And that company would be . . . ?" I inquired.

"The Clone Arranger."

With amazing effort I managed to forgo reacting physically, or so I hoped. "Then that would make your deceased friend —"

"Maybe you heard about him on the news. Earl Knox."

CHAPTER SEVEN

Ten minutes later I sat across from Tom at a nearby popular and overpopulated coffee shop. His staff was caring for Odin and keeping an eye on Lexie. He'd assigned an assistant vet to his appointments while we went out — after checking to ensure that no scheduled pet seemed to be coming for anything more major than a checkup and shots. He'd taken off his blue lab jacket, revealing a nice white knit shirt and dark slacks.

How to play this? I liked Tom. Didn't want to lie to him.

Didn't want to lay the whole truth before him, either. I mean, I wanted all the info I could glean about his friend Earl, not to mention Tom's own now-revealed relationship with The Clone Arranger. But I preferred to keep to myself that I just happened to have been at that particular place of business recently, conducting my own little investigation into whether anyone there knew what had happened to the genuine investigator who'd been snooping around them: Jeff.

I doubted that Tom would give a damn about the fate of the guy I'd indicated had won my heart. But the fact that a lady who was a mother figure to Jeff had a grudge against the cloning company, and most especially the murder victim, might be of interest to the saddened vet with whom I sat and sipped a double fat-free latte.

Somewhat surprisingly, and definitely discombobulating me, Tom said, first thing, "I saw on the news about Jeff Hubbard's car being found in the water near Palmdale, Kendra. I haven't heard anything about him, though. Has he been found?"

"Nope, but I'm assuming he's on an undercover assignment and will show up just fine one of these days." Oh, Lord, did I sound pathetically perky!

"Well . . . I hope so, for your sake." A kind thing for him to say, and he even sounded sincere. Nice man, Dr. Tom Venson.

Still, I needed to change the subject — for the sake of my psyche, as well as to obtain answers. "So, you actually do work for The Clone Arranger?" I leaned forward as if I was all ears. Which I was.

Did the fact that a man as kind and intelligent as Tom had gotten involved with this company mean it was a credible cloning source? That would mean that its failure to clone Lois Terrone's part-Akita was a possible fluke.

Or was Tom too credulous, as Lois had initially been? Though Beryl Leeds had seemed ecstatic over the duplication of her first Lab, that didn't mean all animals were well and successfully twinned.

"Yes, I do." Tom sounded all sincerity as he sipped his unsweetened, un-anythinged simple brewed coffee. He watched me with brown eyes that both smiled and seemed to undress me even as we had this serious conversation.

Not long ago, my libido might have responded with interest. But at this moment, since it missed Jeff, my body simply squirmed.

"Not that I get involved with the cloning," Tom continued. "They have specially trained scientists for that. Plus, the process is proprietary, so they don't want people who aren't actually employees of the company to learn how it works. But as part of their procedures, and to ensure they don't do anything improper to the dogs to be cloned, they've hired me to come in to provide weekly checkups. More veterinary care, if necessary, of course, like in an emergency."

"The whole concept of cloning is really fascinating," I told him. That was said in all sincerity. What if I actually could get a duplicate of my dear Lexie? Would I do it? Well . . .

"I'll say," Tom agreed. "But they do warn people who want their pets to be cloned that a biological duplicate doesn't necessarily mean they'll get an identical new animal." I'd seen that in The Clone Arranger's contract and promotional pages. "And not just because there's always the possibility of gene mutation. Like with people, environment is important in an animal's development, and things never stay the same. Even if someone tries to treat the two pets identically, just having the older one around could make a difference. Or a new home, or even the possibly more loving reception for this new animal who's designed to try to take the place of the first — an infinite number of possible alternatives."

I nodded, signifying understanding, but I wasn't entirely convinced. "If the animals can't be identical, do you believe that cloning's a good idea — and that it actually succeeds, biologically, at least?"

Tom gave a small shrug of a nice-size shoulder. "I can't comment scientifically on the effectiveness of what they do, but they fit a niche for people who want to try to have their pets duplicated. And they're acting responsibly about care of the animals entrusted to them. They've hired me, haven't they?"

His grin was wry and somewhat sexy. *Damn, Kendra, stop noticing such stuff.*

Hating to burst his balloon but needing some answers, I said softly, "How well did you know that poor man who was killed yesterday? And what was his position with the company?"

Sure enough, Tom's alert demeanor disintegrated into something more stoop-shouldered and sad. "Earl was one of the main guys I worked with there, since he was one of the people assigned to make sure the animals in their care were treated well and cloned properly. He was also a bit of a salesman, convincing interested people to give it a try. Actually, he was a blowhard, but on the whole an okay guy. I was really upset to hear he'd been killed, and especially being poisoned, injected with an anesthetic I often use on animals."

Really? Interesting. That hadn't been made public — or at least I hadn't heard.

112

What was it?

And how easy was it for anyone besides a vet to obtain?

Or had it just been sitting out there, readily available to anyone at The Clone Arranger who also worked with animals — or even to a visitor like Lois?

"At least the cops appear to have a suspect," Tom continued.

I nodded sagely and said, "Yes, the news said it was a disgruntled customer who didn't like the way the cloning had been handled with her now-dead dog. Had you met her?"

"No, but I did see her dog when she was there to be cloned. The animal was pretty old and not in great health. It's a shame she died before a successful cloning could take place. But that was no reason for the owner to kill Earl."

Who should she have killed? I wondered, then mentally gave my cheeks a sound slap. Lois shouldn't have killed — and didn't kill — anyone. Or so I wanted to believe, given her relationship with Jeff.

Jeff. I couldn't easily ask Tom, subtly or even straight out, if he'd seen my lover snooping around The Clone Arranger.

On the other hand, if he had seen Jeff lurking, he surely would have told me by now, wouldn't he? Or even the cops, since he knew Jeff was missing.

But . . . could Tom have somehow been involved in Jeff's disappearance?

The sudden suspicion nearly pulled me to my feet. That would be one sound reason Tom wouldn't mention seeing Jeff prying around The Clone Arranger.

But he would hardly admit it to me, would he?

"Is something wrong, Kendra?"

Obviously my unexpected mistrust must be showing on my face, so I did my utmost to eradicate it. "Something just passed through my mind," I admitted with absolutely no intention of informing him exactly what it was. "The ethics of the whole thing. I mean, some people believe cloning is sinful, and even if one has no religious hesitations, what if the technique can be used to clone people? Do you believe that's okay?"

This time both his shoulders lifted under his snug white shirt. "I'm a doctor, Kendra. I come from a scientific background. I guess one could say, even if religious, that if the deity in charge didn't like cloning, he wouldn't allow mankind to discover how to do it." Hadn't Lois said something similar, but from her own theological leanings? "And duplicating people has the same

114

drawbacks as duplicating animals. Plus, there are already so many other ways of conceiving children these days besides the tried, true — and fun, by the way — method."

He gave me a big wink that would have turned my insides suddenly steamy if I was allowing myself to think sex in this man's presence — which I absolutely wasn't.

"Ethical?" he continued. "Heck, I don't know. But I'm all for scientists' rights to experiment, and to profit from their successes, too. How about you?"

"Let me get back to you on that. But you've certainly piqued my curiosity. I'd like to know all the additional stuff about the scientists at The Clone Arranger and what they do. How did that poor man Earl interface with them? In fact, tell me how their whole system works. It sounds fascinating."

Tom took a sip of coffee and stared at his foam cup, as if attempting to ascertain if the answers he sought were written within the design of the coffee company's logo.

"You know" — he looked up at me, some confusion in his eyes — "I perform exams and even do quality control for the company's animal care. But I really can't say how the whole thing functions. All I know is that they promote their services a lot to people

115

who could become their customers. People who want pets cloned come to the facility to have animals evaluated to determine whether they're good cloning candidates. If they are, those animals stay for a few nights while DNA is removed and preserved in the manner proprietary to The Clone Arranger, whatever it is. They made it abundantly clear I shouldn't pry into it, no matter how interested I might be. You're a lawyer, so you'd understand. They made me sign one heck of a confidentiality agreement."

"Not surprising," I said soothingly, wondering, at the same time, who might have drafted it — and how ironclad it really was.

Could I convince Tom to tell me more? As a vet, he had a scientific background. That had to include deep interest in all things arguably along that line. Consequently, I assumed he'd been as nosy as me and examined all information hidden within company computers or otherwise, just to satisfy his own curiosity.

"Anyway, after that proprietary magic is performed, the animals go home," Tom continued. "In whatever time frame it takes, the client is either told to expect a new baby similar to the existing pet or informed it didn't work this time."

"And how did those whose clonings failed

generally react?"

"Don't know." Tom shook his head. "I'm seldom there when the pets' owners drop them off or visit, and I check them over in the clinic area."

"Then tell me something about the people who work for The Clone Arranger."

He peered at me in a manner that suggested I was stoking the curiosity I was certain he had. "Why are you asking so many questions, Kendra? Are you seriously thinking about looking into Earl's death for me?"

My turn to move a shoulder beneath my pretty pink print blouse — not nearly as wide as Tom's or as decisive in its shrug. "I've gotten involved before for friends, and I consider you a good friend," I said with as winsome a smile as I could muster. And hoped I wasn't laying it on too thick. Or kicking him vicariously in his most treasured parts, by referring to him as a friend instead of a potential lover. Even though he should know and accept that by now.

"But I thought your interest was generally in clearing people you considered unjustly accused of murder," he responded.

He was absolutely accurate. I'd gone into my own investigation of murder cases mostly because I didn't believe the suspects the cops had zeroed in on were the real perpetrators — any more than *I'd* been a few months back when accused of a couple of intentional killings.

In actuality, that was my main interest in this case, too. Well, one of them. I'd adore proving that Lois Terrone was innocent, because of her motherlike relationship to Jeff.

And if my inquiry ferreted out what Jeff had been up to in his investigation of The Clone Arranger for Lois's sake, and that somehow assisted in locating Jeff himself — alive, of course — then I would come out of this situation ecstatic.

But all that was for me to know and Tom never to learn.

"That's how it's been up to now," I acknowledged, sipping my latte as I determined how best to finesse my explanation. "But I've always stood for digging up the truth. This time, you've gotten me interested because of your relationship with The Clone Arranger and Earl Knox. I'm sure the authorities have unearthed evidence against that woman who seems key to their investigation, according to the news. And maybe it was her. If I dig in and nose around" — an image that brought Pansy the potbellied pig to mind — "I won't want to get in the cops' way, anyway. Maybe I'll be able to assist them. Or not, if I discover evidence to the contrary. But I'm not working on exonerating any friends or acquaintances at this moment, and though I enjoy the practice of law, it's less exciting these days if I'm not investigating a murder." Not! But that sure sounded good, even to me, along with all the other lies. "So, tell me the cast of characters at The Clone Arranger, and then I'll see what strands I can pull together to find out who determined Earl's fate."

I all but batted my eyelashes. Too much? So I feared at first.

But Tom soon spilled a bunch of data he'd amassed in his mind about the personnel affiliated with this incredible cloning outfit. I took copious notes on the pad I always, as a listophile and lawyer, carried in my large purse.

A short while later, I sat in my rental car going over my jottings, with Lexie riding shotgun and Odin resting in the rear. I'd get Althea to confirm what she could online — which, knowing her, meant everything and then some. Besides, bits of this info might be legitimately posted on The Clone Arranger's website.

And whatever wasn't, Althea would know

how to nose it out.

But would it help find out what had happened to Jeff? That wasn't something even the best hacker — namely, Althea — could guarantee.

I bit back my sudden resumed fear and sorrow and went over the names Tom had proffered. I'd already met The Clone Arranger's CEO, Mason Payne. Other company officers Tom had met included Mason's sister, Debby Payne, as well as the chief public relations person, Wally Yance, and a top cloning scientist, Melba Slabach — or at least I imagined that was how to spell the name Tom spit out.

And then there was the mysterious poison that had been used to dispose of Earl. Could Althea learn what it was by hacking into some of her favorite official sites? I jotted that down, too, then closed my notebook and stuck the key into the ignition. . . .

Which was when I noticed the Escalade just passing me on the road.

Not a big black one, as Jeff's had been, but gold. There were probably plenty, especially in L.A.

But I got a glimpse of the guy driving it. He sat tall in the driver's seat, as Jeff did. He had light brown hair and big shoulders, and he wore sunglasses, so I couldn't get a glimpse of the angularity of his face.

Yet he sure as hell resembled Jeff. And as he drove away, I found myself following.

CHAPTER EIGHT

It took a couple of turns and a red light before I could maneuver the car up close and personal enough to get a good look at the guy.

Just because he had similar features and posture didn't mean he was Jeff.

Just because he was in an Escalade didn't mean he was Jeff. In fact, no way could this be Jeff's Escalade.

And what would Jeff be doing way out here, in Tarzana, near a coffee shop not far from Tom Venson's veterinary clinic?

Hell if I knew. But just in case, squirrelly as it seemed, I had to see for myself if this could be my missing lover.

At the traffic light, I looked, sideways and up, at the guy. He looked down, still wearing his shades. And smiled as if he thought I was flirting with him, the egotistical SOB.

Which revealed a row of teeth smaller, yellower, and more irregular than Jeff's, planted behind much skinnier and less sexy lips. Plus, the hairline was all wrong — too much brow — and the color not a light enough brown. And —

Well, you get it. This wasn't Jeff.

Had I genuinely expected it was? My damned imagination was much too full of hope, I supposed.

Okay, Kendra, you fruitcake. Even if Jeff was alive, this wasn't his territory. Best case, I was hallucinating. Worst . . . well, maybe I was nuts. Utterly looney, like Lorraine, a woman who'd been involved with the very first murders in my life. She'd been locked up in a very nice facility for the mentally unhinged. Was that where I belonged?

Or was I simply being too damned hard on myself?

I didn't even reveal to the dogs how my mind had been working. I made myself concentrate on driving, instead of on fears for my sanity, as I headed for my office.

My dismay must have been tattooed on my face, since the first thing Mignon chirped from the receptionist's desk was "Are you okay, Kendra?"

"Absolutely," I assured her, juggling the dogs' leashes as they dashed toward her in greeting.

"Okay." She definitely sounded dubious.

123

But then, petting the pups, she perked up again, as she was always wont to do. "You just got a call from Shareen Hayhurst of Show Biz Beasts. I forwarded her to your phone mailbox."

Oops. I hadn't focused much on this client's matter since I'd taken it on earlier in the week. Time to zero in on reality instead of speculating so much over Jeff and his issues. "Thanks, Mignon," I said over my shoulder as the dogs and I headed for my office.

A short while later, we headed out once more. I'd spoken with Shareen, and she'd promised, if I came to their offices, to show me more of the documentation Show Biz Beasts handed to prospective clients, as well as a training demo. A real training demo, with real dogs. My dogs — Lexie and Odin, if I wanted.

Did I ever! Not that I anticipated either would take on a film career, any more than my assistant Rachel would suddenly drop her day job with Critter TLC, LLC, to become a full-fledged star . . . I hoped. Even so, the show biz bug suddenly buzzed in my ears.

And, fortunately, Odin's injury was probably healing okay. He hadn't chewed at it, and the bandage remained securely in place without appearing to bother him.

Our drive to Valencia, home of Show Biz Beasts, was utterly uneventful. I saw no Escalades at all. Imagined no pseudo Jeffs piloting any other vehicle on the 5 Freeway, even though this was a primary route toward the engulfing aqueduct.

The animal training facility was located in a fairly nondescript stucco building at the end of a fairly nondescript industrial park in which all the structures looked the same. In fact, if I hadn't been given directions to head for Building B, I'd never have found the place.

Or so I initially thought, until I exited the car and commenced traversing the parking lot with the dogs. No edifice besides Building B had barks and howls emanating from it.

And right over the door hung a subtle sign: SHOW BIZ BEASTS. I'd arrived at the right spot.

Lexie and Odin certainly seemed to think so, the way they planted their noses against the glass and sniffed. And sniffed. Until I pushed the door open and we all three strode into a small waiting room that resembled one in a veterinary office. The floor was covered in beige tile, the walls were painted a slightly darker neutral hue, the benches were pseudo leather, and a large sliding window proclaimed where the greeter must sit.

I approached that opening and introduced myself to the twenty-something guy behind the glass, who said he was Larry. Unsurprisingly for a place like this, a dog sat beside him — a mutt whose heritage I couldn't immediately figure out, but he was short-haired, long-muzzled, and a deeper beige than the walls. He immediately barked hello and rolled over. I laughed as he sat up again, watching me as if awaiting praise, which I of course provided.

"That's Dorky," said Larry, who wore jeans and a white T-shirt that proclaimed Show Biz Beasts were the best. "He's been in ten dog food commercials and a film for training firemen how to save pets' lives." The guy stood, drawing himself up to his not-so-tall height, but it was enough to provide some sort of signal to Dorky, who sat at attention. "Play dead," Larry commanded.

Dorky didn't just keel over. His big brown eyes widened. He jerked as if shot, which definitely drew a sympathetic reaction from me. But the walls surrounding them prevented me from providing any help. And then Dorky groaned and sank to the floor on his side, eyes closed.

"Is he okay?" I demanded.

Larry grinned. "Okay? He's the greatest. Okay, Dorky, play alive." Sure enough, the dog opened his eyes, rose, shook himself, and sat panting — with an expression that suggested he was laughing.

"He *is* wonderful!" I agreed, just as I saw Shareen Hayhurst come through the waiting area door.

She looked less frumpy and middle-aged here in her work clothes. Designer jeans and a T-shirt similar to Larry's somehow seemed more appropriate to her mussy blond hair and wrinkly face. Or maybe just being on her home turf suited her.

"Glad you could come, Kendra," she said, then knelt to greet the canines I'd brought with enthusiastic hugs, which both Lexie and Odin lapped up. "They're sweet. What are their names?"

I told her, and explained the fortunately minor nature of Odin's injury.

"Well, Lexie and Odin, you're in for a treat — or hard work, depending on how you look at it. Come on." She reached for their leashes, and the pups trotted amiably at her side, as if they'd done so dozens of times.

Larry had brought Dorky in first. The

well-trained dog sat calmly in a corner of the large room. Odd, how this place didn't look like a soundstage from outside but essentially was one, whereas The Clone Arranger's unique lab environment was disguised to appear similar to a film industry structure.

The floor here was concrete — the better to be able to take on whatever appearance was necessary for the scene a studio was filming, simply by overlaying a compatible covering. Doggy nails clicked on the slick surface, but no canine appeared uncomfortable.

The walls, too, were nondescript. The ceilings were high enough to allow installation of lighting. The aroma was surprisingly dank for L.A., and somewhat musty.

A fair representation of a place an animal might visit, should it be chosen to star in a genuine Hollywood production, I imagined.

"Okay, Larry," Shareen said. "Run Dorky through his paces."

That dorky little dog was absolutely adorable. On command, he sat, stayed, stood, rolled over once more to play dead, jumped, crawled, did everything but don bifocals and read Shakespeare.

Shareen had handed me their leashes, so Lexie and Odin were beside me. They stood

128

still, as if stunned.

As Dorky finished, Corbin Hayhurst joined us. He wore khaki slacks and a white, untucked cotton shirt that had started to wrinkle — giving a dorkier impression than Dorky. He greeted my dogs nearly as effusively as his wife had, petting them with his pudgy hands.

"I'll take Dorky back to his room and give him an extra treat," Shareen said. "Larry and Corbin can demonstrate a training session for you, and I'll bring back some stuff we didn't leave at your office — a more detailed list of which of our students have actually gotten roles, and some notices we've sent out when we've become aware of auditions."

For most of the next half hour, I had charge of Lexie while Larry worked with Odin and Corbin issued instructions. The simple stuff, like sitting and staying, Lexie got right away, since I had trained her that much as a pup. Of course a prolonged stay was out of the question, since she was much too energetic to remain in one location for more than a few seconds at a time.

Odin, on the other hand, listened intently. When he was told to stay, he didn't move a muscle, except his eyes, until Larry said he could budge. Then Larry issued identical commands to him with sign language, and Odin got that just as fast.

Lying down provided Lexie with a wriggly assumption that she was about to get her tummy rubbed. Odin, on the other hand, lay where he was told. Even rolled over.

Hey, I had a budding canine movie star in my charge — and it wasn't my own cute but disobedient Cavalier. Nope, a really bright Akita named Odin might someday be given credit on the big screen. Or even moderate-size TV screens. Who knew?

Of course that presupposed I was prepared to do the audition thing with him.

Or Jeff would, when he came back. . . .

Oops. I shouldn't have allowed my mind to veer in that very dangerous direction. I was suddenly all solemn, fighting as my eyes considered becoming teary.

Fortunately, that was also when Shareen sauntered back into the room, hands filled with file folders, and I used her as a distraction. I approached and asked to look at the contents, ignoring Lexie leaping at my side.

"Did you read the agreement I left with you on Monday?" she asked.

Fortunately, I had. "The disclaimer seems appropriate," I said. "You make no guarantees that your students will land film roles."

"Exactly. That's on our website, too. But that hasn't stopped that horrible woman with the pair of Bichons — and they were the hardest dogs of all to get disciplined enough even to audition — from getting a bunch of our students' owners together to sue us. I've got her application and other information in that packet, along with photos of her little white monsters."

"Good," I said. "And the class this afternoon really gave me better insight into what those who are casting animals may be looking for. Probably not Lexie, unfortunately, unless someone's simply after cuteness without obedience." That pup leaped onto my leg at hearing her name. "Now, Odin on the other hand —"

"He's a natural," Larry assured me. "Of course I can't guarantee anything, but I'd like to take his picture and have our agency represent him. Send him out on auditions, whatever."

"I'll need to consider if that's a kind of conflict of interest, since I'm acting as your company's attorney in anticipation of litigation. It absolutely would be if I represented the other side, but it's most likely okay. Especially since I don't even own Odin."

"You don't?" Corbin was the one who

appeared upset. "Then why did you bring him?"

I had no intention of getting into a sorrowful explanation, so I simply said, "I'm watching him for a good friend. I suspect it would be okay with his owner if he got into films."

"Can you sign a contract for your friend?"

"Unfortunately, no," I said. I'd had Jeff execute one of my official Critter TLC, LLC, animal care contracts, which gave me the authority to get Odin veterinary care if needed, but signing agreements for film roles was above and beyond anything it reasonably anticipated.

"Is your friend somewhere that we could e-mail an agreement to him? Fax it?"

Hell if I knew. "He's out of touch right now." I had started to get all antsy. I really didn't want to delve into details. Instead, I said, "I need to leave now. Thanks for the demo and additional information. If you happen to learn of a role for an Akita, I might have a way of getting consent from a relative." Jeff's mom, Irene, might agree, although she probably had no better official authority than I did. "Meantime, I'll contact plaintiffs' counsel and see if we can resolve this whole thing amicably."

"Without paying them anything, Kendra,"

Corbin said sternly. "We didn't do anything wrong."

"Let me find out what I can about their claims, and then I'll be in touch," I told them. I said goodbye to Corbin, Shareen, and Larry, and told them to convey our farewells to adorable Dorky. Then Lexie, Odin, and I got on our way.

Traffic was anything but terrific as we headed home. Not that it was unusual for L.A., but the congestion really soured my state of mind. It was one of those occasions when I kind of comprehended road rage. I mean, the traffic reports on the news radio stations didn't mention obstructions or accidents on the 5 Freeway or the Hollywood, but both were backed up enough to keep my car crawling nearly the entire way.

As a result, I was in too taut a temper for any kind of nonsense by the time I arrived at my first pet-sitting destination.

Fortunately, Piglet the pug gave me no guff. In fact, he seemed pleased to be visited by Lexie, Odin, and me, and to be taken on a three-dog walk along his residential street. I gave him a huge hug and an extra treat when we departed.

And much to my surprise, Abra and Cadabra, Harold Reddingham's usually aloof felines, met me at the front door, rubbed their sweet, furry sides against my legs, and even purred. I'd of course left the canines briefly in my car in the shade, since they didn't play well with cats. I nearly purred back as my mood mellowed and I stroked the kitties' backs before feeding them and dealing with their litter box.

Then there was Stromboli, the shepherd mix, who yapped and pranced in apparent ecstasy to see my dog companions and me. Next door, Maribelle Openheim came outside her cottagelike house, Meph at her side.

"Any more need to borrow my boy here?" she asked. She smiled fondly down at her little dog, then back up at me. Her well-styled short hair appeared mussed, and her outfit, too — dark slacks and light shirt — seemed to have been donned hurriedly.

"Not today, but soon," I said. Then, "Is everything okay?"

"Couldn't be better," she said. "I've got a new guy in my life. I'm making a home-cooked meal for him, so I'm a little frazzled, but I saw you and wanted to say hi."

"Great!" I responded, meaning it. I'd introduced her to the judge who hadn't worked out some time ago. I knew widowed Maribelle craved male companionship, so I was delighted she had found someone — hopefully with more staying power than the difficult jurist.

"What about your love life?" Maribelle inquired softly and sympathetically. After all, I'd previously poured out my problems to her. "Any word about Jeff?"

I shrugged sadly. "Not yet." I attempted to insert optimism into a pseudo-perky tone. "But I haven't given up on him."

"Hell, no," Maribelle agreed. "Hang in there."

A short while later, after Stromboli was settled for the night in his home, Lexie, Odin, and I headed . . . where? Would we stay at my place or Jeff's that night? Maybe I'd feel more alive at Jeff's. Or would I worry even more about whether he was okay?

On the way, I parked to call Rachel for a status report on her pet-sitting availability, in case that made a difference.

"Things are just great, Kendra."

My young employee sounded extremely gushy, so I had to ask, "Any auditions coming up?"

"Next week. And tomorrow I'm taking Beggar back to Methuselah Manor. Other people will be around with animals to cheer up the residents — and I'm so excited! One is a producer who's casting for an independent film in a few weeks."

Methuselah Manor was her nickname for MediCure Manor, a senior citizens' residence where she'd been bringing her Irish setter for visits. Not long ago, she'd been accused of stealing from the inhabitants, but we'd straightened that out and she'd continued her mission to cheer up the animal-adoring elderly.

"Sounds encouraging," I said. For her, not necessarily for me. This young lady was so determined to make it as a Hollywood actress that I'd little doubt that she'd succeed someday, out of sheer willpower.

"See you soon," she said, as if there wasn't an inkling of indecision about where I was heading. I suddenly realized she was right.

Hey! A car suddenly made a right turn and nearly hit me. I glared at the driver — a guy. A good-looking guy. A good-looking sexy guy with light hair and sharp features and — a nose much too large and chin much too small. Or so I thought in the instant of our eyes meeting.

Not Jeff. What a surprise.

But the experience made me stare more into other autos. Lots of women drivers around. And the men were of many races and ethnicities, as typical in L.A.

I saw some Escalades, including a black one, but of course it wasn't Jeff's drowned car.

And was relieved finally to get to my place, push the button to open the gate, and pull into my designated parking space beside my garage-top abode.

I sat for an extra instant to regain my composure. Then I allowed the dogs out for a romp while I returned to the gate. A mini-van with a What's the Scoop sign on the side was parked on the street. Plus, there were flyers for that same company stuck in some neighbors' fences, and one hung from my mailbox. I pulled it out just as Rachel sashayed down the walk from the main house, beautiful Beggar beside her.

"Hi, Kendra. Glad you got here this soon. I need to go out for a while" — her jeans seemed dressy and had a nice cotton shirt tucked into them — "and I hate to leave with one of our poop scoopers here behind our fence, unsupervised. Dad's left town again, as usual." Scouting for a film, I assumed, which was his exciting career. "The guy's over there." Rachel pointed toward the far edge of our large yard, in an area with lots of pretty green grass that attracted dogs to squat. Only then did I notice movement in the vicinity of the house.

"Okay, thanks. I'll keep an eye on him," I said, feeling sort of sorry for someone who made a living collecting feces.

I stood outside as Odin and Lexie leaped in the guy's direction.

"He always carries lots of dog treats," Rachel said. "To make friends with his real customers. He told me so. Beggar got his before. I need to put him in the house and go."

I stayed in the yard as Rachel put her pup inside and got her nice, used blue sedan — a gift some months back from her successful dad — from the garage. I stood near the lawn to ensure that Lexie and Odin didn't get near the driveway, and waved to my young assistant as she drove away.

I headed a few steps in the direction of the poop scooper. "Hi," I called, then stopped. What did I have to say to this older, stooped guy with a big plastic bag and metal collecting tool nearly as tall as he was? Oh, yeah. "Thanks for helping out around here."

"No problem," he shot back in a shrill baritone, barely looking at me from beneath the big straw hat that shaded his face. He gave the dogs something from his pocket as they continued to cavort around him. "Is that dog okay?" He pointed to Odin's bandage.

"Just a slight altercation with another dog," I said. "He'll be fine." But as the guy handed them additional treats, I said, "Thanks, but no more for now. Come on, Lexie and Odin." They seemed disinclined to obey. "Now. Come." And then I said the magic word that captured their attention. "Dinnertime." As anticipated, they hurried my way. I stared at the poop scooper for a long moment before I turned and walked toward my apartment.

Tears filled my eyes, partly in pity for myself. I really was losing it. Because I'd really lost Jeff? No! But I'd thought I'd seen him at least once on my way home, and that had led to my seeking him in the faces of the drivers of nearly every other vehicle.

Pitiful. And now, somehow, I even thought I saw a resemblance to him in this swarthy-faced senior citizen who was clearly of Hispanic background.

Get a grip, Kendra, I admonished myself as I climbed the steps.

At the top, I picked up a plastic bag full of mail, a common method of delivery from Rachel who acted as our address's sorter-in-chief. I pulled out envelopes till I reached a middle-size manila one, larger than the general junk and incessant bills I invariably received. I glanced at it — and froze.

The thing was battered, partly open, and entirely a mess. It had been used before, but the prior address was scratched out and unreadable. The new address was mine. The handwriting was scrawly, nearly illegible . . . yet amazingly familiar.

Couldn't be.

I pulled it farther open and extracted two sheets of paper — and on reading one, I no longer doubted who the sender had been. The note on it said, "Dear Kendra, Put this in a safe place. Looking forward to you moving in. Till then —" And that was all. No signature or anything else.

The other sheet had been folded and contained a speaking schedule from one of Jeff's trips earlier this year. He wanted me to put it in a safe place? Sure, but why?

I examined the postmark. Jeff had sent it the day he'd disappeared. Why? To say goodbye? Sure didn't sound that way.

Even so, it just might be the final communication between the two of us.

Inside the door I fell to my knees and cried, as Lexie and Odin attempted in vain to comfort me.

CHAPTER NINE

After their extra-loving attention to the wreck that was me, I fed the dogs a little bit more than their typical dinners that night. Me? Well, I wasn't exactly sick with starvation. In fact, what ailed me kept me from feeling much hunger at all. Even so, I forced down crisp toast slathered with strawberry jelly, figuring I didn't really want to get ill.

Not with so many answers to unearth.

I ate while watching the TV news, sitting on my comfy beige sofa, a dog sandwich between Lexie and Odin, who watched my every reluctant bite as a reminder that they'd gladly relieve me of the enormous task of eating.

No news worth listening to, a good thing. Nothing about submerged Escalades. Nothing about dead Clone Arranger employees or suspects in the killing.

Nothing to take my mind off my misery.

So, if I couldn't beat it, I'd join it. After

eating — and handing over unnibbled crusts to the pups — I poured myself a glass of ice water and resumed my seat in the living room, my pad of paper containing my current lists on my lap.

Items to ponder: Jeff's disappearance. His trip beforehand. His return with no notice, thanks to his contact with his local "mom," Lois Terrone, concerned about the inconsistencies between cloning and her church. The only sign of his having popped up in L.A. at all: the discovery of his Escalade at the bottom of the aqueduct canal.

My awful craziness, looking for him in every male face. *You gotta get a grip, Kendra.*

Okay, next page. The Clone Arranger, the outfit Jeff had apparently been investigating without informing even his own skilled security staff. Why? Did he believe enlightening them — and me — violated his vow to Lois?

Lois had been less than pleased with how her attempt at obtaining a cloned pup turned out. Quite a contrast with an obviously pleased customer, former TV star Beryl Leeds, who'd had her chocolate Lab, Churchill, cloned and now also owned his match, Cartwright.

Then there was the public, one-sided

quasi argument Lois had had with The Clone Arranger employee Earl Knox.

Earl's murder. Lois a suspect.

Who else might have had something against him strong enough to off him? His boss, Mason Payne? Maybe, but who knew? Not I.

The last I'd heard in the news, Tom's speculations about how Earl had died were confirmed — injection with a substance that, ironically, was sometimes used as an animal anesthetic but was also a designer human drug: ketamine. Really?

And, in all this, how did Jeff's disappearance relate to Earl's demise? Did his mostly empty envelope mean something I didn't understand?

By then, my head spun as if I'd slurped too many margaritas. Too bad I actually hadn't. I decided to head for bed. Shower first.

And when I got out, my phone was ringing. *My phone was ringing!* And this was the time of day I always heard from Jeff when he was out of town.

"Hello?" I said breathlessly, listening for the voice I eagerly anticipated.

"Hi, Kendra. It's Tom. I hope I'm not calling too late."

I stopped a second to swallow my disappointment. But I wasn't entirely disappointed. I was glad to hear from Tom . . . wasn't I?

Sure. It wasn't his fault he wasn't Jeff.

"Too late?" My voice was an octave too shrill, and I swallowed again to lower it. "No, though if you'd been five minutes later, you'd have caught me in bed." *Oh, come on, Kendra.* That sounded as if I was flirting with the guy, skirting around a suggestion of sex.

He caught on immediately. "Well, if I headed your way now, then there's a good change I *will* catch you in bed, right?" He broke my sudden silence by saying, "Sorry. I couldn't resist."

"Hold that thought," I said, trying to sound upbeat but not overly interested. "So . . . how are things?" Like, let's change the subject.

"I actually had a reason to call," he said. "I was wondering if you'd thought about what we discussed this afternoon."

Oh, yeah, I had. Of course. I absolutely intended to try to figure out who'd killed Earl Knox. To help Lois — assuming she didn't do it. I knew that was what Jeff would do if he was here.

Not that he'd want me involved. As if he'd ever been able to discourage me from butt-

ing into a murder investigation when someone I knew was accused.

And now, the stakes might be higher.
Somehow, this situation might resolve itself
by leading me to locate *him.*

"I've thought about it," I informed Tom,
"although I haven't determined the right
approach to my kind of investigation."

"How about meeting some people Earl
knew? I'm sure no one at The Clone Arranger could have killed him, but probably
someone there knows the person who did.
Not that they're aware they know that
person, of course, or they'd have informed
the police, but you're amazingly good at
solving murders, Kendra. You know the
right questions to ask. Tomorrow's Saturday,
and I've arranged to have my afternoon free
at the hospital. So, come with me then and
ask some of your special questions, okay?"

"At The Clone Arranger?"

"Sure."

I almost jumped up in excitement. But
before getting overly frenzied, I had to
admit, as casually as I could, that I'd actually been to The Clone Arranger earlier this
very week. He'd find out tomorrow anyway.
Somebody was likely to recognize Kenni
Ballan. It wasn't as if I'd gone there in
disguise.

"I visited on behalf of a friend," I explained. "A pet-sitting client's interested in having her cute terrier mix cloned. She wanted me to take her pup there to get my opinion before she decided whether to go forward. I just got a little information and left."

"Really?" He sounded a smidgen frosty, not to mention skeptical.

"As I told myself before, this world is full of amazing coincidences. Like so many people I know either knowing murder victims or becoming suspects these days. Isn't that wild?"

"Yeah, wild. Look, Kendra, maybe we'd better forget —"

"I'm so excited about helping you figure out who killed your friend Earl," I gushed, trying to head him off at the pass of words before he could tell me I couldn't come. "I met him, you know. He seemed nice."

Nice and sleazy, sort of, but I didn't say that.

"You met him?" Suspicion grew even thicker in Tom's voice.

"I hardly talked to him. And I certainly didn't know him well enough to kill him." I kept my tone light, even as I anticipated what he was thinking.

"Of course not," he said, although his tone

suggested he wasn't completely convinced. "But if you've already been there. . . ."

"I didn't learn enough about cloning to help my friend. And I'd much rather help you. And your poor buddy Earl. He deserves justice, doesn't he?" Okay, I was laying it on awfully thick.

Fortunately, Tom seemed to buy it. "Well . . . sure. Okay, but —"

"Great! What time should I meet you there?"

Unsurprisingly, I didn't sleep well that night. I arose early and forced food into myself after allowing Lexie and Odin to romp in the fenced-in yard of my rented-out mansion. After all, there was now a poop scooper on staff prepared to pick up what they left.

A poop scooper who might have been the one on our grass yesterday was across the street at Phil Ashler's when the dogs and I left to do our morning pet-sitter rounds. Obviously, Phil's new dog, Middlin, pooped enough to require some scooping up behind him.

I really stared at the scooper this morning. Definitely the same guy as yesterday — stooped, face shaded by a broad-brimmed hat, somewhat swarthy and broad featured.

147

A resemblance to Jeff? Only in my wildest imagination — the one I'd let loose yesterday in my misery.

Okay, then. Mostly I made the same visits as yesterday. On my way after caring for Stromboli and waving hello to Maribelle and her Meph, my cell phone rang. "Kendra, hi. It's Avvie."

"Avvie! Good to hear from you."

And it was. Avvie Milton was a sometime friend, an associate at my former law firm of Marden, Sergement & Yurick. She'd taken over as the mistress of my former lover, the middle partner, Bill Sergement. Their business, not mine — although I wondered whether Bill's wife would consider it her business, too. They hadn't been married when Bill had seduced me as a new, young attorney at the firm — bad judgment on my part. I'd extricated myself soon afterward, chalking it up to my horrible pre-Jeff judgment about men.

Since I now worked for Yurick & Associates, the old firm had been renamed Marden & Sergement — a much smaller outfit, since Borden Yurick had resigned and taken his prodigious roster of clients with him.

"I've been meaning to call you forever, and now I have a good excuse. I know something about your current law practice

— Bill talked to Borden a few weeks ago. Are you still pet-sitting, or can you recommend someone?"

"I'm doing both, since I still enjoy the pet-care part as much as lawyering." I turned my car from a residential street onto Moorpark, a moderately busy commercial avenue.

"Honestly?" She sounded completely amazed.

"Consider choosing between dealing with picky clients who probably did everything the other side accuses them of and lie through their teeth to make you take their case — or a cute dog who wants only attention, no strings attached except for going for a nice, long walk on a pretty day, and getting fed. In my mind, there's no question."

"Well, if you put it that way — where do potbellied pigs fit into that picture?"

"How's Pansy?" I inquired about Avvie's adorable pet.

"Fine, but Bill and I are going on a business trip to Sacramento next week, and I need someone to take care of her. Can you do it?"

"Absolutely, and if not, I can get my young assistant to help out."

"You're busy enough to have an assistant?"

"Sure thing."

"That's great!" She actually did sound impressed, which suited me just fine. We made arrangements for me to come to her house for a reintroduction, instructions, and keys. As I prepared to hang up, she belatedly inquired, "How's Lexie?"

"Cute as ever," I said, aiming my gaze at that same Cavalier, who started wagging her tail as she stood on the seat beside me, annoying Odin, who lay there looking bored.

"And — are you still seeing that great-looking P.I., Jeff?"

My heart crunched, but this was simply small talk, without a huge amount of genuine interest attached. "Whenever possible," I told her, and with that I firmly said goodbye.

I headed onto the freeway for a few miles and got off at the ramp closest to my law office. Sure, it was Saturday, but I had a few hours to kill before meeting Tom. And what better way to spend time than working?

Not that I buckled down right away when reaching the office. First of all, Borden himself was there and, with Odin and Lexie hovering attentively at our feet, we chatted in the reception area about cases . . . and then about my missing guy.

"You handling this okay, Kendra?"

"I'm trying." I didn't mention my investigation into The Clone Arranger's possible relationship to Jeff's disappearance — or the murder of its employee.

"Any time you want to talk, or take some time off, that's fine. You know that."

"As always, I appreciate it, Borden." Impulsively, I stood on my toes — Borden was inches taller than my five-five. As always, he wore an aloha shirt. I kissed his cheek, and he flushed sweetly as I backed away.

The dogs trailed me to my office, where I shut the door and called Althea. "Hi, Kendra. Any word?"

"Well, one word is frustration," I told her. "Another is hope. Have you found anything about anyone at The Clone Arranger? I'm going there with a friend this afternoon and need to know the lowdown first. Also, any details about that ketamine that was used to kill Earl?"

"I'm just now compiling all I've got — haven't checked out the ketamine yet, though, just the people. I'll e-mail what I've got momentarily. That okay?"

"That's perfect," I told her.

I was ready to go meet Tom Venson about an hour later. By then, I had Althea's info printed out and stuck in the pockets of my notebook, along with my lists.

The names all sounded familiar after my conversation yesterday with Tom: Mason Payne was the CEO and founder of The Clone Arranger. His sister, Debby, appeared to be his second in command. Earl Knox, the dead guy, had been their chief salesman and all-around manager. Then there were scientists and P.R. types.

I was ready for this meeting. Or so I thought.

First, though, I took Lexie and Odin to Jeff's, which, in Sherman Oaks, was closer than my home or Darryl's Doggy Indulgence Day Resort. Then I headed for The Clone Arranger to meet Tom.

When I reached the secluded facility, Tom was waiting in the parking lot, dressed in a yellow Henley shirt and dark slacks. He looked good, especially when he gave me a big smile, which I returned. And a bigger kiss, which I didn't . . . exactly. I didn't want to seem unfriendly.

No potential cloning clients waited in the brightly decorated lounge today — a shame, since I'd hoped to run into Beryl Leeds and her Labs again.

Almost at once the inner door opened and Mason Payne entered. He was clad in a striped shirt and khaki cargo pants, and he immediately approached Tom and held out his hand. Then he looked at me, both recognition and confusion entering his gaze.

"Hi." I headed toward him with my hand outstretched. "We met earlier this week. I'm Kendra Ballantyne. I was hoping to find out about your cloning program for a friend, so I'm afraid I used a little subterfuge. Now, though, since I was impressed, I'm here to learn more."

More about his operations. His people. His — and their — motives for perhaps killing their comrade Earl.

And most especially, to learn if Jeff had actually been around, and if anyone here had something to do with his awful vanishing act.

"Well, welcome, Ms. Ballantyne. If you're a friend of Tom's, you're a friend of ours. Please, come inside."

Despite his kind words, Mason looked at me a little askance, his light brown eyes shadowed by shaggy silver brows. I smiled brilliantly at him, and he talked to Tom as we strolled into the inner sanctum.

The hallway we entered looked like a hospital corridor: gleaming composite floor, white walls with photos of generic outdoor scenes posted here and there — what, no doggy pictures?

We passed several closed doors that matched the walls. I wondered what was behind them.

Jeff?

Come on, Kendra. Stay cool. And sane.

"I've got the dogs for you to examine in the usual room," Mason said to Tom as we neared a bend in the hall. He looked quizzically at me.

"Can you show me any of your facility?" I inquired with an ingenuous grin. "I'd love to be able to tell my friend more about the cloning process, and whether it would be a good thing for her to continue with the idea of obtaining a duplicate of her dear dog."

"There's a lot that's classified," Mason said worriedly. "Most clients who come back here have already signed secrecy agreements."

"I doubt I'd understand anything scientific," I told him, trying to sound rueful. Legal, yes. Scientific, no. But though I wouldn't hide the fact I was an attorney, I didn't intend to volunteer the info.

Tom had no such compunction. "Her background's in law, Mason, not science or technology."

"Law?"

I gave a small shrug. "Nobody's perfect."

"I don't think this is a good idea," Mason said uncomfortably, as a door opened and two people emerged. Both greeted Tom effusively, then looked at me, as if expecting an introduction.

Which Tom quickly provided, before Mason could object. "Kendra Ballantyne, this is Melba Slabach, The Clone Arranger's chief scientist, and Wally Yance, head of public relations."

"How do you do, Kendra?" Melba said formally as she shook my hand. She was one tall lady, with dark hair pulled back severely from a face that suggested she wasn't long out of school. A plain-featured face, with small blue eyes and dominated by a broad, blunt chin. Unsurprisingly, she wore a long white jacket that made her appear even more like a scientist on duty.

"Great to have you here," Wally Yance said. He looked more military man than spin doctor, with short hair and stiff posture beneath a beige shirt and deep green slacks. His enthusiasm in shaking hands suggested he was all about appearances. Especially since he had no real idea who I was and why I happened to come calling.

"Glad to meet you both," I said effusively. "I'm really interested in the idea of cloning and would love to learn as much about it as

you're able to tell a member of the fascinated masses. Is there some place we could
talk while Tom tends to the dogs he's supposed to examine?"

I didn't even hazard a glance toward the
obviously hesitant Mason. And before the
others could answer, another door popped
open and a beautiful brunette around my
own age sailed out. "Tom!" she exclaimed.

And suddenly she was in Tom Venson's
open arms, planting one heck of a huge and
sexy kiss on his obviously eager lips.

Who the hell was she?

CHAPTER TEN

This wasn't the first time a guy with whom I'd formed some sort of romantic attachment had another lady in his life. Which of course simply supported my multi-exampled assumption that I had a huge chasm in my character when it came to choosing the right men.

Last time, it was Jeff. His ex-wife, Amanda, had barged back into his space, claiming she needed his expertise as a security guru to save her from a stalker. She'd eventually vowed to stay out of his life if I helped to clear her from suspicion in that same stalker's murder.

At least with my old law firm lover, Bill Sergement, it had been no more than poor taste, naïveté, and misplaced ambition that had attracted me to him.

Now, I simply stood there, withdrawing as much as possible with my back pressed tightly against the unyielding wall, watching. The woman continued to kiss Tom so hotly that I thought they might drop their drawers right there, in front of The Clone Arranger staff who gawked along with me in that hallway that suddenly seemed a lot too skinny.

The woman's moans of ecstasy seemed to reverberate everywhere. *Eeew! Let me out of here!*

Mason Payne cleared his throat. When that wasn't successful in separating them, he said, "Okay, Debby. Enough already."

He apparently knew her. Of course he would, since she was here in this secure facility.

And then it dawned on me. I'd heard the name Debby before, most recently in my discussion with Althea. She was Mason Payne's sister, an executive of The Clone Arranger.

Interesting development. Dr. Tom Venson, who acted as the organization's chief vet, had more than a medical reason to be there: a relationship with one of its primary people.

Which got my mind racing in all sorts of fascinating directions, assumptions . . . and suspicions.

But before I determined how to direct them, the couple finally pulled apart.

I didn't know Debby Payne, of course, but to me she seemed radiant. On second glance, I guessed her to be a year or two older than me, and a bit bulgy — well, curvy. Maybe not as attractive as I'd first thought, either, if I attempted to assess her rationally rather than emotionally. On a scale of one to ten, rated against me, I'd be about eight and she'd barely make seven. I always admitted to myself that although I wasn't the ugliest person in the universe, neither was I the most gorgeous.

"I'm so glad to see you, Tom," she gushed unnecessarily.

Tom glanced at me and had the grace to turn beet red beneath his widow's peak. "Er . . . Kendra Ballantyne, meet Debby Payne. We were engaged last year but decided it wouldn't work out."

"We're much more compatible when we're not committed to one another," Debby said with a girlish giggle inappropriate from someone of her advancing age.

Can the cattiness, Kendra, I ordered myself. *It doesn't become you, even when you keep it to yourself.* I walked forward and held out my hand. "Good to meet you, Debby. I identify with your attraction to Tom, but I'll remember not to get too committed for fear it'll end." *Meow!* And I was infinitely exaggerating my current interest.

Oh, but I got a bunch of pleasure from the sour expression that appeared on her slightly flawed face — some unfunny laugh lines at the corners of her light blue eyes, the hint of divots punctuating the area around her mouth. But then she smiled. "Hey, I love to compete. How about you?"

"Back off, both of you." That was Tom, who scowled and took several steps away from where Debby and I faced each other.

"Yeah, do that," Mason chimed in. "Tom, please go see to those dogs I told you about. Kendra . . . er . . ." He obviously was uncertain what to order me to do.

I made it easy for him. "Like I mentioned, I'd love a tour of The Clone Arranger's facilities — everything unclassified, of course. And I'd like to hear all that you can tell me about it."

Mason appeared slightly panicked until his eyes lit on Wally Yance, the P.R. person. "Wally, could you show Kendra around the client areas and answer some of her questions?"

Oh, great. I'd definitely get the spin spun to the public from him. But that didn't mean I couldn't lob a lot of cogent queries at him. A few might stick enough that I'd get some only partially devious answers that

I could follow up on.

"Of course, Mason," the man said smoothly, almost gliding up to me along the shining hallway floor. He was a little shorter than I'd initially thought, but his military mien lent him the air of more height. "This way, Kendra."

I aimed a glance toward Tom to see if he, too, was being accompanied around the facility — by his obvious admirer Debby. In fact, he was — along with Mason. The three of them headed in the opposite direction from the way Wally led me. Melba joined us — a potentially helpful thing, if I could get the group's head scientist talking. Maybe I'd learn something about why the cloning system hadn't worked for Lois. What it was that Jeff had been investigating. What he'd possibly learned that he shouldn't have . . . assuming someone here had something to do with his disappearance.

That, I couldn't ask. But I could assume some ingenuousness and address what had happened and had been on the news.

As we walked down the hall, the P.R. guy and the lady scientist on either side of me, I suddenly felt a frisson of unease. Tom knew I was here, but he was more a part of this group than I'd known. Althea understood I'd be coming here, and Lois, too. But if I happened to disappear like Jeff, who would know? Who would care?

Especially now, when I was more than a little aware that Tom's allegiances most likely didn't lie with me.

But so far, my fears were unfounded . . . I hoped. I decided to pretend they didn't exist. Still, I'd absolutely stay alert.

"You know," I said in a conspiratorial tone, "I met that poor man Earl Knox when I was here the other day. I was so surprised to hear that he had died — and even more that he was *murdered*." I stressed the word as if I was some naive member of the public impressed by the news I heard. "Do either of you know what really happened to him?"

"If we did, we'd have told the police," Wally said, as if he was being as truthful with me as with the cops . . . or the media. His expression looked utterly frank as well, as if he was on camera. "But of course we can't help thinking it was the woman who'd been talking about suing us because her dog died before her cloning was successful."

"Yes, it was really unfortunate," Melba said, sliding her hands into her lab coat pockets and shaking her head somberly. "But the poor thing was already elderly when she brought her here, and we weren't successful in our DNA extraction the first time. The client was so angry. . . ." The woman jutted her blunt chin out as if she were totally defensive and distraught about what had occurred.

I decided this was a good time to change this particular subject, or at least skew it, since I didn't want them, or anyone else, to zero in on Lois as the sole suspect. "That's what the news implied," I said. We had reached a closed door that apparently opened onto something not verboten for nobodies like me to see, since Wally reached beyond me and turned the knob. "But I also heard speculation that some people who worked with Earl didn't really like him. In fact, some were upset by the way he was telling some untruths to the people he was trying to sell cloning services to."

Wally froze and leveled a very non-P.R., angry stare at me that made me swallow. "Who told you that?"

"Oh, I heard it on one of the TV channels," I said airily. "Were you one of the people who didn't like him?" Though nervous as an animal about to have DNA extracted, I made myself smile as if half joking.

"Earl and I got along fine," Wally asserted.

I threw my glance toward my other side,

where Melba stood and fidgeted. "You, too?"

"If it's any of your business," she said icily, "yes. Earl and I were friends. I didn't talk to those horrible media people who hung around here, but they really should look into Earl's real enemies, like his awful ex-wife. Or the guy who owns the company he worked for before he came here, who claimed he stole some of their proprietary technology and turned it over to us. Which he didn't, of course."

"Of course," I said. *Yes!* I thought. Now we were getting somewhere other than in Lois Terrone's locale. "Interesting that the media didn't find out about those. Does his ex-wife live around here?"

"I doubt it's your business," Melba said in a tone filled with utter irony, "but yes. Her name is Edwina Horton. And before you ask, the company Earl used to work for is CW Ultra Technologies, located in Arcadia. Its founder and CEO is Clark Weiss. Now, do you want to see our facilities or not?"

"Absolutely." I made a detailed mental list of what I'd just learned. Sure, it was finger-pointing in a direction to thrust any suspicion away from them or anyone at The Clone Arranger, but these were new avenues to explore.

Now, if only I could ask if they'd been explored before.

By Jeff . . .

Wally had thrust the door open, and I preceded both of them through it into a vast room that was gleamingly clean. One side was lined with small, fenced-in areas, and three contained puppies!

"How cute!" I cried, dashing toward them. And then I stopped and looked back at the people who'd accompanied me here and asked the obvious. "Are they clones?"

"Yes." Melba sounded as proud as if they were her own offspring. In a way, since she was chief scientist, I supposed they were.

"They're nearly old enough to go home with their owners and older siblings," Wally said in a tone that suggested he shared a lot of satisfaction in this achievement. "That's one reason we can show them to you. All the proprietary procedures are handled in other areas of the lab. There's a lot of work that goes into creating clones, but with these little fellows that work is just about done."

I'd reached the pens and looked in at the three adorable puppies. One was a Lab, not very unlike Beryl Leeds's, but it was black instead of chocolate, so it clearly was unrelated to her older dog, Melville. Another was the sweetest tiny Yorkie. The third was a boxer that could have come from a litter raised by Marie Seidforth, a client I'd assisted in a situation where her home-owners association might have required her to forgo further boxers. As always in pet-related disputes I dealt with, I'd used ADR in Marie's situation — usually used in le-galese to mean "alternative dispute resolution," but defined by me as "animal dispute resolution."

"May I pet them?" I asked.

Permission was granted, and one by one I picked them out of their pens and hugged them.

They felt like regular puppies. Acted like regular puppies, frolicking on my lap as I sat on the cold lab floor, licking my chin, yapping, and attempting to leap away.

I laughed — a whole lot more than I had in the last couple of weeks. They were ador-able.

From the stuff I'd read, the technology behind cloning made it difficult, but not impossible, to clone dogs, at least for an arguably affordable price. But clients like Beryl Leeds obviously had the funds. Lois Terrone? She said they'd claimed to have charged her a bargain price — because they intended to harm her dog? More likely, to build up clientele and get their company established.

And some clonings clearly worked. If these endearing darlings were the result, then The Clone Arranger definitely would get public recognition soon.

Still . . . I needed more info that I hoped to get from Tom, which meant I had to keep speaking to him even after his effusive greeting by Debby Payne.

I'd initially figured Tom wasn't a legitimately likely suspect in Jeff's disappearance, since my affections were an unlikely motive. But what might Jeff have learned to undermine the apparent wonderful success of The Clone Arranger? And how would Tom have reacted to that?

And Tom had even admitted to having professional access to the drug that been used to kill Earl.

I stood, finally, and dusted myself off. "Can you tell me anything more about how cloning is done?" I asked. "As you can tell, I'm really amazed. In awe. These puppies are wonderful!"

"Come into our office and I'll give you an informational brochure," Wally said with a smile that suggested relief. I'd obviously said the right thing — implied I was impressed enough not to embarrass them or cause any trouble.

I was sure, though, that I'd get the same info that had been sanitized for public consumption, probably what I'd picked up before.

It wouldn't give me the answers I really needed: Who killed Earl Knox, and why? Had Jeff actually been here investigating, and had it led to his disappearance? If so, why?

Who was involved?

And at this moment, at least, Dr. Tom Venson wasn't just on my list of suspects. He'd taken a place of dishonor right near the top.

CHAPTER ELEVEN

There wasn't a whole lot else for me to see at The Clone Arranger that afternoon. Or at least there wasn't a whole lot else that Melba and Wally were willing to show me, considering the apparent size of this warehouse-huge facility.

I got to see one sample lab fitted out, they told me, nearly identically to the ones where DNA samples were taken from the animals to be cloned, then treated in the outfit's proprietary manner for storage or for immediate replication of pets, whatever the owner had paid for.

What they showed me was a room that could have come from a showroom of ideal veterinary paraphernalia, for all I knew. A tall table with a shining metal top sat in the middle. Pristine, presumably locked, cabinets sat at the room's periphery, and counters jutting from them contained an array of technical doodads I had no hope of

identifying. I had the sense of rarefied air —
purged of all L.A. smog or other contami-
nants, not even the usual aromas of animals
or disinfectants present in places where pets
were generally found or handled.

I received a clearly sanitized explanation
of what went on in here: a detail-free
overview of how samples were extracted and
stored and, gee, how after that they were
taken to some other very special and secret
rooms in this facility to be put under a
magic spell so, soon, someone would wave
a magic wand and say "poof!" and the result
would be an embryo of a creature identical
to the one from which the DNA had been
removed.

Well, forget the magical part. This was
solely scientific, or so they told me in a
manner designed to wow laypeople like me
without really revealing diddly squat.

"Is it true," I asked, "that the DNA has to
be removed from a living animal, like the
woman suspected of killing Earl claimed
she was told here? I've heard that it doesn't
matter in some processes, and there are
cloning companies that even preserve DNA
from dead animals for future duplication."

"It matters in our special process," Melba
confirmed without explaining the intrica-
cies, leaving me completely curious.

Eventually, I'd seen everything they'd permit me to view. I was through here . . . at least for now. Time for me to hurry out and make some notes.

Except that I couldn't depart without saying something to Tom. Something like goodbye, sure. As in *Goodbye forever, you two-timing louse.* But he wasn't actually two-timing at all, since I'd never even given him a chance to one-time with me. And one kiss, even as hot as the one Debby had laid on him, didn't mean there was much between them now. And most important of all, I'd made it clear I wasn't interested in him romantically, especially now.

But the louse part . . . well, with his involvement with The Clone Arranger, and The Clone Arranger's personnel's possible connection to Jeff's disappearance, it wasn't a huge stretch to keep Tom on that list of suspects I was about to embellish and reorganize, as soon as I got a moment to myself.

As I was very obviously being ushered toward the door, I stopped and said to Wally, "Where's Tom? I'd really like to say goodbye to him. And to Debby and Mason, too, so I can thank them for their hospitality." I was really pouring on the bread-and-butter politeness, but hey, courtesy and

171

etiquette might get me invited back, if I needed to perform further research here.

Or not, if they suspected what I actually was up to.

But since I sort of dug in my heels and refused to be herded outside, Melba said, "You can't go in the examination room where he's looking over some of our prospective clone subjects, but if you wait here, I'll go get him." Her features appeared pinched at the prospect of having to humor me, or maybe it was just because of how tightly her dark hair was pulled back from her face. Whatever, she turned her back and hustled down the hall.

We were just outside the entry lounge, and Wally insisted that we wait in there. "Might as well be comfortable," he pointed out in too boisterous a voice.

Aha — alone with a Clone Arranger at last! I agreeably entered the lounge and sat on one of the less-than-comfortable yellow-upholstered metal chairs, staring first at the one beside me and then at Wally till he got the message and took a seat. "How long have you worked for The Clone Arranger?" I asked, as if I'd searched for something to start a conversation. Which I had, sort of. Only, I had a motive for this particular madness.

"About a year," he said. "I worked for a veterinary supply company before that, also doing public relations." What a surprise.

"Do you like it here? I mean, if you worked in a similar industry before, I assume you like animals. What do you think about cloning — both scientifically and ethically?"

I knew what his canned response would be. "The Clone Arranger provides a wonderful service to pet lovers," he said, much too mushily. But he was, after all, in P.R. "And ethics? Well, I know there are controversies about cloning, especially the possibility of cloning people, but it's simply a different approach to regular old genetics. Assistance in reproduction has been around for a while, and it's a good thing, don't you think?"

Sounded somewhat like Tom's canned response. Had he learned it here? Most likely. And Wally was trying to turn the tables on me, regarding me expectantly with small, focused brown eyes, as if readying a positive response for anything negative I might say.

I decided that something argumentative wasn't in my best interests in this conversation, so I responded sort of sideways. "Well, as I said, I came here first because a friend wanted my take on cloning in general, and The Clone Arranger in particular. I'm still not sure I can form a fully informed opinion, but for the moment I can say I'm really impressed with the place and the professionalism of all of you." Not Debby Payne's libido, though. Or the fact that I didn't know enough to clear even one person from the suspicion of having killed Earl Knox.

And the whole Jeff situation? Well, I absolutely hadn't enough data to determine if there was anything related to his disappearance around here.

Before Wally could attempt to respond, the door opened once more and Tom came in — by himself. He rushed toward me and stopped as I stood. He took me by the shoulders and regarded me with an intense look that suggested he'd plant one of those sexy kisses on me, too, if I was receptive.

I wasn't. I stepped back. "Time to get on my way," I said lightly. "I wanted to say goodbye — to Mason and Debby, too." I peered around as if searching for the brother and sister behind him.

"They're on a conference call with a client," he said. "And I have one more dog to examine in the back. But, Kendra, I want to make sure we get together soon. Tonight, if possible, or tomorrow, for dinner. I want to make sure you understand that Debby and I are history."

From the corner of my eye, I saw a movement as Wally reacted in some manner — nodding or tossing his cookies, I couldn't tell at this angle.

But I made myself look up nonjudgmentally at Tom's earnest expression. "I have to say I was . . . well, not exactly thrilled," I said, as if it made all the difference in the world to me that he hadn't been entirely up-front.

Maybe, under other circumstances, it would have. But at this moment, I intended to impose invulnerability onto all my emotions. I'd have to block them to ensure I could continue with all that was on my agenda.

And since one of those things was to interrogate Tom further about his Clone Arranger involvement, I had to put on this act of innocence and hurt.

"Even so, you can call me later," I told him. "It's the weekend, and pet-sitters never rest, even if attorneys sometimes do. But I'd love to get together with you . . . I think." With that I sailed out of the lounge with a final thanks tossed over my shoulder to Wally.

My head spun as I sat down in my rental

car's uncomfortable driver's seat. Feeling eyes on me from the lounge — even without visible windows — I didn't stay to work on my lists but instead headed away from the place. As soon as I found a fast-food joint's parking lot, I pulled in, dragged out my notebook, and began jotting names, including the people I'd just met and the ones I'd been told had possible grudges against the deceased Earl Knox. I also noted impressions of the place and its facilities.

And the cute puppies I'd seen in the cloning holding area.

And then I wrote in great detail how I imagined Jeff might have approached the place had he been conducting one of his P.I. investigations. How he might have, with more skill, gone undercover as a potential customer. His assumed impressions of what he saw and who he met.

How any of them could have seen through his meticulous cover. And lured him up north to the aqueduct area and forced his Escalade into the canal.

And done — what — to him?

Imagined? Heck, I envisioned it, with each individual as a villain, or several or all as coconspirators.

Only then did I realize I was weeping. Again.

Hell! I was accomplishing nothing besides increasing my suspicions with nothing at all to hang them on. I needed facts.

And so I placed a cell phone call to the person most likely to ferret out all the facts, available or not, about the people whose names I'd noted. But it was, after all, Saturday, and Althea unsurprisingly didn't answer the office phone. She didn't answer her cell, either.

So it was up to me to do what I could myself. I had access at my office to all sorts of online databases, after all. I hurried first to Jeff's home, where I had left the hounds. I needed some loving company, which Lexie and Odin gave unstintingly when I knelt and took their furry, squirming bodies into my arms.

We took a short but successful doggy walk on Jeff's street. I cleaned up after them myself, wondering where the new poop-scooping outfit's closest employees might be. "What do you think?" I asked the dogs. "That group appears to be becoming ubiquitous, and I might get spoiled if they follow us around to take care of your leavings."

Lexie barked enthusiastically in response, almost as if she understood. Odin seemed slightly more aloof, but definitely alert, as if observing the residential neighborhood around us while looking for the poop scoopers in question.

And then the three of us squeezed into the car and headed for the Yurick offices.

Unsurprisingly, I was the only attorney there so late on that Saturday. All other lawyers at the Yurick firm were senior legal beagles who'd joined Borden because of his humane approach both in ignoring the age of his compatriots and bringing them on for their experience, and in practicing law in as enjoyable a way as possible, which usually meant no weekend work at all.

That also meant support staff was seldom around on Saturdays unless there was some real reason to be there — not just increasing anyone's billable hours.

I checked first, though, using my key to enter and finding all the lights off inside. Even so, I shouted out, "Hello? Anyone here?"

No response, not even a cry from Gigi, the sometimes resident Blue and Gold Macaw who'd belonged to a now-deceased attorney, Ezra Cossner, and who was now the pet of another proud attorney, Elaine Aames. But neither Elaine nor Gigi was here. Nor anyone else, for that matter.

Which gave me unfettered leeway to bring

in my canine companions. Not that I generally stinted anyway.

I kept Lexie and Odin leashed until we reached my really nice corner office, then let them loose after shutting the door.

I'd used Borden's database subscriptions with his okay even before joining his firm. Now, I was fully entitled to do so. And so, one by one I typed in all the names I'd gathered, and gleaned all the info I could: on Mason Payne and Debby Payne. On Melba Slabach and Wally Yance. On the people I hadn't met but who had been mentioned: Earl Knox's ex, Edwina Horton. And owner of Earl's former employer, Clark Weiss, and his company, CW Ultra Technologies.

I'd already gotten some info on Earl, but I checked him out again. And also The Clone Arranger.

I printed out a substantial amount of data. I even did some additional research on cloning and how it was supposed to work.

But I didn't get the answers I sought. And so I was relieved to finally hear from Althea.

"Kendra, sorry I didn't call you before, but I was up in the Palmdale area trying to get some more information about that damned aqueduct and anyone who'd dived into it and emerged alive."

My heart rate quickened as I leaned so hard against my desk that Lexie, now on my lap, moaned in complaint. "Sorry," I whispered, giving her a gentle hug. Then, into the phone, I said, "And what did you learn?"

I heard nothing but a sigh initially, and then, "Nothing helpful, except that my cell phone carrier apparently doesn't get a good signal up there. How about you? Have you found out anything at all?"

My turn to give her a rundown of my visit to The Clone Arranger, then of my feeble attempt at doing what she excelled at: on-line research. "I'd love for you to dig into all those much more helpful sources you have," I said to her.

"Dig . . . or hack?" she responded with a laugh.

"Whatever." When she said she had pen and paper in hand, I gave her a list of everyone and every company I'd already searched for. "I found stuff on all of them, but by the looks of it they're all model citizens with nothing to hide — and no proclivities for making P.I.s who might be investigating them disappear." My eyes welled up, and my throat all but closed.

"Yeah," Althea said, also suddenly sounding hoarse. "Well, I'll see if I can find anything more useful."

We hung up shortly thereafter, and once again I sat and started nearly to sob. Damn, but this was getting old. I hated hurting this way. But until I had some closure about what happened to Jeff . . . Hell! Closure suggested that he was gone for good, and I wasn't about to accept that.

I was grateful when my phone rang again, needing this newest diversion. It was Avvie Milton.

"Hi, Kendra," she said. "Sorry it took me so long to get back to you. Could you come now and get the key and info for watching Pansy?"

"Sure," I said, "but give me about an hour." I wanted to drop Lexie and Odin off at home.

I bundled my printed prizes from my computer searches, determined to take them along and scan them in greater detail later, in case I'd missed something important about anyone. And then I bundled the pups into the car with me.

And damned if I didn't see another Escalade as I drove out of the law firm's Encino parking lot. The driver? Looked like a lady from here.

But often, as I drove, I stared at the occupants of nearly every automobile, as if, somewhere inside one, I'd see a sign of Jeff.

CHAPTER TWELVE

No Jeffs in any car around me. I thought I counted an unusual number of small, cute, blunt-butted hybrids, mostly silver Toyotas, as I took the dogs to my place, then headed down Coldwater Canyon toward Avvie's. But these days, with the price of gas, I knew a lot more people were buying vehicles that used less of that smelly, pollution-promoting liquid.

Avvie lived on the city side of Coldwater, in a charming, small blue house with diamond-paned windows that always reminded me of a quaint European cottage. After I parked and headed up the walk toward the front door, I saw yet another silver hybrid car scoot by on this narrow but nice residential street. As I'd been doing, I checked to see if the driver happened to be Jeff.

Yeah, right. I shook my head as I rang the bell.

Avvie answered the door nearly immediately. "Kendra!" she cried, enfolding me in a hug.

I hadn't gotten together with Avvie for a while. She hadn't changed much from the attractive, coolly confident attorney who'd been my protégée way back when, at the Marden firm. I'd helped her learn to dress with elegant sophistication instead of the girlish silliness she had initially effected. She'd kept her later look, today clad in designer jeans and an attractive lacy blouse. Her highlighted hair was sleekly styled.

I glanced down at my own pale blue slacks and darker tunic top. Not bad. Conceivably even more lawyer-at-play than pet-sitter-at-work. Not that I was in competition with Avvie here and now. Or ever, even at my former firm. At least not in the dress department.

"I'm so glad to see you," she said.

"You look great, as always," I countered.

In Avvie's living room, which was decorated with an assortment of antiques, sat Pansy, the potbellied pig. She was fuzzy in black and white, porky in girth, and adorably porcine of snout.

"Watch this, Kendra," Avvie said. "See if your Lexie is as well trained." She reached into an old china tureen on a carved table beside her even more carved sofa with red velour cushions, and pulled out some kind of piggy treat. "Pansy, sit."

Pansy sat, much to my surprise. Pigs did doggy stuff? She hadn't seemed so well trained when I last pet-sat for her.

"Lie down."

She did that, too, right on the old-appearing Oriental rug in the center of the well-polished hardwood floor.

"Play dead."

"You gotta be joking," I said, even as the cute little pig collapsed into an immobile heap of ham. And I do mean ham — as in an actor who emotes too much. For nearly as soon as Pansy crumpled into stillness and even closed her eyes, those same eyes popped open, and damned if she didn't seem to smile. "Adorable!" I exclaimed.

After another minute, Avvie waved me to join her on the sofa, and we both sat. Pansy lay down by our feet.

"So how have you been, Kendra?" Avvie asked, looking at me with obvious interest in her hazel eyes. "Do you really enjoy practicing law with Borden?"

Her tone suggested a smidgen of disgust, which was how all remaining Marden lawyers seemed to regard the boss I adored, Borden Yurick. None of those high-powered, high-stress sorts seemed at all interested in enjoying the rest of life while practicing law. Neither had I, actually, until a rest was forced on me by the awful circumstances that had included accusations of unethical conduct followed by suspicions of murder.

But now, I wouldn't trade my usually enjoyable existence for even double the lucrative salary I'd brought home as a high-priced litigator for the Marden firm.

Well, maybe I'd like a little more, so I could afford to live in my rented-out house. Much as I enjoy Rachel and her dad, Russ, I want my own, bigger digs back one of these days.

"I get some interesting cases for Borden's senior citizen clients," I informed Avvie in response to her inquiry. "And my own animal advocacy stuff — can't beat it!"

"Not even with your pet-sitting?" Avvie sounded amused, in a manner suggesting mild tolerance of someone incredibly eccentric.

"That's fun, too," I admitted with a huge grin.

"If you say so. And I'm glad you do, since I want you to watch Pansy again for me." At her name, the pig lifted her head from the floor and regarded Avvie as if she understood every word. And then Avvie asked, as she had on the phone, "So, are you still seeing Jeff?"

Avvie had met him some months ago. She knew I was seeing him not solely on a professional level.

Even so, I wasn't prepared to respond.

I found myself blurting, "He's been missing for a couple of weeks, Avvie. His car was found submerged in an aqueduct canal up near Palmdale, but I just can't — won't — believe he's dead, no matter what the authorities think."

"Oh, Kendra, I'm so sorry." Avvie and I had been good professional cronies, but not of the close and huggy sort. Even so, she leaned over and gave me a squeeze. "What happened?"

I wasn't about to relate any complicated details or suspicions, so I simply wailed, "I wish I knew," and burst into tears.

Avvie sat up, then told Pansy to keep an eye on me for a minute. She returned nearly as quickly as she'd promised, large glasses of red wine clutched by the stems in her shaking hands.

"Here. We both need this — mostly you." She thrust a glass toward me, and I took a deep sip of the fruity, pungent stuff as if I was parched and it was water. So what if it was only afternoon? It was Saturday. My mind didn't have to be sharp enough to spiel legal arguments, only alert enough to drive skillfully and take excellent care of pet-sitting clients.

And stay wise enough not to reveal too much, even to this obviously sympathetic friend.

Still, I told Avvie more of the emotional stuff. It's a girl thing, I guess, to want to confide some of the hurts inside. I told her how I'd come to feel as if Jeff and I could share a future. I explained about his going off on one of his frequent trips to conduct an investigation, lecture on security, or install a security system, and how he had failed to call me — or even his office and close-knit staff — when he returned.

And how his Escalade had turned up at the bottom of the canal near L.A., when no one even knew he'd been back in town.

No one? Not necessarily true.

"You poor thing," Avvie said, her eyes filled with sympathetic tears.

"Enough about me," I made myself say. "How are you? Tell me about your big business trip with Bill this week."

Big globes of wetness suddenly cascaded down her cheeks, and she thrust them away with the backs of hands whose nails were elegantly polished, as I'd taught her. "It's a huge conference for litigators in Napa Valley. Sightseeing and wine tasting planned between continuing legal education sessions." She sucked in her breath. "Lots of attorneys are taking their spouses and significant others. Bill's wife is coming, too." She said this last with what was obviously forced brightness. "I've been too busy for a social life lately," she said, as if I'd buy into the fiction she'd created long ago when she'd first started sleeping with Bill, wife or not. "So, I'm going on my own."

"Oh, Avvie," I said. My turn to turn on the sympathy. "I'm really sorry." And I honestly was. Not because the day I'd predicted to her many times in the past had actually come to pass, but because I knew she, too, was hurting.

What a couple of sorry people we were at this moment. Good thing pets are prime in cheering humans up. Pansy rose and snuffled up to her best friend. Avvie reached down and gave her a hug.

Time for my delayed departure. Avvie handed over her keys and pet-sitting instructions.

"My contract's the same as before," I said, handing her a couple of copies, which she signed immediately, having already seen it. So did I, giving her one for her records. I'd started off sitting without using any of my legal skills — no official, asset-protecting company, no signed agreements with human customers — but when I realized that this was going to go on for a nice, long time, I formed a limited liability company, Critter TLC, LLC, and papered it with all the stuff I'd advise a client in similar circumstances to use, including insurance.

"I'm taking off first thing tomorrow morning," Avvie said.

"Have a good time," I told her. "In fact, have a great time. There're bound to be some hunky unattached male attorneys at this conference who'd love to engage in wine tasting with a lady lawyer as lovely as you." I tossed a sideways smile at her. "Imagine how much it'll gall our buddy Bill to see just how wonderful a time you're having."

"Yeah," Avvie said, appearing pensive. And then, "Yeah! Absolutely. Kendra, you're the best. And I'll keep my fingers crossed that Jeff will be back safe and sound right away."

"Thanks," I said. "Me, too."

Okay, I admit my head wasn't perfectly clear as I slipped into the car. I hadn't imbibed overly much of the wine Avvie had generously served me. As much as I thought I'd enjoy drowning my sorrows, I kept focusing on that word . . . drowning. Which kept me from wanting my mind to get totally muzzy. Slightly muzzy was more than enough.

I glanced around Avvie's pleasant residential neighborhood, which I'd visit a lot over the next several days. Unless, of course, I enlisted Rachel to spell me. She'd enjoyed her previous stint of playing with Avvie's adorable potbellied pig. In fact, I suspected she'd insist on an opportunity to visit here again when she learned of our latest Avvie assignment.

For late on a Saturday afternoon, I couldn't say the area was abuzz with activity. I didn't notice any of the neighbors out . . . except, at the home catty-cornered across the street, was that — Hey, it sure seemed to be.

I scanned the vehicles parked on the street. I didn't see any adorned with a What's the Scoop sign. But the person apparently picking up dog poop from the front yard facing Avvie's next-door neighbor sure resembled, from this distance, the younger guy I'd seen near my home the day Rachel had pointed out the newest poop scooper on our street. Not that I was certain — especially with my mind, despite my best intentions, a bit wine-clouded. But that's what I thought from the way he moved and his similar outfit, including frayed jeans, although his muscle shirt du jour wasn't white but gray.

Heck, he could be someone else altogether, even the person who lived there, out clearing his own premises of poop. But the metallic tool he used resembled those I'd seen in the hands of the What's the Scoop staff.

With a shrug, I drove off toward this evening's first pet-sitting gig: Widget, a cute terrier mix. Rachel had been his caretaker not only for midday walks, but also for morning and evening visits during a few days this week. Now it was my turn to drop in and feed and walk the adorably energetic pup, whose owner lived in a small stucco home in the northern Valley. That meant a bit of a distance to drive, but I stayed on Coldwater heading north, soon reaching the straight and flat area beyond the canyon.

I was at Magnolia Boulevard when my cell phone rang. Of course I immediately grabbed it from my purse and put it on speakerphone. I hadn't yet gotten myself a hands-free or Blue Tooth to chew on in the car even though talking on a cell phone held to your ear while driving was illegal in California.

I checked caller ID, which I recognized immediately. Not someone I wanted to speak with, but what else could I do?

"Hello, Amanda," I said formally to Jeff's ex-wife, who'd promised to stay far away from him when I kept my own promise and helped clear her of a murder accusation.

"What's going on, Kendra? Why didn't you tell me Jeff's missing? It's one thing for me to keep away from him, but that doesn't mean I don't care. I'm holding you responsible, Kendra, since he's yours now. Where the hell is Jeff?"

CHAPTER THIRTEEN

I wished I had some kind of canned response to toss out now, each time Jeff's name came up, although I would of course obtain a very different reaction from Amanda Hubbard than I had from Avvie Milton.

With my wine-misted mind, and even mistier eyes, I decided to move to the side of the road. Fortunately, I saw a small shopping center, so I pulled in and parked.

"There's not much I can tell you, Amanda," I told her. "How did you find out about Jeff?" Corina Carey's, or her cohorts', blatant attempts to blast the Escalade escapade into the news? But that was a few days ago now. Maybe Amanda had missed it, since she sounded as angry as if this was all new to her.

"Your friend the police detective, Noralles, came to my house to try to detect something," she spat into the phone. "Naturally,

I couldn't answer any of his questions. I didn't even know there was a problem, let alone have an idea of a solution. Now tell me, Kendra, what's going on? Even if you can't explain where Jeff is, you were at least aware he was missing."

"Yes," I said sadly. No use rubbing it in that she could have learned about it sooner had she paid attention to the brief media flurry. I related what little I knew, up to and including the location of his Escalade submerged in the canal up north.

"And you were going to tell me about this when?" she demanded.

"How about . . . never?" I intoned. "It really isn't your business any longer."

"Bitch!" she screeched, then hung up.

I sat for a few minutes without moving — except for those damnable tears rolling down my damp cheeks yet again. At least this confrontation had been by phone and was brief. With luck, this would end my contact with Amanda regarding this situation.

On the other hand, my luck these days was decidedly awful.

Still, as I sat there, an idea snuck into my mind. I dug into a pocket of my enormous purse and — yes! There it was. The business card handed me by Beryl Leeds at The

Clone Arranger.

I didn't imagine she lived in her P.O. box, which had a Beverly Hills zip code, but for ease of retrieving her mail, she might have selected to have it sent there because she actually resided in that upscale L.A. area.

She'd had some apparent success with The Clone Arranger. She knew the cast of characters, even the deceased Earl Knox, though she had been shown out of the visitors lounge by a more august executive, Mason Payne.

Even though I'd introduced myself under an alias to Ms. Leeds, might she nevertheless allow me to visit her and her cloned pup? I called to find out.

The answer, almost to my utter surprise, was yes. She gave me her actual address, and even directions, when I called her, so I headed there, back over the hill once more.

Unsurprisingly for someone who'd once had a starring role in a popular TV show, her house was huge, although perhaps not by Beverly Hills standards. It was on a wide residential avenue, surrounded by substantial peers. I saw it through the light-colored metal of the gate anchored into a tall wall that appeared to be marble. I parked on the nearby street, and at the gate I pressed a button on an intercom and announced myself.

The gate swung open automatically, and I trod over artistically arranged concrete pavers to the front door. There, I heard a bunch of barking while a housekeeper allowed me in and showed me into a vast living room with a vaulted ceiling, oil paintings on the walls, and burgundy leather furnishings atop a tight-woven pink rug. On one of the multiple sofas sat Beryl, surrounded by several Labrador retrievers.

Wearing slender blue jeans with a loose, lacy top, she rose gracefully at my entrance, and the dogs slipped onto the floor and approached me. "So you're Kendra Ballantyne, and not Kenni Ballan?" she inquired with a laugh. Her arched brows, slightly darker than her pale brown, well-styled hair, rose in apparent amusement. "Why the subterfuge at The Clone Arranger?"

I had stooped to pet the pups. Two were pale in color, one full-grown and one clearly young — original and clone, I supposed. The third was the chocolate Lab I'd met before, Melville. He seemed to take stock of who I was — a friend, Beryl reminded him when he didn't act especially sure at first. Then he settled down and let me pat him. Beryl confirmed her fur kids' identities and the pup's origin before I responded to her question.

"I'll be frank, Beryl." I waited while her housekeeper served us steaming, strong-smelling coffee in floral china cups, then left the room. I continued, "I'm an acquaintance of Lois Terrone, the woman identified in the media as a person of interest in Earl Knox's death."

Any semblance of amusement immediately disappeared from Beryl's attractive, midforties face. "Then why should I speak with you?" she asked as coldly as if the room suddenly swirled with snow.

"Because I'm seeking the truth. If it helps to clear Lois, all the better, but if not, that's the way it is." I took a sip of coffee. Definitely strong. I felt the caffeine skateboard through my veins, eradicating any remaining effects of my earlier sips of wine. "I was at The Clone Arranger that day with a friend's dog, since I wanted to learn about the business. Lois was upset because she believed they had something to do with the death of the beloved dog she had brought there to be cloned. Meeting you, and hearing how satisfied you were with their work, made me more inclined to believe that what happened to her dog was unfortunate but unrelated to her handling there." Not entirely true, but it made Beryl's frozen features start to relax, allowing her accordioned crow's-feet to loosen up.

"That's right," she said softly. "I'd heard from Mason and some of the others about that poor woman, their lack of success in that particular cloning, and how upset she was when her dog died. But you can see how wonderful their results can be. Come here, Cartwright," she crooned to the Lab puppy with the large feet. Cartwright wriggled his way over to his mistress, his DNA-identical dad, Churchill, right behind.

They did look alike, despite the difference in their ages. Both were similar shades of off-white, with alert brown eyes, slim builds, and adorable and intelligent faces.

"And you didn't have any trouble with Churchill about having his DNA removed, however they do it, or health issues afterward?"

"Not a one," Beryl replied firmly, with Labs on her lap once more. "And that woman — Lois? She talked about making trouble for them, and I, for one, was really perturbed. I'd planned on doing testimonials, not just on their website — whatever was necessary to help The Clone Arranger keep doing its wonderful work. We've even discussed my doing an infomercial on their behalf."

"I understand," I said. Then had to ask, "Since you're a treasured customer of long standing, did The Clone Arranger ever explain their method of cloning to you?"

She scowled. "Even if they did, I'd hardly tell you, Kendra. It's highly secret." She brightened once more. "But my expertise is acting, so I doubt I'd understand the finer points of cloning anyway. I just paid them, then received my darling duplicate puppy dog. And believe it or not, they charged less than some other outfits I heard about, including one that went out of business. In any event, I'm expecting a baby and I'll be able to bring it home in a few months, assuming everything went well with Melville, and so far I'm told it did."

The chocolate Lab, who'd stayed with me while I stroked behind his ears, apparently heard his name and headed for his mistress.

I had only one more question to ask. "Did you happen to see anyone at The Clone Arranger who might have . . . well, perhaps been jealous of Earl? Or angry with him? Or —"

"You mean, my dear," she said drolly, "did I happen to see anyone who had it in for him enough to kill him, to take the heat off your friend Lois? The answer is no. Everyone got along fine."

Not exactly the answer I'd hoped for, but I had gotten a lot out of my interview with Beryl Leeds. As I'd believed before, she was one happy customer of The Clone Arranger. She'd seen suitable results.

Did that mean Lois's complaints, and Jeff's ensuing investigation, had been inappropriate?

I wasn't quite willing to go that far . . . at least not yet.

On my way back from Beverly Hills, I received another cell phone call. Okay, I was a lawyer. Getting a call from a frantic client, even on a Saturday afternoon, wasn't entirely unanticipated. It definitely acted as a distraction from all the other, worse stuff churning around in my life.

It was Corbin Hayhurst of Show Biz Beasts, who said they'd been contacted by some of their unhappy customers and were told to expect service of an official lawsuit complaint the following week. "What should we do, Kendra?" he all but wailed. "I thought you said there wasn't any basis for someone to sue us."

"No reasonable basis," I confirmed. "The thing is, under our legal system, people can sue each other for unreasonable stuff, and it's up to the defense to show how stupid it all is."

"Then you'll fix it?"

"I'll certainly do my damnedest," I equivocated as I pulled the car up to my first late-day pet-sitting spot. "But nothing in the law is certain." At his silence, I said, "Tell you what. I'll come see you tomorrow and we'll talk about it some more."

"At my expense at your hourly rate," Corbin grumbled, but we nevertheless set a time, late morning. So what if it was Sunday? Weekends meant little in the la-la land of L.A.

The distraction of that client call assisted me in temporarily ignoring the whole Jeff situation — or so I told myself. In fact, I enjoyed my pet-sitting, then my post-dinner games with Lexie and Odin. Odin's injury still seemed to be healing well. At least it looked good, and certainly didn't prevent him from playing.

Later, we got together with Rachel and Beggar at my rented-out abode, and Rachel and I compared notes for our animal care the upcoming week.

Fortunately for me, and sadly for her, her exciting upcoming auditions had been postponed. But at least her dad, Russ, would be back in the area, which was always a good thing for her development of additional film industry contacts.

No post-shower phone calls that night, so my heart rate remained stable. My sleep quotient stayed low, though, so I got up and worked on my lists of anything new I could think of relating to Jeff and his vanishing act — which at that point wasn't much. I booted up my computer, too, but mostly played solitaire, as I soon realized I'd already researched the same old stuff on my lists: cloning, The Clone Arranger, its personnel, Jeff Hubbard, Hubbard Security, Lois Terrone . . . I was fast running into a rut.

So what else could I get into? My legal cases, of course. My favorite involved my relatively new attorney avocation of ADR: animal dispute resolution. What could I do to get the dissatisfied customers of Show Biz Beasts to calm down and call off their proposed lawsuit? Nothing sailed off the computer screen and into my tired mind, but at least I'd set my subconscious back onto that particular path . . . I hoped.

Eventually, I snuggled into my bed, solo except for the cuddliest of canines, Lexie and Odin. The next morning, I intended to take my charges along on pet-sitting so I wouldn't be alone in the car. As we prepared to pile into my rental car, I noticed my neighbor across the street, Phil Ashler, out walking his relatively new rescue dog, Middlin — middle-size and a middling shade of brown. I hurried to the wrought iron fence to say hi — about the same time he was greeted by the older poop scooper who was exiting the minivan with the Where's the Scoop sign on the side. Where was he working around here this morning? I assumed that Rachel had intended that he clean up on my property only once a week, and same thing with Phil and Middlin.

"Hi, guys," I called out as Lexie and Odin leaped against the fence beside me, obviously excited at the sight of Middlin.

"Kendra!" exclaimed Phil. My retired neighbor wore a baggy yellow T-shirt that emphasized his sallow complexion. He approached the fence with Middlin, which caused Lexie to slink into submission, but the more assertive Akita, Odin, stood his ground. Good thing the fence wouldn't let any of the canines get closer together. "Good to see you," he said. "How've you been?"

"Just fine," I lied. Our buddyship remained more of a social acquaintance, so I didn't intend to tell him about the awful stuff in my life just now.

"Have you met Juan?" he asked, nodding toward the gray-haired, stooped guy in the straw hat whom I'd seen poop-scooping before.

"Not officially, but I've seen him at work." I stared at him, although Juan was clearly reluctant to meet my eye. There was something about him — something besides his smelly profession — that captured my attention. "My tenant has hired your company, Juan, although someone else was working here the other day."

He nodded, shooting me a smile that showed stained teeth, then hurrying to open the back of his van.

"Maybe I'll see you here," I called out, wondering why I bothered to bother the guy.

"I don't think he speaks much English," Phil confided softly. "But he seems to do a good job."

I nodded, said goodbye to Phil, and collected the excited dogs for our morning's activities. But my distraction of the previous night had somehow been disturbed. Why? What kept bringing the missing Jeff to the forefront of my mind?

Gee, Kendra, could it be that you care about him?

Okay, I told my sarcastic self, *enough.* But that didn't keep me from staring at nearly every driver or pedestrian I passed, just to see if there was any resemblance to my missing lover.

I gave Stromboli a whole lot of extra attention that morning. Piglet the pug, too. And I even played piggy games with Pansy, since I hadn't turned the potbellied pig over to Rachel as one of her charges just yet. But even with Lexie and Odin along, my emotions kept swirling sadly.

As a result, I decided that human hugs were in order before facing my law clients at Show Biz Beasts with as few answers as I had, so after we completed our pet-sitting rounds, we headed for Doggy Indulgence.

Sure, it was Sunday. But several months ago my buddy Darryl had caved in to film industry pressure and started opening on weekends. After all, filming occurred all the time.

His staff was smaller on weekends, though, so my skinny buddy in the Doggy Indulgence shirt — one in bright red for a change — himself manned the front desk in the vast room with its multiple canine corners. "Kendra!" he cried as the dogs and I came through the door. "Good to see you . . . what are you doing here?"

"Damned if I know," I said sadly, releasing the hounds so they could join the other

doggies doing whatever they wished —
within reason.

"Ah, that tells me a lot. Hold on." Threading his way among doggy clients who surrounded his feet, he made his way out of the main area toward the kitchen. Soon, he emerged with a couple of employees who took his place near the entry. "Come into my office," he said. And then, when we were seated, "You look even more awful than before. Kendra, you either have to find Jeff and figure out that murder fast, or forget them both."

"Tell me about it," I retorted dejectedly.

"I just did. Look, isn't there anything else you can work on to take your mind off them?"

"That's one reason I'm here. The first reason, by the way, was that I was seeking sympathy from my best friend."

"You got it, kiddo." He rose from behind his desk and held out his arms. I walked into them and was enfolded in a big and comfy bear hug.

"That helps," I said to him as I backed off a bit. "The other reason I'm here is that I thought you might enjoy coming along to the law clients I need to visit now."

"Who's that?" he inquired, with frank curiosity shading his brown eyes behind wire-rimmed specs.

"You referred me to them: Show Biz Beasts. I'll have to hold a confidential attorney-client session with them while we're there," I warned, "but —"

"Count me in," Darryl exclaimed.

As before on her home training turf, semi-frumpy Shareen seemed almost elegant in slim jeans and a sleeveless T-shirt as she led a pack of dog owners in training their pets to pull loads. Prospective on-camera mushers and Iditarod hounds who would most likely never come in contact with the real ice-cold terrain of Alaska nevertheless took to harnesses and commands as if they truly raced along Arctic routes. Never mind that their trail was in fact one end of the large industrial soundstage-like building that housed Show Biz Beasts, and their turf was artificial grass hidden under mounds of fake scenery ice and snow.

I'd brought Lexie and Odin on their leashes, and, amazingly, my adorable Cavalier appeared to recall her lesson here the other day. When I signaled her to sit, she sat.

Odin, on the other hand, the true scholar the other day, appeared excited to join the class and pretend to be a strong sled dog. I first ran him fast through the paces he'd learned, to show Darryl his skills. Then he gave a few good yanks until Darryl showed him who the alpha dog was in their two-member pack, and shoved him gently back into the sitting position.

We watched the pseudo sledders slide through their paces, including Dorky, the dog who belonged here. Darryl's grin appeared as large as mine felt. What an appealing display of doggy derring-do. Round and round the staging area they raced, their owners shouting and acting as if they were out to win the most renowned of all icy races.

Eventually the race ended, and only then did I realize that the musher at the head of the pack was Corbin Hayhurst himself, his short height and wide girth hidden beneath his costume of heavy parka, boots, and bulky slacks — not exactly de rigueur L.A. wear, even inside a mock soundstage.

He handed off his team of hounds to an attendant and approached me, as his wife Shareen did the same.

"This is fantastic!" Darryl exclaimed. "I knew you trained animals for all kinds of shows, but this . . . this beats everything I've ever seen on TV or otherwise." He seemed so excited that Odin stood up on his hind legs and issued a shrill bark, not something the staid Akita generally did.

Lexie, still on the leash I held, looked askance at her companion, as if unsure how to take his reaction.

Soon, I left the dogs in Darryl's capable care as I followed Shareen and Corbin out of the training room and into their office. Unsurprisingly, considering the kind of business it was, the walls were covered with photos from all kinds of films, from independents to big blockbusters. Each had animals involved, mostly dogs, but also cats and birds and even an iguana, which earned an extra smile from me as it reminded me of Saurus, a pet I'd sat for and who'd been the subject of a petnapping that was successfully resolved.

We discussed the latest salvo from some of their dissatisfied customers since Shareen and Corbin had been informed that a lawsuit complaint had been filed and would be served next week unless Show Biz Beasts anted up and got all their former students placed in films.

"Which isn't going to happen," Corbin exploded from behind his shiny black metal desk. He'd shed his outdoor outfit and looked more comfy, in loose blue jeans and a muscle shirt that revealed his flab.

"You know we always tell people in advance how fickle the industry is." Shareen shook her head. Her frown emphasizing parallel wrinkles in her forehead, she sat in an uncomfortable gleaming metal chair that matched mine.

They said nothing new, and I'd no assurances to comfort them with. "We'll just need to look at the complaint when it's served," I said, "unless you think of a way to appease them with film or TV appearances, or even just auditions."

Which was when the germ of an idea started to percolate deep within my mind. I wondered . . . well, I'd run the thought by my down-to-earth friend Darryl before I mentioned it to the Hayhursts, or followed it up by contacting other people I knew.

"That's all?" Corbin sounded extremely miffed. Of course I knew why — or at least part of it.

I didn't want to get his hopes aroused, but I did say, "Tell you what. Today's visit here is on me, especially since I really enjoyed watching the end of your class. But I need to do some research regarding an idea I have about your case. Okay?"

"Okay," Shareen said hastily, aiming an irritated glance at her husband, who was obviously about to protest.

"Just keep the billable time under control," Corbin grumped, and I assured him I would.

A short while later, Darryl and I again occupied the front seat of my car, with the dogs settled in the back.

I told Darryl what had come to my mind, and he whistled. "I love it!" he all but shouted. "Not only that, I've got some suggestions, too." And they were all extraordinarily good ones that encompassed an even greater solution than I'd imagined. One that could have far-reaching effects for a whole lot of people I knew.

"But like Shareen said, we all know how fickle the industry is," I cautioned him after we'd brainstormed for a while.

"Yeah, but it helps to have contacts," he reminded me. "And both of us do."

I laughed, and for the rest of the ride back to Doggy Indulgence I felt a whole lot lighter in spirit than I had for many days.

But as I left Lexie and Odin off to spend a few hours enjoying themselves at the doggy resort, I realized that my now uncharacteristic cheerfulness was extremely fleeting. In fact, it fled as I returned alone to my rental car.

There was a potentially extremely unpleasant place I needed to go . . . right now.

CHAPTER FOURTEEN

Okay, *needed* to go was a little strong. *Wanted* to go wasn't exactly accurate, either. *Felt compelled to go* . . . that was most precise.

I had learned from Melba Slabach, head scientist at The Clone Arranger, about a couple of people who'd had it in for Earl Knox but had nothing to do with that company. One was Earl's ex-wife, Edwina Horton, and the other was his ex-employer, Clark Weiss, owner of CW Ultra Technologies. I'd obtained information, including contact data, about both of them on the Internet, confirmed and enhanced by Althea.

Since it was Sunday, I didn't anticipate the CW behind CW would be at his offices. That meant my visit would need to be to Edwina.

I forbore at first from calling her from my cell phone as I sat in my rental car in the Doggy Indulgence parking lot and pondered my moves. I was a whole lot uncertain how to play this particular interview. How to get the woman to confirm she was home. How to get her to talk to me, when I'd no genuine credentials beyond being an attorney and pet-sitter. The latter wouldn't get me any kind of audience unless she had a pet that might require sitting. Even then, if I came on an ostensibly uninvited sales call, it wouldn't necessarily get her to open her door, let alone open up about her relationship with her ex — and any remaining motive to dispose of him.

If I admitted I was an attorney? Then perhaps I'd have to profess to represent someone with an interest potentially adverse to her. Or an estates and trusts expert representing an estate from which she was likely to inherit?

Earl was deceased and could have left an estate. But I didn't have enough info on him or his assets to make a credible, if fraudulent, claim of representing his heirs.

Before I came to any kind of conclusion, I called Althea.

She sounded more down than ever before. Afraid to ask, I did anyway. "Have you heard anything about Jeff?"

"No. Have you?"

"Unfortunately, no. But I'm not giving up,

215

Althea, and neither should you." I glared out my windshield at the cars slinking by on Ventura Boulevard. A big commercial cleaner's van. An SUV as large as an Escalade but of a foreign make. A little silver hybrid — another one. Sedans of many makes and colors.

Nothing worth watching.

"Of course not," Althea said a whole lot too heartily, so I knew that was the direction she was diving into. And if always upbeat Althea thought Jeff wasn't coming home . . .

No! I still wasn't about to go there. I wouldn't make any assumptions about his whereabouts. I'd consider him gone forever only when — no, *if* — the authorities came up with an identifiable corpse. And that wasn't going to happen.

"Hey, I called for advice and a favor," I informed her. I explained my dilemma about Earl Knox's ex. "I've acted as an apprentice private investigator before, under the aegis of Jeff's license. Can I do that when the guy holding the credentials can't vouch that I'm a student?"

"Sure," Althea asserted. "A couple of the guys here were close enough to get their licenses, and Buzz Dulear has already applied."

"Really?" He hadn't mentioned it on our outing to see the drowned Escalade. "I thought his expertise was in security equipment."

"It is, but he figured it would be a good thing to become an official P.I., so he's been working on it. Now, it's even more critical, so he's started pushing. I'm sure he'd be willing to say you're working for Hubbard Security on this investigation. Heck, the cops aren't doing much good. We need all the help we can get to get our head honcho back in the fold again."

"Amen." I told her I'd keep in touch.

And then I placed my call to Edwina.

She lived in a condo in Pasadena, near the bustling area of Old Town. When I was growing up in L.A., the area was old and run-down, but it had been restored and was now a really popular locale.

Which meant Edwina's penthouse condo might have cost as much as my rented-out home. No matter. I wasn't here to compare assets but to extract information.

The opulent lobby, complete with plush rug, silk-upholstered seating, and crystal chandeliers, had a security desk that must have been manned full-time. When I identified myself to the uniformed lady guard and gave the name of the resident I was there to see, she immediately placed a call. After a few words into the phone, she smiled and pointed me toward an elevator whose door was just opening — thanks to her control, I presumed.

I doubted it would stop at any floor but the top, which was where Edwina's flat was located. I didn't bother pushing any of the other buttons, since my curiosity was less intense than my need to talk to the woman.

Did I imagine she'd offed her ex-husband? I sort of hoped so. Domestic quarrels were most likely to lead to a killing. But my research and Althea's had indicated the Knoxes had been divorced for three years. Court records — Althea's bailiwick, not mine — showed that the property settlement had been handled then, and there'd been no resurrection, at least not officially, of any gripe or unhandled claim. There'd been no kids, so no complaints about custody or support. Edwina and her current husband owned a franchise for a tony clothing store. No apparent need for her to demand spousal support, at least not now.

So if there'd been some kind of disagreement that might provide a motive for murder, I'd have to try to figure that out by digging as deep as possible into Edwina's soul, since nothing stood out on the surface.

The elevator door slid open almost silently, except for the *ding* signaling my arrival on the designated floor. I stopped outside the appropriate entry and pressed the doorbell.

"Who's there?" resounded a voice via an intercom. Heck, she knew who it was. The guard downstairs had already announced me.

Even so, I played along. "This is Kendra Ballantyne, Ms. Horton. We spoke on the phone about an hour ago." *As if you didn't know.*

"Just a moment," she said, but that moment grew into a minute, then three. Was this a kind of game to assert alphaness like a canine? Well, I was alpha enough myself to play along — then nip when it made sense to take control.

Finally, the door opened. The woman who stood there was slightly shorter than me, slightly younger than me, and a whole lot more stylish, despite the fact that I was wearing jeans I'd paid a fortune for and a pretty, silky top. Oh, she had on jeans, too, but they were so worn in strategic areas that they screamed of a high-end label. Her blouse all but flowed in its exotic floral print. A sweet yet spicy designer scent filled the air around her. All products from the trendy store she owned with her current hubby? A logical assumption — and I was nothing if not a logical lawyer. And prime pet-sitter. And intelligent pseudo investigator.

"Ms. Ballantyne?" she said in a low and dramatic tone. "Could you please state your business again?"

Come on, I wanted to say. No way would she have forgotten our earlier conversation. But telling her off wouldn't get me inside her door. Instead, I said in a tone worthy of the excellent litigator I was, "I'm here to discuss your former husband, Earl Knox. I work with Hubbard Security, and we're conducting our own investigation into his untimely death. May I come in? I don't think this is the kind of conversation you'll want to have in a hallway."

She blinked shifty brown eyes that were skillfully made up to look larger than they were. Her mouth was all shimmering pout, and I suspected that Botox and she were not strangers. "Earl and I divorced several years ago. I doubt I can tell you anything helpful."

"Please let me be the judge of that." Since she had neither invited me inside nor moved beyond her entry, I figured I'd do what was most inclined to embarrass her. "Okay, then, suppose you tell me how you met Mr. Knox in the first place."

To my great delight, a neighbor's door opened and an older couple started inching down the hall. They'd get an earful if I didn't get my entry invitation.

Obviously, Edwina thought so, too. "Please come in," she all but huffed.

"Thank you," I said, oozing earnest etiquette.

Inside, her condo looked as if it had been decorated for drama, all decked out with gorgeous, modern furniture that could have been featured in an issue of *Architectural Digest*. And maybe it had been. That wasn't a magazine I went out of my way to indulge in. Most of the stuff was in shades of white, which suggested that she either had no pets at all, or that what she had was white, too — a Bichon Frise, or a mini-poodle, perhaps. A snooty white kitty would fit, too. But nothing came out to greet or sneer at me. And I'd learned in my life that I thought a whole lot more of people who loved animals than those who didn't.

Edwina's gait was all grace as she waved me toward her pristine living room and onto a white sofa. This woman had been married to the unsophisticated promotional person

221

from The Clone Arranger? An odd match. No wonder it had come to an end.

She lowered herself into a chair that actually had some color to it — pale pink, a fitting foil to the plainness of the other stuff. "So what can I tell you, Ms. Ballantyne?" She looked at me expectantly until her brow puckered in a small frown beneath her short, well-highlighted hairstyle. "No, wait. You tell me first who hired you. Is it that woman who threatened Earl's employer because they supposedly hurt her dog?"

"I'm sorry," I said, "but I'm not at liberty to reveal my client's name." I kept my expression neutral, trying to interject professionalism. "I'm also an attorney, and confidentiality is paramount in this situation."

"I'm not sure I want to talk to you then." She crossed her arms stubbornly and leaned back, her smug face conveying a challenge similar to her words.

"That's certainly your prerogative right now," I said. "But of course if litigation results, you'll be subpoenaed, and then you will need to respond. On the other hand, if we receive the kinds of answers that lead to conclusions other than those we believe are in order, there may not be any litigation, and therefore no subpoenas."

My turn to shoot her a smug look. Which

obviously worried her, since she frowned again.

"All right, ask what you want, and I'll decide whether to answer."

"Fair enough." I started slowly and way in the past, asking about how they'd met: in college. He'd been a computer science major, and she — big surprise — had gotten a degree in fashion design. They'd fallen for one another. Who knew what caused serious vibes between two so different people? They married. They fought. They divorced.

Nothing extraordinary there. Nothing suggested that this woman had any emotions strong enough even to consider slaying a former mate, for any reason.

Still, I started asking her about Earl's prior job with CW Ultra Technologies and his former boss, Clark Weiss.

Suddenly, Edwina's demeanor darkened. "That bastard! You talk about a horrible person, someone Earl could have killed — or even I could. He screwed Earl over horribly, and then accused *him* of stealing. Go ahead, Ms. Ballantyne, if that's why you're here. Ask me who I think killed Earl."

"Okay," I began. "Who do you think —"

"Clark Weiss. If it wasn't that nutty woman who had a grudge against The Clone Arranger, then it was Clark Weiss who killed poor Earl."

CHAPTER FIFTEEN

Well, hell. I knew Edwina could have been making up a motive for Clark Weiss to have killed Earl simply as a ruse to remove herself from my list of suspects.

Even so, I bit — or at least allowed her to believe so. "What do you mean?" I tried to sound as if I was in utter shock.

"If you're really an investigator, you've got to know something about Earl's background. Right?"

"My investigation isn't complete," I retorted defensively. "If it was, I wouldn't be here asking questions, would I?"

"How should I know?" The woman flicked manicured fingernails toward me as if she didn't give a damn. "But if you were any good, you should have done your homework. Earl worked for CW Ultra Technologies before joining The Clone Arranger. CW stands for Clark Weiss."

"That part I got," I responded dryly.

"What did Earl do there?"

"The company is an umbrella composed of many separate businesses, mostly to do with medical research, including pharmaceuticals. They raise private funds and invest in other organizations conducting research. More important, they figure out areas where knowledge is needed but lacking, find people skilled in those areas, and hire them to come up with the next generation of . . . whatever. That includes things like DNA duplication for medical purposes, and testing for law enforcement forensics, for example."

Aha! DNA. I perceived the link between CW Ultra Technologies and The Clone Arranger.

"I can see from your expression that you see where I'm headed, Ms. Ballantyne."

"Kendra," I corrected. I'd learned that I'd elicit a whole lot more from people when we seemed to be on a friendly, first-name basis.

"Whatever." She waved pink-polished fingernails toward me again. "Anyway, Earl started with a pharmaceutical sales company and worked his way into management, and that background is why Clark Weiss hired him. But Earl was fascinated by DNA research and technology. He hung around the laboratories where CW scientists worked with DNA and cloning research, coming up with all kinds of ideas for going forward with the stuff. But Clark got upset with Earl for not sticking to what he'd been hired to do — sales and management for existing technologies, not research and development. Clark even took away some of his vacation days that he claimed Earl owed him for wasting company time."

"Then Earl helped to develop their DNA technology?"

"I don't think so," Edwina contradicted, "but he wanted to. Since the DNA stuff intrigued him, he left when he found a job at The Clone Arranger, where they weren't as structured as CW. He still excelled in sales, but he was allowed to make suggestions about the company's direction. Of course, The Clone Arranger had its own technology already."

"Really?"

"That didn't keep Clark from making claims against Earl that he'd stolen proprietary processes from CW. Even threatened a lawsuit."

"But if Clark thought he had enough evidence to pursue a legal claim against Earl — and, presumably, against The Clone Arranger — why would he kill Earl?"

Edwina glared as if I was the stupidest person in the room. Which in this instance, on this topic, she might be correct — not that I'd admit it to myself, let alone her. "Because a lawsuit would be slow and expensive, and the outcome wasn't guaranteed. But when Earl talked to my husband, Marty, and me about what he was doing at The Clone Arranger, at least at first, he got all happy, the way he used to when we were married and he wanted to rub my nose in something he thought he knew more about than I did."

She frowned and stuck that small, possibly artificially reduced, nose in the air. Okay, sue me for cattiness, but I was definitely amenable to criticizing this snotty — er, snooty — lady.

"Only at first?" I asked.

"Oh, you know how things go after the honeymoon period is over, even on jobs. And I didn't talk to him a lot. But when I did, he never complained about his new company — not much, at least."

I slipped in several more questions, but I thought I'd heard nearly enough. One thing I felt a little deflated about was that she had seemed genuinely caring in this conversation about her ex-husband. Friendly, at least. I couldn't quite conceive of her offing him.

Too bad her current husband wasn't there for me to interrogate. If she had stayed mightily fond of her first mate, husband number two could have considered he had a real reason to off Earl.

"Oh, one more thing," I said, shrugging as if I actually intended this most telling question of all to be offhand. "Did Earl ever mention to you anything about an investigator, maybe hired by Clark" — or anyone else, such as Lois Terrone — "snooping around The Clone Arranger?"

Edwina once more furrowed her forehead, then quickly wiped away telltale crinkles along with any facial expression. "He did mention that once The Clone Arranger's promotion started to work, there were always people nosing around, wanting more information — the media, outfits that had started cloning before The Clone Arranger, even others who thought cloning was against the natural scheme of things. Some apparently went so far as to hire people as snoopy as you." Her grin was more than a tiny bit sly.

"Everyone wants in on a good thing," I said with a smile I hoped was equally slimy. I rose and started for the door. "Thanks for speaking with me, Edwina. I'll be in touch again if I have any more questions. Oh, and I'd love to visit your boutique. Do you have a card?"

Do dogs under my aegis poop, even at inopportune times? Just as silly a question. Of course she did, and she even had it handy, in a small holder on a table near the entry.

But if I ever elected to visit said shop, I'd arrive only after a prior phone call to see if Marty was available to talk. And without a credit card. That way, I wouldn't be tempted — much — to interrupt my talking time by shopping for high-end apparel I couldn't afford anyway on my limited, unlucrative law-and-pet-sitting income.

Back in my way-less-than-Beamer rental car, I called Althea's cell phone, despite the fact that it was Sunday.

"Where are you, Kendra?" she demanded, then asked the usual. "Have you learned anything about Jeff?"

"No," I said sadly. "I gather you haven't, either." But I didn't wait for her negative response before asking, "Can you give me the address for CW Ultra Technologies?"

Sure, it was Sunday and the business was unlikely to be open. But if it happened to be on my way, or not too far out of it, I'd drive by just to get a sense of how successful it appeared from the outside.

Althea informed me that its office was in Arcadia. That upscale town a little east of Pasadena was not far from my current locale. I decided to drive by and scope the site out for future, deeper scrutiny, then head back to pick up the pups and take off on the evening's pet-sitting.

I got onto the freeway once more. I had to travel only two exits, then head about half a mile on commercial surface streets.

The structure that housed CW Ultra Technologies was a typical three-story office building in an area filled with similar ones. With all its windows, it didn't resemble a laboratory at all. Except for me, the parking lot was empty, and I supposed that even if the place had a guard instead of a security system, I wouldn't be able to talk myself in . . . would I? But then what? Even if I assumed that digging into unknown files could yield useful results, I needed a better sense of what I'd be looking for. That meant speaking with someone — such as CW himself — first. But if I alerted him to my quest, might I ever have an opportunity to get this near to the place again, let alone snoop in the paperwork?

Before I reached a real decision what to

do, I saw in my side-view mirror yet another silver hybrid vehicle. It hadn't turned into the parking lot, as I had, but stayed on the street, in a spot along the curb.

Boy, that kind of car was proliferating around L.A. — or was I seeing only one? The tinted windows and distance to where I sat prevented me from scoping out the driver. Not that I'd necessarily be able to compare him or her with any previous hybrid driver who'd come into my view lately. But with Jeff's disappearance and Earl Knox's killing, paranoia had asserted a major appearance in my brain.

Was I being followed? If so, why? And was I in any danger?

Heck, how could I assume otherwise with everything else that had happened?

I pulled my cell phone from my purse to keep it handy. The area was too deserted to expect any assistance from a Good Samaritan passing by. Sure, there was a beige mini-van parked ahead along the street, but I didn't see its driver. My nervousness seemed way misplaced. Even so, I told myself to keep a cool head and a realistic path for flight. I scoped out the parking lot and saw an exit on the opposite side from where I'd entered.

In case the person in the hybrid could see

me better than I could see inside that vehicle, I pretended nonchalance, checking my makeup in the cosmetic mirror on the visor — and also using it to see if there was any possible assistance behind me.

Not.

All I viewed was my own wide blue eyes. Was that fright I perceived in them? Well, yeah — sunken into their sockets in my face that seemed a lot more plain than usual in its pallor. Oh, well. Beauty wasn't a prerequisite for getting out of a potentially perilous situation. Assuming all this wasn't my own overactive imagination.

Which it most likely was. So what if the car was still there?

Even so, as fast as I could, I shoved up the visor and at the same time turned on the engine, gunning it until I sped out the far side of the parking lot and onto the nearest street. There, I ignored any speed limits and hied my low-powered rental vehicle as fast as it could go back onto the freeway.

Where, wisely or not, I felt a whole lot less threatened. Safety in numbers and all that, since traffic was typically horrible, even for late on a Sunday afternoon.

I kept my eyes open to my surroundings and the occupants of all the autos around me as I headed back toward Studio City.

Did that guy in the dented red pickup truck have a resemblance to Jeff around the strong chin? Nah, not really.

How about the fellow in the jade-colored Jaguar who passed me as if I was standing still? Which I was, in this traffic. Who could tell, at his speed?

My emotions were clearly overwrought.

Talk about keeping an eye open for a would-be rescuer — well, that would have been Jeff, had he been somewhere reachable. Now, I was simply grasping at flimsy straws of fading hope.

I turned on the car radio and listened to a modern middle-of-the-road station to help calm my shattering nerves.

And soon reached the exit closest to Doggy Indulgence. At last.

The light turned red at the bottom of the ramp, so I stopped and stared into my rearview mirror.

No silver hybrid. Thank heavens.

I headed toward Ventura Boulevard and Darryl's delightful doggy spa. I dared to relax and consider my plans for the pending evening. At the next traffic light, I thumbed through my pet-sitting journal to remind myself of which clients required visits and the kind of care they anticipated. Evening meals? Of course, for everyone.

In a couple of minutes I pulled into Darryl's parking lot. It wasn't filled, at least not as much as on weekdays, but I gathered there were still sufficient seekers of doggy day care on this Sunday to merit its staying open.

I parked in the area I always preferred, toward the far end of the lot, where my Beamer had been less likely to get dinged. If only I'd anticipated its smashing fate. . . .

As I turned off the engine, I saw a movement toward the boulevard and glanced that way.

A silver hybrid car parked there, blocking the only viable exit.

Coincidence? Could be. If not, who was in it? What did they want? Was I about to somehow share Earl Knox's fate? Unlikely. It was too far away for the occupant to inject me with ketamine. And there was no viaduct near here for anyone to attempt to drown me, although the Los Angeles River was nearby — or at least the dry channel where water flowed during the rainy season, which seldom included May.

Darryl was my closest friend, in more ways than one at this moment as I sat outside his building. If I was in genuine danger and not simply hallucinating, I didn't want to involve him.

The cops were a better idea — I could at least invoke Ned Noralles's name. I started to press in 911, when I noticed that a beige minivan had pulled close behind the hybrid and started honking its horn. Surely not the same one I'd seen on the street before.

No, it was probably someone coming here to drop off or pick up a pampered dog. I only hoped that person wasn't imperiling him- or herself with impatience.

Whoever it was, the noise apparently got to the hybrid driver, and the car took off.

I watched for an additional minute without moving, intending to thank the minivan driver — and maybe even walk inside with that now-adored, impatient person. But that vehicle didn't pull into the lot. Instead, it sped off, too.

Slowly regaining my breath, I stayed a short while longer, observing the area in an attempt to ensure I was safe.

No reason to assume I wasn't, especially when a few of Darryl's employees meandered outside with some of their visitors of the day on a leash for a late-afternoon constitutional and potty break.

There was no apparent danger to them, and I used their presence to go inside.

"Kendra, are you okay?" Darryl all but dashed toward me from his post at the sign-in desk. "You look awful."

"Gee, thanks," I said, but my heart wasn't in my usually glib sarcasm, and I sounded almost serious. I stooped immediately as Lexie and Odin barreled toward me from different parts of the huge doggy room and leaped on my legs for attention. I buried my face first in Lexie's fur, then Odin's.

"Come into my office," Darryl ordered. I was too stressed to disobey.

I noted a stain on the collar of my friend's Doggy Indulgence shirt that suggested he'd hugged a drooling dog. Not an unusual state of affairs for this caring caretaker.

He pointed me toward a chair facing his cluttered desk and ordered, "Sit."

Once again, I did as he said.

"Tell me what happened," he commanded. He was obviously alpha that afternoon, so I complied. And when I was done describing my day's difficult activities and imaginary hybrid stalker, he stood and all but growled at me. "Kendra, you've got to cut it out. I know you're stressed about Jeff, and worried about the woman who was apparently so close to him, but you have to start caring more for yourself. If you don't, I'll start playing stalker myself and shadow you to make sure you stay safe."

"No need," I responded hurriedly. "I was

freaked out enough today to learn my lesson. I'm backing off." Fortunately, my hands were in my lap and I doubted he could see them over the stuff on his desk — so my crossed fingers weren't in his line of vision. What else could I do? I was involved, like it or not. And I especially didn't like not knowing where Jeff was. How could I keep my nose out of a situation when I was so much in the middle of it?

"How about hanging out around here tonight, till I leave?" Darryl asked, his voice a whole lot more gentle. "We'll go out to dinner, then you can stay at my place. Lexie and Odin, too."

"That's really sweet, Darryl," I replied. "But —"

"I knew there'd be a 'but,' " he grumbled.

"I have pet-sitting to do. And I'll be fine. Honest. I'm going to call Jeff's assistant Buzz Dulear and see if he can keep an eye on things. I might even call Detective Ned Noralles, too, just to let him know that I think I'm being followed."

Not that I anticipated Ned would immediately send a fleet of squad cars full of cops to act as my bodyguards. Still, some backup might make me feel better. Buzz was the best bet for that.

Only, when I got back to my rental car

with the pups and made those calls, Ned was off duty. The dispatcher promised to get him a message, but I wasn't holding my breath.

And Buzz didn't answer his cell phone.

So, I was on my own. But I was alert. I kept my eyes wide open as I went through all my pet-sitting duties, jotting notes in my official journal and watching for hybrid cars in all the neighborhoods I visited.

And saw none, thank heavens.

I decided that if I was being followed, whoever it was would be more likely to watch for me at home than elsewhere. Which also meant that, by heading there, I was more likely to endanger Rachel and her dad, Russ. I therefore told the dogs, when I got back into the car after my last pet visit, "We'll stay at your house tonight, Odin. What do you think about that?"

He wagged his curled tail eagerly, as if he understood.

I headed for Jeff's Sherman Oaks abode, parked in the driveway, and hurried the dogs inside. As they eagerly ate their dinners, I peered out the windows of the front hallway, toward the street.

Nothing out of the norm there. Jeff's lawn was empty, a few familiar-looking cars were parked at the curb — none hybrids — and across the road I saw one of the poop scoopers at work. From here, it appeared to be the older Latino fellow, but I wasn't sure.

Of course the dogs desired their evening constitutionals when they'd finished gulping down their dinners, so I leashed them and headed out the front door. They'd been walked together often enough that I didn't have any difficulty getting them headed in the same direction, and we went left on the sidewalk.

I might have heard the roar of an engine from another kind of car, but hybrids tend to be quieter. Even so, I did hear some kind of sound behind me. Before I could turn too far, something — or someone — hit me hard, and I went flying toward the nearest house.

Just as a hybrid car streaked by, right in the spot where I'd been standing only an instant before.

I screamed and yanked on the dogs' leashes to get them away from the street. And then I looked down at the ground, at the form of the straw-hatted poop scooper who'd dashed from across the street to protect me.

Only . . .

Okay, Kendra, I told myself. I'd been hallucinating all over the place lately. I'd even assumed I'd seen what I now imagined when looking at this senior Hispanic-appearing man before.

But now I could see the skin of one leg that had been bared as his jeans tore.

I could see the light hair peeking out of the silver at the back of his head, below his hat, as he rose to his knees, face toward the ground.

I could see a hand close up, one that wasn't gloved.

And now that he wasn't standing and stooped, I could see, from an odd angle, his actual height.

I gasped and grabbed at the hair at the back of his head, making him look right into my eyes.

Well, sure, he wore damned sunglasses, so I couldn't completely tell their color. But their expression was angry — yet wholly familiar.

Before I could say anything out of my stupidly gaping mouth, the man said in a raspy tone, "Get back in the house, Kendra, and take the dogs with you. Now."

Today was my day for obeying orders from the men I cared about most, I guessed. In any event, I responded in a scratchy voice of my own, automatically keeping it low. "Okay, Jeff. See you inside."

CHAPTER SIXTEEN

To say I stumbled into the house would be a humongous understatement. Especially since my canine companions kept leaping joyfully toward the man who followed me up the sidewalk, yanking at their leashes . . . and my horrified heart.

Traitorous Lexie and Odin. Oh, they'd tried to tell me the truth previously during the last week or so, in their own puplike ways. But every time they'd acted excited about the ersatz poop scooper, he'd been in a situation that explained it — covered with fascinating other-dog smells. Or feeding them treats. Or . . . who knew?

And I . . . I'd visualized a semblance of Jeff, somehow, in this person. But I'd imagined seeing Jeff in nearly every male I'd observed lately, especially as the driver of almost every other car on the road. I'd assumed I simply missed him so much that I willed him back into my life, genuine or not.

Well, now, here he was. And the insides of my anatomy were churning and flip-flopping almost as much as my anxious mind.

I all but sat down on the shining hardwood floor in the entry. Hey, I told myself, I was okay. No need for a drama queen performance. Whatever Jeff had attempted to accomplish over the past painful days by his amazingly absurd, extremely inconsiderate, and agonizing act, I'd deal with it.

I hoped.

I stood, held my head high, and gracefully walked down the steps into Jeff's sunken living room.

Was I ready to violently detach his previously handsome head and burn it in the lovely old stone fireplace that was the room's focal point?

Perhaps. I'd think about it. Murder magnet that I was . . . But so far I'd always been an advocate for the innocent.

For now, I stepped gingerly onto the southwestern-style area rug, maneuvered around the loglike rustic coffee table, and lowered myself onto the closest piece of the white sectional sofa. I glanced toward the wide-screen TV along the wall, turned off for now.

Where was my old nonfriend and media

personality Corina Carey now, when I needed her? I hadn't heard from her for a whole day or two. Did she already have the scoop on this situation: *Mystery solved — or magnified? Expanding his duties as a new poop-collection organization's chief executive officer to include acting as senior scooper is none other than a local P.I. who had supposedly disappeared. Film at eleven.*

And did those disloyal dogs come to sit beside me and offer affection, compassion, and understanding?

No! They took their excited places around the man who plopped down on the other end of the couch. Considering the condition of his ratty clothing, that same sofa, at least at that end, would soon be *formerly* white.

"Okay," I said, oh so snidely cheerful after many long moments of staring in his direction, "care to tell me what's been going on, Jeff? I mean, that poop-scooping outfit is certainly a charming costume, and the way you've camouflaged yourself by graying your hair and wearing hats and slathering on that swarthy makeup — I was aware you were one great P.I., and I know now that includes being a master of disguise." He opened his mouth as if to respond, but I raised my hand to restrain him for one more minute. "It's great, Jeff. Honest. Whatever's gone on . . . well, how about explaining it to me? No matter what it is, I'll handle it. All I want to know is . . . why?"

To my utter horror, I suddenly realized that my voice had risen several octaves and was headed into hysterical mode. That was coupled with the torrent of tears that flowed unchecked down my cheeks. Attempting to get control of every aspect of myself, I shut up and covered my face with the palms of my shaking hands.

Which made me utterly oblivious when Jeff rose and drew near. Suddenly he was kneeling on the floor before me, gently removing my trembling extremities from my face.

I stared through the stream from my tear ducts. He'd removed his dark shades so I could see his deep blue, sympathetically damp eyes. His complexion still seemed overly dark despite the bathing his skin was taking. His cheekbones remained higher than those of the Jeff I knew, and the flesh of his cheeks was sunken, as if he had sucked it in.

Maybe he had. This was, after all, a disguise, probably complete with prosthetics — wasn't it? Or had I lost my mind altogether, assuming this fellow who'd somehow, possibly coincidentally, hung around in several neighborhoods with me, and who'd just saved my life, was the man I wished he was?

Bullshit. This was Jeff.

Well, hell. I suddenly found myself engulfed tightly in his familiar and comforting arms. Felt him raining kisses on my mouth. I had an immediate urge to tear his clothes off. Mine, too. Whatever was going on, he was alive . . . and so was I.

Damn, but it felt good to be touching him.

But before we got too far into our mutually hedonistic hug, I stiffened. So did he, and not only in his most sexually strategic locale.

What the hell had been going on with him? And did I really want to leap into bed with him without further explanation?

No!

I pulled back. "Okay, Jeff." I attempted in vain to rein in my heavy breathing. "Explanations first. Sex later. Maybe." *No way!*

"Damn it, Kendra," he responded in Jeff's familiar tone, except a whole lot huskier, "there's stuff I can't tell you. Some I don't even understand — at least not all of it. Just know that one reason I started What's the Scoop so fast and hired a few guys I knew to help out was that I was worried about you. Wanted to keep an eye on you. Protect you. But the thing is . . . that doesn't mean I can trust you."

"What!" I all but shrieked. "What are you talking about? Why in heaven's name would it even cross your mind for a split second *not* to trust me?" I suddenly had a nearly irresistible urge to kick this incomprehensible and frustrating man right in his formerly beloved balls.

The dogs obviously sensed something seriously wrong with their dearest humans, and they crowded around Jeff on the floor, as if to protect him. From me.

Well, hell. He'd given himself reason not to trust me at this particular moment . . . by accusing me of not being trustworthy.

"Okay, Jeff," I continued more serenely, "sit down." I patted the nearest section of the sofa without grimacing at all at the sorry state of his poop-scooping outfit. So what if the upholstery wound up needing to be cleaned or replaced? I'd touched him and his clothes, and survived without showering . . . yet. "Let's discuss this rationally." *Like, where the hell have you been, you big jerk? And not trusting me . . .*

"Okay." He sat where I'd indicated, and the traitorous dogs leaped up beside him.

"So," I started once more, assuming a

completely false conversational tone, "how about beginning with telling me why you initially disappeared, and where you were before you showed up to pick up pet feces?" There was a lot more I needed to know, but we had to begin this disturbing discussion somewhere.

"I won't tell you everything, Kendra, so don't press me. But . . . tell you what. Did you get the package I sent?"

I suddenly smiled sappily, notwithstanding my irritation. "You mean that sweet note? It helped me get through the time you were missing."

"Good. And the other thing inside. Did you examine it?" He regarded me so suspiciously that my smile evaporated like ice tossed on a sizzling grill.

"Your speaking schedule? It was interesting, but I'm not sure why you wanted me to hold on to it for you, since by the time the package reached me the dates had passed."

"The other item in the envelope!" he exploded. "The one the schedule was wrapped around, to protect it. That's what's important. As if you didn't know."

"If there was anything else," I said as reasonably as I could despite my increasing ire, "it must have fallen out before delivery. The envelope was a mess, the address all scratched out with mine scribbled on top, and it wasn't entirely sealed. What else was supposed to be in there?"

"If you didn't receive it, why do you care?"

I felt as if he'd slapped me square in the face. Who was this unmasked man? Not the Jeff I thought I'd known. But there was something strange in his altered attitude, and I needed to understand everything.

I made my mood chill once more. "Let's start with this whole trust issue, then," I said with utter calm. "You won't tell me everything because you've somehow lost confidence in me. Please explain." As if he could.

"I'll tell you two things," he said in a voice as remote as Antarctica. He lifted his hand. Now, on second scrutiny, I realized it looked similar, but was unidentical to Jeff's. Makeup made his skin darker, and areas that had formerly been smooth seemed calloused — presumably because of the unfamiliar tools he'd used to scoop poop. "First, I have reason to believe at least one person I trusted betrayed me. Second, I don't know everyone involved — or much of anything else. I was injected with something. Ketamine, probably — or another one of those designer or date rape drugs. Or maybe a combo of some kind that included ketamine. Some was found in my system when I finally got myself into an emergency clinic under an alias. I was all scratched up from going out the car window, too."

I nodded, knowing what he meant . . . and hiding my horror. Not that I thought he'd been assaulted in a sexual way. But Althea's and my research had revealed nasty things about that ketamine stuff.

It was the same drug believed to have been used to murder Earl Knox. Jeff could have been killed.

At least the blood inside his Escalade had been explained.

"Whatever it was left large gaps in my memory. Plus, I know who drugged me and tried to drown me, but I don't know who was conspiring with him." His eyes met mine once again and didn't let go. That clearly meant he hadn't dismissed me from that particularly nasty list, at least not the last part.

Well, screw you, I thought. *And I don't mean sexually.*

Even as I admitted to myself that his attitude honestly hurt like hell.

A little later, we sat at the round wooden table in Jeff's tiny kitchen. He intended to depart shortly after eating. Though this was actually his home, he had appearances to maintain.

What if a neighbor saw him shove me out of the way of that speeding car? Sure, I might be freaked enough to invite the most lowly of yard care helpers into the house while I regained my composure and sense of safety. Might even feed him dinner as part of my thanks for his help.

Which I did with Jeff, by the way. Fed him, I mean. No Thai takeout, of course. Nothing to stoke any sensuous feelings toward him — as if I could work up any such sensations under these circumstances. Not this night. Not anymore.

Not with a man who'd recently claimed to love me, couldn't quite keep his disguised and arguably disgusting hands off me, but apparently couldn't clear me of involvement in a plot to dispose of him in an aqueduct canal.

I thawed and cooked frozen chicken breasts, and dished out a premade salad — all fare I'd fed myself lately when I'd come here with the dogs. Not gourmet, but good enough to feed a pseudo poop scooper. Plus, I had a bottle of inexpensive but still tasty wine I'd bought a few days back to drown my sorrows, then hidden so I wouldn't imbibe unwisely. I opened it right now and poured us each a small libation.

Jeff puttered about the house as I prepared our meal. I was extremely conscious of his presence, even when I couldn't see him. And full of anticipation for our impending conversation.

Was he about to reveal anything useful? Something to make these past weeks comprehensible? Diminish my awful agony?

Soon I served dinner. Jeff sat and started right in to eat. I took a few bites, too. Sandpaper. Sawdust. Chili peppers. No, I hadn't used any of the above as seasonings, but I might as well have. I didn't taste a thing, and what I swallowed abraded my throat and settled hard in my suffering stomach. Wine helped to smooth the path, but I wasn't about to drink much and mess up my mind before I got some answers.

"Enough, already," I finally said. "Tell me what you do recall, or make up a story. Whatever. Let's start at the beginning. Do you remember leaving L.A. on your trip?" *After all but finally convincing me to move in with you . . . ?*

His nod barely budged his artificially silvered hair. "Of course. That was before I was drugged. I had a couple of assignments out of town. One was to supervise installation of a nice security system in a new state government building — in Pennsylvania. I arrived there and saw things get started, but then got a hysterical call from Lois — I know you've met her now."

I nodded, forbearing from berating him for not introducing me before to someone who obviously meant a lot to him. Or even mentioning her — at least I still didn't recall that he had.

"She was so upset and said she needed me to conduct an investigation right away. A confidential one."

I nodded sagely. "She's told me about her internal conflict between The Clone Arranger and her church connections."

"She did?" He appeared surprised. "Well, okay, that opens up some of what I didn't think I could say. I figured I could come back here, talk to her, then dash to handle my second assignment, a seminar in self-defense and company security in Phoenix."

"And you didn't tell me you were back in town because . . . ?" I didn't intend to sound so huffy, but, hey, the guy had claimed to love me. Wouldn't it have made sense just to give me a hint he'd be around, even if all I could do was blow him a kiss from a distance?

His eyes locked on mine, and he gave an ironic shrug. "Easy answer? As I said, I'd

253

promised Lois confidentiality, so I didn't figure on telling anyone, even you or my own employees, that I was here. I didn't intend to stay long anyway, but to learn what was really wrong and assure Lois I'd handle it when I got back."

"I'm a lawyer, among other things," I informed him unnecessarily. "I understand confidentiality, and wouldn't have dug for details if you'd told me to butt out. And you know that, so I gather there's also a not-so-easy answer."

"Well, yeah, and your attitude right now shows me I was right." I opened my mouth, but he didn't allow me to voice even a syllable of contradiction before he pressed on. "The biggest reason I didn't tell you was that I was sure you wouldn't be thrilled to know I was around and didn't have time to see you. I figured that what you didn't know wouldn't hurt you."

"But it did hurt me," I shot back in painful protest. "And you, too, I gather."

"Maybe."

"So, okay," I said in an attempt — futile, I figured — to see his side of things. "You didn't tell me for a reason." Right. "But what about your own employees — Althea? Buzz?"

"I did talk to Althea early on, on my cell,

though I didn't tell her everything. No need to explain where I was or what I was up to, or so I thought. I felt a little dumb, actually, for getting involved in what I figured was a fool's errand for family. Sort of family. I checked in, said I'd seen things start off okay in Philadelphia, and was working on my seminar presentation. I had no idea then that I wouldn't show up there."

"I see," I said slowly, because I didn't exactly see at all.

He scowled beneath his poop-scooper makeup, as if reading my irritated thoughts. "Like I said, I felt dumb. Anyway, this is where things start to get . . . well, difficult." He laid his fork so loudly on the plate that both pups stood and wagged, assuming he had purposely sought their attention — possibly for tossing them a treat. He smiled as if happy for the distraction, and did indeed find small pieces of chicken to drop into the two eager mouths.

"Enlighten me as easily as you can," I said dryly, taking a substantial sip of wine.

He did — sort of. Surreptitiously, at least with respect to the rest of us who cared about him, he'd visited Lois and learned the reason for her plea of confidentiality because of her cherished church affiliation. He listened to her tale of how she'd wanted a duplicate of her almost-Akita Flisa and had gone to The Clone Arranger. Something hadn't worked, and while they'd been trying, Flisa died. She was certain it hadn't been natural causes.

Despite his generally good powers of persuasion, Jeff hadn't convinced her to wait till his return to start his investigation into the outfit. Giving in to her pleas, he agreed to spend just one day taking a peek. He'd assumed he still had an extra day available before he had to head off to present his seminar.

He'd been the one to give me instruction in private investigating, so it wasn't any big surprise that he had acted pretty professionally on his own — except for one big lack: backup. Wisely, he decided not to burst in on the business and tell the people at The Clone Arranger that he was probing their practices to see if they'd done something awful in their work with Flisa. Unwisely cocksure of himself, he told no one at Hubbard Security but had taken a quick trip undercover on his own.

Unlike me, he hadn't shown up there with a pet supposedly to be cloned. Instead, he had brought out some of his cache of fake credentials and pretended to be there from the state to inspect the facility.

He stared at me sheepishly. "Apparently, I wasn't undercover enough. I talked to some of them. One guy in particular. Playing my government role, I scared him into telling me stuff he shouldn't. Even got him to . . . well, never mind. I did some more looking around and . . . anyway, next thing I recall was being sprawled in the backseat of my Escalade. I wasn't entirely conscious, but knew enough to suspect I'd been drugged. Someone in the front seat was talking on a cell phone. I wasn't awake enough to hear everything, but I heard enough to know I was in big trouble."

"What do you remember?" I asked, intrigued and horrified at the same time. I was fairly certain I knew what happened next — an apparent car accident, with the Escalade and Jeff winding up in the California Aqueduct.

He frowned, as if in concentration — an expression I remembered well on the old, undisguised Jeff. I'd found it sweet and sexy. But now, I refused to allow myself to feel anything . . . didn't I?

"Well," he said slowly, "the driver raised his voice, which was probably what woke me up. He was angry he'd been forced to do the 'dirty work.' That's how he phrased it. But he promised to take care of things on his end. Argued with whoever he was talking to and said something like 'You got to someone in this clown Hubbard's own operation this fast, like you promised? That's great — his girlfriend? You'll be the one to follow up on that after I do this, right?' I guess the answer was affirmative, since the guy said 'great' again."

"You were drugged, unsure of what you were hearing. Yet you took this to mean you couldn't trust me?" A sense of utter outrage made me want once more to kick the guy across the table from me. But sense and self-preservation took over. He might look like a fragile senior citizen, but under that dumb disguise he was hunky, muscular Jeff.

"I didn't know what to believe," he said, sounding exhausted. Looking that way, too, but I refused to allow myself to feel sorry for this sorry excuse of a former boyfriend. "And then . . . well, I must have fallen unconscious again. Next thing I knew, I was in the Escalade, underwater. Fortunately, good Boy Scout and security expert that I am, I kept a tool inside the car that allowed me to break the window and escape. I floated for quite a distance, I guess. I wasn't sure where I was, or when it was, when I finally pulled myself out of that cold canal. Wasn't even sure who I was and how I got there for a while, either. And then, when I started to remember bits and pieces, I wasn't sure what was real. Who I could trust. Or whether what I'd heard meant you were in danger, too — without my knowing from whom."

"I get it," I said solemnly. And I did. He had been drugged. Whether or not he heard what he recalled, he'd become confused.

Only . . . that was now a couple of weeks ago. Why hadn't he figured things out in between?

And another thing had started to bother me. "Do you know who the driver of the car was?" I asked.

"Yeah," he said, and his hands made fists on the sides of the table. "I'd met the bastard first thing at The Clone Arranger. It was Earl Knox."

The guy who'd been murdered soon thereafter. A guy whom Jeff — who'd been drugged, confused, and furious — obviously had issues with.

Had Jeff been the one who killed him?

CHAPTER SEVENTEEN

I didn't enlighten Jeff about this latest ugly suspicion of mine — that he had recently gotten revenge for the attack on his person and Escalade by disposing of the attacker, Earl.

Instead, I continued to ask questions that I hoped would help him straighten out what appeared to be continued confusion in his mind. And felt strangely pleased that, even having endured all that, he had still managed to worry about me — maybe.

I took a sip of wine and went on conversationally, as if we were discussing something simple, like how to pat a puppy. Which I did, after putting my glass down, since Lexie and Odin now sat on the floor on either side of me. My dear, doggy protectors.

Assuming they'd take my side over Jeff's should I need an actual defense — a major and likely misguided assumption. My sweet little Lexie undoubtedly would, but a bigger, broader, more alpha Akita like Odin — who just happened to be Jeff's?

"So," I said, "Earl agreed to do 'the dirty work,' which I assume meant getting rid of you."

Jeff nodded. "That's what I figured."

"But you don't know who he was talking to."

"Probably somebody at The Clone Arranger."

"The owner, Mason Payne, or someone else?"

Jeff shrugged. "That's what I need to know. And, before you ask, no, I still don't know who he referred to or what he meant when he said the person he spoke with had 'gotten to' someone in my operation — or my girlfriend. I've been looking into The Clone Arranger even more since my return — although less directly. What's the Scoop, and my working outfit" — he gestured at his current disguise — "give me a lot of latitude to show up all over the place and still stay invisible. And I've hired some guys I taught in classes in other Southern California cities to come here fast and scoop poop with me, while observing your house and mine and other pertinent places." He waved his hand in the air to silence me as I opened my mouth to comment. "And before you say anything, it wasn't simply to spy on you or the others, but to protect you, in case what they'd meant was that they intended to harm you."

"Even after they thought they'd gotten rid of you?"

He nodded. "Especially after . . . well, Earl was killed, and I'm sure one of them did it. Plus, I'm fairly certain I know why. But the who still eludes me."

"And you're not telling me why . . . why?"

"Because if you're part of their scheme, you know why. And because . . . well, if you aren't part of their scheme, you'd already have told me something I was anticipating you'd say, to convince me you weren't. Handed it over."

"You mean that important and extravagant speaking schedule? Well, gee, I'll go get it for you." I stood as if to head for the office to retrieve that stupid envelope and its supposedly critical contents. "Oh, wait. I'll bet you mean that other mysterious and supposedly missing insert."

Jeff stood, too, and shook his head, looking more stressed than I'd ever seen him. And it wasn't simply his makeup job that turned him into a stranger. "I can't believe this! Oh, hell, sure I can. I did a lot of things wrong in this situation, Kendra. I can't even begin to tell you. . . . Well, yes, I can. Do you know, I was actually in the clear. I got what I needed my first time in that damned place, amazingly enough. I thought I did the right thing by sending it to you, but now you . . . And then, a little while after I left, Earl called me to come back for even more evidence, and I was stupid enough to go. That's when all the crap happened. And yet, there I was, a career cop first, then what I thought was a pretty smart P.I. — but I still fell for it. Fell for *you.* Damn!"

He slammed his fist down on the small table, rattling the empty dishes so hard that Odin growled and Lexie slunk away with her ears down and tail between her legs. Poor, uninformed babies.

And I included myself in that. Too many holes and painful implications in Jeff's story.

Too many unanswered questions that I decided not to ask now, mostly since I knew he wouldn't care to comment — even assuming his muddied mind had any answers. But the circularity of his conversation suggested to me that whatever the drug he'd been given, whatever else had happened since then, he was one hurtfully confused P.I.

Unless this was all part of his undercover act.

"Don't be so hard on yourself," I asserted as mildly as I could. *Or on me.* "Dessert?" I felt my face color after that inquiry, since it could clearly be taken as an invitation for something sexual. And if he took it that way, I'd simply have to disabuse him of the idea.

Not now. Maybe not ever again, if we didn't get through the current murky morass of misinformation and mistrust.

"No, thanks. I'd better get going." His ire had deflated to obvious misery, and he stared down at the floor, clearly dejected.

His leaving was a good idea. Even so . . . "This is your home," I reminded him. And I hated to see him go while obviously so sad.

"But it's not the home of the owner of What's the Scoop," he said. "And that's the person I was when I came inside."

"No, you were a worker who helped to save my skin from the rampant hybrid car." All the more reason to keep this man around. The car was still out there somewhere. So was its unidentified driver.

Jeff hadn't been pleased earlier when I informed him I'd often seen the car around me lately, but never had the right angle to obtain a license number. Of course, he theoretically had the opportunity to do that himself today, but was too busy scooping poop and keeping an eye on his house, and then shoving me out of the way, to accomplish that basic little investigative act. And hadn't he been driving that now-familiar beige minivan that forced the hybrid car away from Darryl's driveway? If so, why hadn't *he* noted the needed license then?

That he hadn't was, in a way, a good thing, since he couldn't castigate me too hard.

But it mostly was a bad thing, since neither of us could single out the person who apparently wanted me squashed.

Most likely the same one who'd wanted Jeff "taken care of."

I slowly walked him toward the door.

"You need to call Ned Noralles right now," Jeff said as he stood in the entry. The dogs sat down sadly at his feet, as if understanding he didn't intend to stay. "Tell him what happened. Insist he send some patrols to keep an eye on you."

"Sure, I'll call Ned." I attempted not to scoff. "I'm certain he'll be really excited now about what happened a couple of hours ago: an attempt on my life without an earlier notification, and nothing to identify whodunit except that it's the driver of one of those new, increasingly popular hybrids.

And since I can't tell him anything about how I really got out of the way . . ."

"Call anyway," Jeff insisted. "Even though it happened out of his jurisdiction, he should be interested that this is related to the Earl Knox homicide."

Which statement bounced right back into my mind my earlier wonderment. And fear.

Could that killer have been Jeff?

Surely not. If it was, why would he be so eager to bring in his greatest nemesis on the LAPD, Ned Noralles?

As obfuscation and cover-up of the truth . . . ?

He must have read the confusion on my face. "I'm really sorry about all of this, Kendra," he said. And then he pulled me into his arms once more, and, to my amazement, I let him.

Beneath the whole senior citizen scooper disguise, I again felt that hard, hot body I'd come to know and adore and lust after so longingly. . . .

He gave me one heck of another desire-stirring kiss.

When he pulled away, he looked deeply into my eyes with his smoldering, sexy blue ones and said, "One more thing, Kendra."

"Yes?" I responded breathlessly.

"I know about your interest in that veterinarian — Venson."

My lust chilled yet again to slush. "That isn't your business. And anyway —"

"He's connected to The Clone Arranger. He's one of the guys on my suspect list. I just thought you should know."

And before I could comment that Tom was also already on mine, Mr. Poop Scooper was gone.

I did as he'd directed, though. I called Ned. Even reached him right away. He was involved in an unrelated homicide investigation, which meant he wasn't exactly inclined to have a protracted conversation with me.

But he did express concern. "You didn't see the driver? Get any identifying information?" The same salvo of questions I'd assumed he would ask.

"Unfortunately, no," I told him.

"Well, I'll get some additional patrols on your street tonight to keep an eye out for this bozo."

"Jeff's street," I said. "Lexie and I are staying here with his dog, Odin."

Ned's voice softened, which I thought was especially sweet for a hardened homicide cop who actually despised the guy he assumed was deceased. "Kendra, you know that the chances of our locating Jeff alive grow smaller every day he's gone."

He's not gone, I itched to shout. *He's alive!* But instead I said what was expected, in the saddest voice I could dredge up. "I'm just hanging on the best I can."

"Call anytime," he said. Nice man, for a cop who hated my crime-solving guts. "Good night, Kendra."

A long time later, as I finally prepared to shower and get ready for bed, my cell phone chimed.

I jumped. This was the time Jeff always used to call. But he had just been here. And I'd thought he was remaining undercover.

When I checked the caller ID, the number was unfamiliar.

Which worried me. Was it the hybrid car driver calling to check to see where I was? Ready to do something nasty to me here? Maybe, despite calling Ned, I should have bundled the dogs and me into my car and headed home, where I might be safer behind my wrought iron gate and the security system in my garage-top apartment.

Of course, Jeff was the security expert. His system should be state of the art and even more foolproof — or had he lost out in that, too?

"Hello?" I said loudly, unwilling to show my inner scaredness to whoever it was.

"Hello, Ms. Kendra," said a voice with a heavy Hispanic accent. "This is Juan."

Juan? Who was that? "Um —" I started to respond.

"From What's the Scoop," he explained. Which made me smile. It was Jeff calling, right on time. And, yes, still undercover.

"I wanted to make sure you are okay," he continued. "After that accident before. And to thank you again for dinner."

I translated all the syllables that remained unspoken beneath the surface. Someone could be monitoring my calls. Or his. Part of his ongoing paranoia? Perhaps. But he was worried about me. Still cared — even if he amazingly considered me a person of interest in the attack on him and whatever other crimes he had suspects in.

"I'm fine, Juan. Thank you. And thanks for pushing me out of that car's way. Too bad the dumb driver didn't stop and apologize." Yeah, right. But this at least gave the impression I thought it was inadvertent.

My lips itched to shout out at him about those last comments he'd made in person — about Tom Venson. None of his business how I felt about Tom. And the fact that Tom had been so close to Debby Payne not long ago that they'd lip-locked so lasciviously, right in my presence . . . well, that wasn't

Jeff's business, either — although, if he was investigating, maybe he should know.

But not now. Not if he thought we were being monitored.

"Yes, too bad the driver didn't stop," he repeated. "Well, I will be back in your neighborhood cleaning tomorrow, or one of my workers will." Next translation: We'll be watching over you. Protecting you.

"Thanks," I said. "And good night."

Despite my irritation about the Tom Venson angle, it was a surprisingly good night, even though the dogs and I still slept alone. Slept was the key word, because for the first time since Jeff's disappearance, that was exactly what I did the entire night through.

When I woke the next morning, feeling refreshed, anger, irritation, and exasperation warred with relief inside me.

My assumptions and beliefs and prayers had been correct. Jeff was alive.

But there was a lot he'd said that grated on my psyche where it really hurt — pride. And deeper emotions, like what I'd assumed was love.

He might be protecting me. But, oddly and hurtfully, he didn't trust me. Suspected me of . . . what? Hiding something? But what?

Did it matter?

Well, silly non-P.I. that I was, I decided I wouldn't let a little thing like Jeff being alive or acting weird stop me from doing what I'd already intended: clear his mother figure Lois from allegations of murder.

I only hoped my finger wouldn't wind up pointing at Jeff.

And that I wouldn't wind up squashed beneath a hybrid car somewhere.

Because I was going to keep up my investigation, following the same clues as before.

Stupid? Could be. But I was nothing if not single-minded when in murder-magnet mode.

But that didn't mean I'd be injudicious and careless about my stupidity.

At least I could direct my inquiries to fewer major questions, now that I no longer had to find Jeff or figure out what had happened to him — only who had helped to cause it. Who had also probably been the perpetrator of Earl's demise.

First, though, I had pet-sitting to do, starting with my own beloved charges. Which meant a quick dash into the backyard and a nourishing breakfast — for them. I wasn't exactly in the mood for eating on this Monday morning. And then?

And then, it was time to take them for a

walk. Yes, outside on this very street where I'd almost been creamed by a car last evening. I doubted Jeff would be there that morning. Too risky for his undercover scheme. Maybe one of his What's the Scoop staff — what had he said? P.I. students from other cities in this state?

Could I risk that they'd be as alert and agile as the guy in senior citizen disguise who, beneath it all, was one strong and fast dude?

Well, no. Nor could I count on Ned coming through with sufficient police patrols to make me feel entirely safe. But I especially couldn't rely on Lexie and Odin to cross their legs till I drove us all somewhere safer — presupposing we wouldn't be followed.

So, I took my chances — all the while staying alert and staring up and down the somnolent residential street in all directions. Using my ears like antennas for all kinds of noises, since hybrids didn't sound like ordinary engines.

Noticed when a minivan pulled up in front of a neighbor's house across the street, and an apparent poop scooper smaller than Jeff got out and gave a slight nod in my direction before getting down and dirty to work.

And heaved a huge sigh of relief when I finally got all of us — dogs and me — in my car, ready to go pet-sitting.

I called Rachel first thing on my cell phone. "Everything okay at home? Have you started your rounds yet?"

"Yes and yes." She sounded exasperated in the way teenagers — even those nearly out of that age range — did so well. "I've taken care of Beggar, of course. And I've also looked in on Abra and Cadabra already. On my way to care for Piglet now. And later on, I'll do my midday walk of Widget. Anything else?"

"I'll let you know," I said. "Just be careful. And stay safe."

"Gee, Kendra, you sound more like my mom every day."

Not exactly a compliment. A while back, she'd run away from her mother, who lived in Arizona, to come stay with her dad.

"Okay, daughter," I said, sticking sarcasm into my tone. "That means you really have to listen to what I say."

At which point I heard raspberries in my ear from the cell phone. I laughed, which caused Lexie and Odin, both in the backseat of this too small car, to start leaping around.

A thought occurred to me. "By the way,

did you find anything that could have fallen from an envelope in my mail?"

"Like what?"

"Wish I knew."

"That's a huge help. The answer is no, although I'll take a look around the area I'd left it, in case there's something lying around."

"Thanks," I said, and hung up.

When I had completed my own pet-care visits to Pansy the potbellied pig and Stromboli and the other adorable dogs, and noted everything in my Critters TLC, LLC, journal, I went to Doggy Indulgence, to leave Lexie and Odin safely in the care of my favorite doggy spa, as well as my favorite human and his staff, for the day. And then, still checking out all other cars on the road — no mean feat on busy L.A. freeways — I headed to my law office.

Where I had frantic phone messages from a couple of clients. Mignon told me so the instant I stepped inside. "I put them through to your voice mail, Kendra," she chirped, "but the Hayhursts really need to talk to you."

I headed down the hall, saying hello to support staff and a couple of the senior attorneys, then shut myself into my corner office, where I called the Hayhursts.

Shareen answered. "Kendra, I've heard from someone who'd signed up his dog for one of our classes but called to cancel. He heard about the pending lawsuit and doesn't want to spend the time and money if we're a big fraud."

"Did he say how he heard about the litigation?" Not that it necessarily mattered. The complaint had been filed and was therefore a matter of public record. But if the news was getting filtered through the media, we needed to know about it, to see if we could try to conduct damage control.

At least this wasn't something Corina Carey had jumped into . . . yet.

"I'll find out," Shareen said. "But Kendra, isn't there something you can do?"

"I'll naturally be a super advocate for you in court, if necessary. But I also have another idea."

"Really? What?"

"I can't tell you yet. Give me another day or so." To follow up on that idea I'd had after earlier conversations about their case. If it came together as I hoped, it would be one hell of a feat of my favorite ADR.

But that remained to be seen. And I had some phone calls to make, to see if there was even the remotest possibility it could be put together.

I hung up after promising Shareen I'd speak with her again soon, but before I could get some of those phone calls going, my office line buzzed again. I glanced at the caller ID. Jeff's office.

I ignored how my heart rate accelerated. It wouldn't be Jeff, after all. Not since he suspected members of his staff of conspiring against him, as he did me.

The paranoid fool. Wasn't he?

I had to take a few breaths and put myself back in the mood I'd been in yesterday at this time. When I had only hope, but no evidence, that Jeff was alive and kicking, instead of still waterlogged somewhere in a canal.

"Kendra? It's Althea. Just wanted to touch base with you." She spoke in the same sorrowful voice she'd used for the last couple of weeks. "Have you heard anything about Jeff?"

Sure have, was what I wanted to say. *He saved my life, and I fed him dinner.* But I'd promised him discretion.

"Sorry," I said. "Can't tell you anything." *But can you tell me whether anything in Jeff's suspicions can be justified?*

"I figured," she said dejectedly as I stood and stared out my office window toward the nearly filled parking lot. " 'Cause you'd tell me if you found out anything I should know."

Which made me feel a whole lot worse as I hung up.

Hell, Althea wasn't the only one I wanted to shout to about Jeff's survival. Surely Lois, despite her own dilemma, would want to know. And how about middle-aged Mother Hubbard? Jeff's mom had appeared to be awfully nice. Shouldn't she be informed that her son was, if not wholly okay and sane, at least alive?

But I'd promised him. And until I either unpromised or understood with absolute certainty that Jeff was wrong, I had to keep my mouth shut.

But how was I going to fix even a fraction of this awful situation? And if I actually figured out who'd killed Earl Knox, and who'd conspired with that particular dead man to attempt to kill Jeff, would any of us who were involved start trusting one another again to restore what had, previously, been a quite pleasing status quo?

CHAPTER EIGHTEEN

Okay, I admit it. I was obsessed with this whole outrageous situation.

Was this obsession different from any other situation when my murder-magnet status had kicked in? Maybe not.

But I suddenly determined where I had to go. Well, not so suddenly, since I'd already figured on heading there today, just not at this exact moment.

"Are you okay, Kendra?" Mignon asked as I headed out the office door once more, sympathy resounding in her voice.

"Sure," I called back over my shoulder. "See you later." My odd mood wasn't, after all, due to the sorrow I'd evinced when I'd shared concerns about Jeff's possible demise. But I still had a lot to learn about the disjointed yet related strings in this whole scary state of affairs.

I pulled my rental car out of the lot and headed for the 134 Freeway east, toward

Arcadia. I intended to follow up on what I'd started doing there yesterday: finding out anything I could about Earl Knox's former employer, CW Ultra Technologies.

Real or not, I imagined an entire armada of vehicles accompanying me: a menacing silver hybrid, ready to spring and slap me off the road. A vehicle sent by What's the Scoop or its leader, Jeff, following along to excavate excrement or protect me, whichever came first. Maybe even an unmarked cop car, if Ned Noralles took me seriously enough yesterday. Well, that last was a stretch, but the others seemed somewhat feasible. That led me to all but crawl in the freeway's slow lane, figuring that only someone who really, really wanted to stay behind me wouldn't pass as fast as possible and sling me the finger. I checked my mirrors often, and though I did see a few of those fingers, I didn't see anyone intentionally shadowing me — which didn't exactly mean I was safe. But neither was there any obvious peril to avoid.

Eventually, I exited the freeway and again glanced around. Still no sign of a tail. Maybe I truly was safe.

And maybe I was five years younger and five pounds slimmer, and . . . Well, you get it.

I soon reached the offices of CW Ultra Technologies. Today, the parking lot outside the ordinary-appearing building was pretty full, but I found a spot for my too small car. There were spaces marked for executives. The one labeled for the CEO of the company made my insides twist in envy. It held a BMW, not aged and crumpled like my own the last time I'd seen it, but brand-new, bright red, and obviously expensive.

I'd always kept a suit coat in my Beamer's trunk for situations where I needed to look lawyerly. I hadn't wanted to ruin anything in this puny rental car's dirty crevasses at its rear. But I had been wise enough to throw a sporty beige tweed jacket over the back of my seat, so I hurled it on over the dark slacks and subtly striped white man-tailored shirt I'd donned today.

Inside the building, I saw that there was indeed a guard desk, manned by a security sort in uniform. He didn't stop anyone or check IDs during this regular workday, but I still bet someone did so yesterday, over the weekend. I glanced at the building directory, noted that CW was on the third floor, and took the elevator.

The hallway was cookie cutter, just like every other office building. A sign on the door identified my goal as CW Ultra Technologies without explaining what that was. I opened the door and walked into a bland, generic waiting room. I gave my name to the young female receptionist, said I was here on behalf of a private investigation company, and asked to meet with Clark Weiss, claiming personal business.

I didn't get to see Mr. Weiss first thing — what a surprise. Instead, a harridan of a secretary burst through the inner sanctum's door and demanded I reveal what I wanted. In a much calmer voice than hers, I explained that I was here looking into something concerning a possible theft of CW's technology, but needed to speak directly to Mr. Weiss about the details.

That apparently got his attention, since I was shown to his office a few minutes later.

The first thing I noticed about Clark Weiss was his huge eyes magnified by his small, black-rimmed glasses. He stood behind his crowded but immaculately organized mahogany desk, and seemed almost scrawny in his baggy white shirt tucked into pale blue trousers.

"Hello, Ms. Ballantyne," he said immediately. "I've heard a lot about you."

That caused me to blink in surprise. "From who?" I asked, complying with a wave from his long fingers to sit in the

281

single, awkward-looking leather chair that faced his desk. To my surprise, it enveloped me quite comfortably.

"I'm interested in The Clone Arranger," he answered obliquely. "I know what happened to Earl Knox from the news. And I'm aware of your involvement with the suspect, Lois Terrone."

The guy might look rather ordinary in his nerdiness, but the look was clearly deceiving. He was alert, sharp . . . and potentially dangerous. I'd watch my step around him.

I was doing that around a lot of people lately, so he could join that list.

"Involvement isn't exactly —" I began, only to be interrupted.

"Because of my interest, and the fact there's reason, however tenuous, for authorities to consider me a suspect, I've dived right in to figure out everything I need to know about what happened. That means I'm aware you've solved murders before. I'll tell you right off that it looks like I had reason to kill Earl, but I didn't do it."

I opened my mouth again to try to say something, but once more he stopped me from speaking with his own speech.

"You've learned somehow that I was mad at Earl. And I was for a while, I admit it, but not lately."

"Why is that?" I couldn't help asking.

"Let me tell you a little bit about us first," Weiss said, settling further into his stiff-looking desk chair. "CW Ultra Technologies is, unsurprisingly, a company specializing in technology, the more offbeat the better. We have labs in various secret locations."

"None right here?" I managed to inquire.

"This is an office building, Kendra," he pointed out unnecessarily. "We mostly keep our management away from the front lines of research to let our scientists feel free to go in as many potentially fascinating — and lucrative — directions as possible."

We, I figured, meaning *him.*

"In any event, some of our medically oriented scientists got interested in cloning. Tried to find a way to make it work easily and inexpensively. Yes, yes, I know about the controversies surrounding cloning, but we didn't let that stop us. We got going in some interesting directions. Put together a really nice protocol that seemed quite exciting, in fact — a whole lot of cloning potential. Earl was head of the team that included that group. He spent more time in the labs than we like our managers to do. And then he left CW. Went to work for The Clone Arranger, and suddenly they're doing exactly what we intended, cloning pets. The timing pretty much clinched things. I was certain that Earl took our scientific breakthrough and sold it to that scumbag outfit he started working for."

"Then you *are* still angry," I surmised.

Weiss's open-mouthed smile occupied most of his face. "Not at all. Well, okay, maybe still less than thrilled, but after Earl left, my scientists took that little germ of an idea and started to really run with it. We've had a major breakthrough, in fact. By the end of this year, maybe middle of next, we'll have a much superior method of cloning cheaply. And that's where this is all going, you know. It's entirely possible these days to clone animals at outrageous prices, but to make any money at it? Maybe you're aware that one leading organization involved with cloning pets went out of business."

I nodded and tried to comment, again to no avail.

"I don't know the facts, but I surmise that it cost way too much, they had too few clients who could afford them, whatever. They were affiliated with another company that clones livestock, which is a great fit, because keeping up a good gene pool in production of animal food products can lead to lots of profits. Those clients are willing to pay a lot more than the folks who might want duplicates of Fido or Fifi in the future. Then there's The Clone Arranger, not totally outrageous but still aiming for either high-middle incomes or above, or people who are willing to go into debt to duplicate their favorite pet. And then there's us. Oh, I know it's just talk right now, but soon I'll achieve my mean-spirited little goal of putting The Clone Arranger out of business — not by suing them or killing their people, but by stealing their thunder. Cloning pets for affordable prices. The fact that Earl bounced out of here with some stuff he shouldn't have? Irritating, sure, but ultimately irrelevant. Does that convince you I had no motive to kill Earl?"

"Well, he allegedly did steal from you in the first place."

"If I intended to dispose of him for that, I'd have done it long before this. Now, anything else you'd like to know, Kendra?"

"I don't think —"

"Well, if you have money to invest, you've come to the right place. We have some really exciting technologies coming up in addition to cloning that will make our investors fortunes — private equity money, so not much government interference. Interested?"

"You lost me when you asked if I have money to invest."

"Oh." That was the first thing that appeared to take the wind out of his overinflated sales pitch.

"But may I have your card and call you if I think of anything else?"

"Sure, Kendra. Anytime. And if any of your friends are interested in an exciting investment . . ."

"I'll keep CW Ultra Technologies in mind, Clark."

My thoughts turned slow and complicated somersaults as I headed back toward my office.

Oh, yeah, I remembered to check my mirrors for any new and dangerous entourage members on my tail. Didn't see any, nor any protectors — which didn't, of course, mean neither was there.

But I multitasked in my mind along with driving slowly and carefully. I rehashed all that CW had said.

His company had made cloning breakthroughs of its own but hadn't yet implemented them.

Earl Knox had been right in the center of them, and then he left and joined The Clone Arranger.

The Clone Arranger's breakthroughs were, in their way, astounding . . . weren't they? Immediate reproduction of pets at high, but somewhat manageable, prices — better, I believed, than anyone else had accomplished so far in this limited market. But who knew what would happen when CW Ultra Technologies introduced their even newer processes?

Were The Clone Arranger's successes wholly based on something Earl Knox had absconded with? And was Clark Weiss consequently lying about killing the thief? Or had he perhaps told the literal truth, yet known who committed the murder because he had commissioned it? Or at least sanctioned it?

I considered much of what he said on the way west to the office. And still wasn't satisfied with what I knew — or suspected. But how could I find out more?

I eventually reached Encino and pulled once more into the busy parking lot outside the building that housed Yurick & Associates.

"Hi again, Kendra," Mignon chirped as I slipped through the front door. "There've been more calls from the Hayhursts. I forwarded them to your voice mail." She regarded me assessingly, with her large blue eyes beneath her bobbing auburn curls. "You look . . . well, better somehow. Are you feeling okay?"

"Well enough." Uh-oh. Was I already starting to look less morose because I was aware of Jeff's survival? I couldn't let anyone know that yet. "I'm trying to get my mind curled around some stuff besides my troubles."

"Oh, I get it," she said, and I headed for my office.

On the way, I all but ran into my boss, the firm's sweet senior partner, in the hall. As always, he was clad in an aloha shirt — bright red today, with birds of paradise adorning it. He peered at me over his bifocals. "You look — well, less awful today, Kendra. That's good."

"I'm trying to get over it, Borden," I said. "Thanks for caring." I gave him a hug, then sidled by. It was a wonderful thing to have so many people worried about me, but it also meant I had to exercise my acting abilities so they wouldn't figure out how I really felt.

Assuming *I* could figure out how I really felt.

I headed into my cluttered office and sat down on my comfy, ergonomically correct chair. I had to admit to myself that somehow my depression of the past days was easing a bit.

Because of Jeff's return? Sure, to some

extent. But I also felt as if I was taking an active role in determining what really had happened. Now, if only I could actually figure it all out. . . .

I turned my desktop computer back on and waited for it to boot, determining what to research now. The logical thing came immediately to mind: I'd look at the CW Ultra Technologies website again.

I saw the now-familiar face of Clark Weiss smiling on several of the web pages, talking up how wonderful the company was, without saying much about what it did.

Very familiar. But he didn't get into the supposed cloning technology, or its possible theft, online.

Well, then, the next place I headed was The Clone Arranger's website. I'd been there before, too, of course. But this time I searched for something specific. Sort of. Something that might help me determine whether some of their technology had originated elsewhere.

Yeah, right. As with most websites, this one was designed for the best possible promotion. Nothing specific was said about the cloning process, only that it was one of the most sophisticated used anywhere, which allowed them to keep costs more reasonable than most competitors. Competitors? Heck, according to them, there were none anywhere within reach. The Clone Arranger ruled!

Sure it did. Even so . . .

I looked over the testimonials from satisfied clients. Unsurprisingly, Beryl Leeds was there with her golden Labs, daddy Churchill and clone Cartwright. Nothing yet about the latest procedure with chocolate Lab Melville, but that might yet follow. And hadn't she mentioned pending infomercials?

There were other clone endorsements, too. I didn't recognize the humans, but their pets clearly were adorably duplicated: a couple of standard poodles. Some Shih Tzus. A pair of pit bulls. Chihuahuas. And even a Siamese cat, a couple of Persians, a chinchilla, and a ferret.

The babies I saw while at The Clone Arranger hadn't made it to the website yet — another Lab, a Yorkie, a boxer — but maybe they'd be here, too, someday.

I thought of poor Lois and her lost part-Akita Flisa. And wondered whether, if I'd been there for a genuine procedure, I could have presented adorable Meph's owner Maribelle with a duplicate adorable wiry terrier mix. I couldn't say that Earl Knox had been a particularly pushy salesman with me, but he had been an absolute advocate of The Clone Arranger's abilities.

Hmmm. My mind was definitely on an upswing today, since some ideas I'd not even considered before had started flooding in. I was developing an honest-to-goodness, truly exciting theory that might provide a motive. For whom? I wasn't sure yet. But could it be that . . . ?

My office phone rang, and I reached to answer it.

"Kendra, this is Shareen Hayhurst. Please, Kendra, isn't there anything you've come up with yet to help us out of this awful situation? We've had more potential students cancel. Some trade publications got wind of the situation, and it's starting to snowball. If this keeps up, even if we wind up winning the lawsuit, Show Biz Beasts could go out of business."

My brain changed direction yet again, but it still was working well. In fact — "I've made some of the phone calls I promised to make last time we spoke, Shareen. But I need to lock in a time to come to your classroom. Just hang in there, and I'll get back to you soon.

I hoped. But the way things seemed to be going, attempting to schedule something a day or so away sometimes was harder than working it out immediately. Assuming that the people I called weren't suddenly on location somewhere far from L.A.

I made those follow-up calls, and was almost astounded that my surmise, at least for today, was correct.

I called Shareen. "Expect a bunch of visitors at Show Biz Beasts in three hours."

CHAPTER NINETEEN

While driving down Ventura Boulevard a little later, I supposed my lucky stars were all in alignment, at least with respect to setting up this potential ADR solution. Otherwise, it would be amazing that everyone whom I needed to be in town actually was.

Even so, would this scenario evolve into something useful?

Maybe not. Maybe my clients from Show Biz Beasts would have to await their day in court and hope the system worked for them. Which couldn't be guaranteed, even with my excellent and experienced litigation skills on their behalf.

Instead, I aspired to achieve some successful ADR for them. And I had to adopt optimism about the possibility. This was Hollywood, after all, and my concept involved the film and television industry. But whether my offbeat seed of an idea would bear TV fruit remained to be seen. And, hopefully, aired all over the place.

I went out of my way to pick up Darryl before heading to Show Biz Beasts. After all, he'd evinced some genuine interest in my potential animal dispute resolution idea.

And Odin and Lexie? Well, they joined us. I hoped they would cooperate in this completely speculative little venture. At least, I figured, Odin might.

"So what's really going on?" Darryl inquired after I'd shoehorned him, along with the dogs, into my little rental car.

"Well," I said, "you can be on the lookout for stalkers pursuing me. Especially in little silver hybrid cars."

"Like aliens from outer space?" My long and lanky friend, who barely fit into the passenger seat, peered at me over his wire-rimmed spectacles.

Lexie and Odin didn't seem dismayed by this conjecture, perhaps because they both stood on the backseat, attempting to smell awful automobile aromas that wafted to their nostrils from the back windows that I'd cracked ajar. I'd also locked the doors, of course, using the switch up front so they couldn't inadvertently push the handles and open them.

"Nope," I said. "Most likely a nasty human or two whom I've somehow rubbed the wrong way, possibly in my quest for justice on Lois Terrone's behalf."

"Any ideas about who killed Earl Knox, if it wasn't her?"

After this afternoon, I feared I had too many ideas in that direction, but I decided not to inform my dear friend Darryl just yet. Not till I'd had an opportunity to digest what I'd learned, mix up my suspicions, and see where it all led.

Which, unfortunately, still might not point away from the very-much-alive Jeff, wherever he happened to be just then.

"I'm working on it," was all I said.

I saw Darryl glance often into the passenger side mirror, as if seeking someone following us. I smiled to myself — more in irony than humor. And hoped he'd see it, or I would, if someone actually was in pursuit.

After taking the 5 Freeway north, we arrived in Valencia, and I headed toward the soundstage-like edifice that housed Show Biz Beasts.

As I'd hoped, the parking lot was filled with vehicles whose drivers milled about outside.

I parked, got the dogs' leashes, and exited the car as the small crowd approached.

I grinned at the group. "Hi, everyone. Good to see you all." I completed whatever introductions hadn't yet been made, including Darryl, who'd heard of them all but hadn't necessarily met them.

Among those present was the current tenant of my rented-out mansion, Russ Preesinger, the redheaded, nice-looking guy who was dad to my Critters TLC, LLC, assistant, Rachel. Right now, I really appreciated his vocation as a location scout for a major studio. And I particularly appreciated that he'd happened to get back to town just in time for today's activities.

Then there was his predecessor renter, Charlotte LaVerne, my very first tenant, whom I'd helped to clear from a suspicion of murder that occurred right in my own leased-out home. She squealed upon seeing me and dashed in my direction, swathing me in a huge, habitual hug. "It's so great to see you, Kendra," she gushed, baring her toothy, white smile. Charlotte looked the same as when she'd rented from me, with a pretty face and a long black braid down her back. As always, she appeared youthful and slim — today, in slinky, tight slacks and a top that bared her midriff. "I'm so excited about seeing this idea of yours."

Since she was the one likely to have the most useful contacts, I hoped she would hang on to that opinion after I proposed my idea to this great group who could turn it into reality — and I did mean *reality.*

I glanced around quizzically.

"If you're looking for Yul," she said in a chilly voice, "he stayed in Nevada with his ferrets." She didn't sound extremely pleased about it. Her boy toy Yul's ferrets had once resided in my house, too — illegally, here in California. They'd been among the murder suspects I'd succeeded in clearing.

Finally, there was Charley Sherman, a law client of Borden's and mine who, in puffy, faded jeans and red plaid shirt, retained a resemblance to the Pillsbury Doughboy. I'd helped to negotiate a fair settlement for him in a suit that turned into a class action. He and his wife were plaintiffs who'd sought compensation after a resort up the coast made promises of luxury accommodations that were patently false. But he wasn't here because of that. Charley was a nearly retired executive of Hennessy Studios — where he had been a trainer of exotic animals.

Soon, we all trooped inside. Shareen and Corbin Hayhurst hovered anxiously around the entry, obviously aware of the conclave in their parking lot. Their assistant and greeter, Larry, stood there, too, appearing ill at ease in his Show Biz Beasts T-shirt, with the resident dog, Dorky, on a leash.

"Did you bring in some neophyte animals the way I told you to?" I asked them.

"We sure did, Kendra," Corbin responded.

"Good. I've brought a couple more." I handed them Lexie's and Odin's leashes. "Here's what I have in mind." And I proceeded to explain to the people I'd asked to meet us here, all in different areas of the industry, my idea for a TV reality show involving animal training.

Charlotte was an alumna of a major reality show who'd gone on to excel in the industry. She was now the producer of several reality show hits. She had contacts. She had clout.

And despite the fact she wasn't a dog lover, she sounded absolutely delighted to participate with the Hayhursts to train some untrained dogs — including my charges, since at least Lexie pretended not to remember her previous lesson — in the basics of sitting, staying, and lying down. Once they had mastered that, the idea I had was for contestants to utilize props from potentially exotic locales — like the sled dog scenario I'd seen here. That was where Russ's contacts could come in.

And then there was the idea of using Charley's contacts to eventually sign up each week's contest winner for a genuine role in some upcoming TV show or film.

Everyone could profit. Everyone could win. And if these folks could put something together, that's what the Show Biz Beasts staff could offer to their disgruntled clients as a compromise. No guarantees of getting on the show, but they could audition at the front of the line. And certainly no guarantees of winning if they got on.

Just what I especially liked: a win-win-win-win, etc., situation, potentially to an infinite number of wins.

And our small sample this afternoon, with Lexie, Odin, and the four other dogs the Hayhursts had assembled — Dorky, plus two middle-size mixed breeds and a golden retriever — made it look like one super suggestion. All six pups, put in a scenario of pretending to be service dogs for some humans who'd forgotten how to walk, did an outstanding job of finding and fetching for them on the hastily constructed pseudo set consisting of a home's living room and kitchen. Even Lexie! Not that she'd have won the top prize in a genuine contest, but perhaps Odin would have.

I was absolutely excited and ecstatic when we were done, since the three Hollywood types were already discussing getting their people to talk with each other and with the

Show Biz Beasts representatives.

"If you'd like to do any filming in a doggy day care center, or if you have animals come to visit from other locales in the future and need a place for them to hang out during the day, you have an unequaled resource right here," I told them all, passing out some of Darryl's Doggy Indulgence business cards.

"What about you, Kendra?" Charlotte asked. "What will your cut of this whole thing be?"

"Well, my legal fees," I said, stealing a glance toward the Hayhursts. "And if I can get a screen credit, and some small stipend for the idea, that would be wonderful. But let's see first if it helps to settle the pending lawsuit."

"We'll probably go forward even if it doesn't," Charley Sherman said.

"If you don't have an agent, Kendra, I can get mine to call you," Russ said.

"I'm an attorney," I reminded him, then stopped. "But I don't know a lot about negotiating this kind of contract. And then there's the old adage, 'The attorney who represents herself has a fool for a client.' "

"Good thinking," Russ said. "I'll give my agent a heads-up."

And as I retrieved Lexie and Odin, I gave

them a huge grin.

I wasn't smiling later, though. The Show Biz Beasts situation could be progressing toward a happy ending. But it wasn't the only scenario into which I'd stuck my nose, and the other main situation wasn't settling down.

I'd dropped off Darryl at Doggy Indulgence and had no sooner gotten back into my car with the dogs than my cell phone rang. Caller ID revealed it was Lois Terrone.

I hadn't spoken with her since finding out for certain that Jeff was alive. Not that I feared a skilled litigator like me might misspeak and give his secret away, but heck, I wasn't an actress. My words might be perfect, but would my demeanor be?

And besides, I believed she deserved to be told the truth.

Turned out my lack of acting ability didn't matter. Lois was the one who set the emotional scene for us. Hysteria shrieked out from her shrill tone. "Kendra? Thank God I reached you. I've been told to come back to the Glendale Police Department for further questioning this afternoon — in an hour."

"That might be a good thing, Lois," I lied. "If they told you to come without sending

301

someone to bring you in, maybe they do just have additional questions. Have you called Esther Ickes?"

"Of course I'd call the lawyer I hired first, but could you come, too?"

I stared out the windshield, attempting to ignore how Lexie and Odin leaped around beside me, eager to exit the car if we didn't get on the road.

Well, hell. Darryl's was still open for a while. They'd have fun playing here while I headed toward Glendale.

Was I really considering showing up at the cops' latest confrontation with Lois? Only partly. "I'll meet you there," I said. "Got the address?"

She gave it to me. "Thanks, Kendra. I know you have experience convincing cops about people's innocence in murders."

"Not because I have superior knowledge about criminal law," I told her. "Only because some of my closest friends and I have been accused. You're in great hands with Esther. And we can confer ahead of time. Maybe discuss some potential exonerating scenarios that Esther and you can suggest. Or if nothing else, come up with the best defense."

"I shouldn't need a defense," Lois wailed.

"Unfortunately, you may," I said. "I'll

meet you outside the police station in about forty-five minutes, okay?"

"Okay," she said with a sniffle.

I walked the dogs right back inside Doggy Indulgence, where Darryl indulgently said, "You just can't stay away, can you, Kendra?"

"Lexie and Odin can't. I've got someplace I need to be fairly shortly." When he opened his mouth as if to ask a question, I headed him off by saying, "I'll fill you in later." And then I hurried out.

Once again I sat in my rental car without driving. I needed to make a phone call. Unfortunately, I didn't have Jeff's current number — one he would actually answer. I'd failed to save it when it was captured on my cell phone. And so, I used what resources I could to track him down.

"Hi, Rachel," I said to my pet-sitting assistant. "Do you happen to have a card from What's the Scoop? I need their phone number."

"Right now?" she said. "It's probably buried at the bottom of my purse, and I'm in line at a Starbucks."

"What better time to dig for a card?" I inquired, unsure about any rationale for her hesitation.

"I'm right by the CBS Studios, talking to

a sexy guy who works there," she hissed almost inaudibly into my ear. In other words, I'd interrupted a potentially important flirtation.

Well, tough. Still, I needed her continued cooperation in many things. And so I said, "Show him how important you are. Say I'm your agent, and I need you to provide a phone number for someone you recently auditioned with from a card you're carrying."

"Oh, right," she said a lot louder and much more happily. "Great idea. And they're interested in calling me back? Then how could you lose their number?" She soon rattled off a phone number in the 818 area code — San Fernando Valley and vicinity — that I assumed was the right one for the poop-scooping and snooping associates.

"Thanks, Rachel," I said. "I owe you."

"You certainly do," she said sweetly, and we both hung up.

The next conversation was almost as odd as that one.

"What's the Scoop," answered a familiar, but obviously disguised, male voice. It was higher, with a hint of an indistinguishable accent.

"Mr. Scoop . . . er, Juan," I started, unsure how to address this alternate version of Jeff, especially since my insides somersaulted just because he was alive and I was talking to him again. Or because I despised him for distrusting me? Probably a bit of both. "I have a situation that might require your services," I said. "A good friend of mine suggested that the area around the Glendale Police Department needs a good cleaning." Was that too oblique? Too obtuse? But I knew Jeff in his former incarnation, pre-drugging and near drowning, would have gotten it.

"I see," he said quickly. "And how soon do you need my services?"

"Right away," I said.

"Got it." And he hung up.

I felt uneasy on the entire drive to Glendale. Not that I noticed any hybrid cars, or any other kind of vehicle, subtle or not, stalking me. But I knew that the reason Jeff acted as he did on the cell phone was that he was unsure if we were being monitored. And since his company phone number and cell phone were new, that meant the person being eavesdropped on would be me.

Could my cell phone be bugged? But how? I never left it far from my person, just in my purse, which was substantial enough in size to be obvious if anyone messed with it.

My car, then? This wasn't my very own bashed Beamer, which I felt almost sorrowfully certain by now was going to be proclaimed a total loss by the auto shop where it had been towed after my non-accident several weeks ago. It was unlikely that the rental car company placed conversation monitors in its vehicles. GPS systems to track them if stolen, perhaps, but bugging their products didn't seem like a good business practice.

Or maybe there wasn't an actual bug anywhere, but Jeff was still being exceedingly cautious, aka paranoid. Which made me want to strangle him. And soothe him — not to mention myself.

In any event, I didn't shout any of my suspicions or anything else into my empty car as I drove to Glendale. There, I parked at a meter on the street, being careful to feed it enough since I was alongside the home of the local police.

Wow! Jeff was fast. By the time I arrived, my fallen, frustrating hero was already there, in his little-old-man-in-a-big-hat disguise, treading slowly, while stooped, along the little bit of lawn near the substantial bureaucratic-style building of the Glendale Police Department. It appeared more elaborate than some of the LAPD edifices

I'd seen, larger and with a lot more style. One side was decorated with long, narrow windows. The entry area, not far from Jeff's lawn patrol, had a metallic sculpture sort of thing adorning it, and three flags flapped on the nearby poles: the country's, the state's, and, gosh darn if the City of Glendale didn't have its own official banner!

The police department building wasn't especially lonely. Similar structures that must have housed additional city functions were located nearby.

Okay, so now what should I do? Approach a poop scooper and ask for the time? Or —

No. As I got near the entry, I saw Lois standing inside, talking to Esther. Lois caught my eye, and I waved for her to come out. What we might discuss shouldn't be for the ears of the uniformed officers I saw behind a glass barrier across the room, apparently the greeters who asked visitors their business before allowing them to pass through to official areas.

Besides, speaking of eavesdropping, that was why I had requested the chief poop scooper's presence, and I doubted that someone in his dress or condition would be allowed inside, notwithstanding the open-air atmosphere of the large, open entry with its high ceiling. Bad smells aren't static, and the cops might assume his would permeate their otherwise awe-inspiring structure.

Fortunately, Lois understood my gesture and headed outside, accompanied by Esther. As always, Esther looked like the septuagenarian she was: short, stooped, silver-haired, and sagging, lined face. But looks are deceptive. She was one savvy lady lawyer, and her bright peach suit suggested she wasn't a wallflower. She'd always been the go-for-the-jugular sort, and I knew that Lois was in excellent legal hands. "Kendra, my dear," she cried as soon as she was outside, and reached out her hand. I took it, and she used it to draw me close, into a snug hug of greeting.

"Great to see you, Esther," I said, feeling underdressed in my business casual dark slacks and flowered cotton shirt.

Lois, too, had come clad in a suit. Hers was more modest and subdued than her counsel's — depression gray, with a plain white blouse beneath. She looked closer to Esther's age than mine, though she had to be right in between. This situation hadn't been kind to her psyche or appearance. The limp I'd noticed earlier had grown more pronounced. Her formerly glowing green eyes had dulled, and her blond curls drooped even more than before, along with the wattle beneath her chin.

Glancing at my watch, I saw that the time for the session with the cops was fast approaching. "Any idea why they want to talk to Lois again?" I asked Esther, keeping my voice loud enough for the poop scooper to hear.

"I gather they think they've amassed nearly enough evidence to take my client into custody," Esther replied grimly. At that same client's sorrowful groan, Esther reached in that direction, grasped Lois's hand, and added, "But not if I can help it." Then she turned back toward me. "Kendra, from what I've seen of your skills in the past, it's a good thing for Lois that you're helping out. One thing I need to ask you, though."

"What's that?" I again ensured that my voice was projecting. "Ask away, Esther."

She looked at me oddly, then said, "My suggestion, my dear, is that you figure out very quickly what happened in this particular murder. Time is running out, I fear, to clear my client."

That client reacted quite strongly to Esther's statement, sinking toward the ground as the poop scooper sped from his nearby chores to catch her.

CHAPTER TWENTY

Fortunately, Lois was just a touch woozy, and managed to avoid being carted off by EMTs in a shrieking ambulance. She simply, and firmly, said no.

We all went inside for a few minutes of rest and relaxation while the attentive authorities in the anteroom notified their upstairs counterparts that their meeting would start a little late.

Okay, so they didn't exclude the cruddy-appearing poop scooper from coming inside and hovering over the frail lady he'd helped to rescue from a fall. And in fact, despite his decrepit appearance, he smelled only half bad. What a surprise.

Jeff played his role well, though, asking often if the lady was okay — and not leaving when she assured him she was, despite the odd stare she shot his way. Did Lois see Jeff inside this awesome disguise? I did, of course, but I'd been a lot physically closer to him than his mother figure — really up close and personal.

Then again, she'd known the real him a lot longer than I had.

In any event, despite curious looks in his direction, she didn't let on that anything might be amiss. And for his part, Jeff stayed, perhaps acting as if he awaited a tip for his assistance, although he didn't stick his hand out. We remained in the lobby for at least ten minutes, sitting in chairs along an outer wall near the windows.

Pretending the cops couldn't hear and the poop scoop guy's English was worse than it was, I eventually responded to Esther's comment to me that had upset her client enough to affect her consciousness. Speaking in a lowered voice, I said, "I'll do whatever I can to find the person who's really of interest in the . . . incident." I looked around again, in an attempt to ensure no stranger was listening. At least Corina Carey wasn't in evidence, taking notes for her miserable *NewsShakers* show. "I have some ideas already."

Lois, whose chair was in the center, looked a shade brighter. "Really?"

I nodded. "Nothing too exciting yet," I warned her. "But I do have some questions for you, and their answers could assist me in getting somewhere."

"Anything," she said, straightening a little. She regarded me expectantly, green eyes aglow.

Which made me feel a bit awful. What if my inquiry was way off base? Still, I had to try.

"Let's go back a ways." I ignored an annoyed gaze from Esther, who was concerned about how long they'd have before the detectives upstairs headed down to round them up. "How did you hear about The Clone Arranger?"

"On a newscast about designer dogs," Lois said. "They were mentioned, along with some places doing research into genetic enhancement of certain pet traits — like a speed gene for greyhounds, I think."

I'd done some research in that direction, too, so I knew what she was talking about. "Okay, then," I continued, "how did you first contact them?"

"I found their website and called for an appointment."

"Did they ask what kind of dog you were interested in having cloned?"

"Where's this going, Kendra?" Esther interrupted.

"I know it doesn't necessarily sound relevant," I responded. "For right now I

312

don't want to explain. Please just play along."

My old friend Esther was usually a pillar of patience, but she didn't seem inclined to take the time today. Even so, she settled back with a bit of a sigh, her head turned so she wouldn't miss a word, even if she didn't comprehend the significance . . . yet.

"So Lois, did they ask anything about your dog?" I repeated.

She shook her head. "I don't remember anything before, on the phone, like that. I just went there, they looked Flisa over, and asked a few questions about her lineage — like, did I know her parents, how much Akita did she have in her, that kind of thing."

Aha! That could comport with my theory.

"Tell me as much as you recall about how that visit went."

Esther rolled her eyes, as if to remind us we didn't have all day.

"In twenty-five words or less," I added.

Lois looked lost. "I don't think . . ."

"I'm kidding," I said. "But we do need to keep this brief."

I'd asked some of this stuff before, but not in as much detail. Now, Lois quickly described a visit that had begun much as mine had as Kenni Ballan, there with "my" little Meph. She had met first with sales manager Earl, who had given Lois some paperwork and spouted similar disclaimers about no guarantees of pups and no assurances of exact twinship if the cloning was successful, especially as to personality. She had gotten a lot farther than I had, though, being granted an audience with The Clone Arranger's science guru Melba Slabach, who'd explained how DNA samples would be taken from Flisa's skin and elsewhere. Yes, Lois recalled meeting Mason and Debby Payne while she was there, and P.R. specialist Wally Yance, too.

"And while you were there, was there any discussion of whether cloning generally worked best with purebred or mixed-breed dogs?" I inquired at the end, almost as an apparent afterthought.

"Well, yes, I think someone said purebred. Melba, maybe. Or Debby. I mentioned my Akita Ezekiel, at home, but said it was Flisa I wanted to clone, at least for now. And —"

"Kendra, I really think —" Esther interjected.

"I'm through," I said. "Thanks, Lois. And as far as how to mount a defense in your discussion up there" — I pointed toward where the elevators sat behind barriers, then let my finger raise a little. "You can tell

314

them, or at least give some good hints, that all wasn't exactly kosher at The Clone Arranger, and other people may have realized it. That could have given a goodly number of other suspects a reason for eliminating Earl. Good luck."

And I watched, the poop scooper standing at my side, as Esther accompanied Lois upstairs.

He stood beside me at my car. "I know what you were getting at, Kendra." He sounded all Jeff, and all furious. I only wished I knew why. And that I could shrug his awful attitude off so it stopped stabbing me. "You do have it, then. Or did you know about it before? Was all that just an act, your supposed attempt to help Lois?"

He was entirely out of character as a poop scooper, which surprised me. At least as far as his demeanor, not his disguise.

"What 'it' are you talking about?" I asked, not for the first time, glaring right back into his icy blue eyes. "The supposed disappearing 'it' from your package?" I was getting angry with his entire act. Why the heck did he choose to continue to mistrust me?

"You obviously know what it is, Kendra, or you wouldn't have asked those questions."

"Circular argument here, Hubbard," I retorted, then slapped my hand over my mouth. Okay, it wasn't any huge surprise whom I was talking to, but I'd promised not to announce it.

"Besides," he continued, apparently unfazed, "don't you see how dangerous it is for you to continue with this? It's taking up a lot of my time protecting you and getting these guys I've hired to back me up."

"Did I ask you to protect me? And besides, I'm sure that most of what you're doing now is spying on me, to see if I come up with 'it,' whatever 'it' is."

"It," he said with a chilly stare, "is a thumb drive, as you obviously know, since you're clearly aware of the information on it."

"A thumb drive?" One of those handy little storage gadgets to save stuff from computers? "If you did actually put one into that envelope, it wasn't there when I received it. As I told you, the package was already open." And just in case, I'd asked Rachel to see if she'd seen any extra dropped-out contents anywhere. At least now I knew what to ask her about. "And *what* information do you assume I know?"

"Don't act dumb," he insisted to me.

Utterly insulted, I scowled and stepped back.

"Look, Jeff, I think the drug that got pumped into your system is continuing to extremely mess with your mind." I'd come to assume that was a reason for his continued paranoia — even if it couldn't explain why he didn't tell me he was back in L.A. in the first place. "Please see a doctor, or better yet, a shrink."

And I refused to shrink under his increasingly furious stare.

"Okay," I continued, "here's how it is with me, whether or not you like it. I started snooping into this situation all because of you. Because I was worried about you, thought you were dead. I began helping Lois because she was important to you. Well, I know now that you're alive." *Even if you're not acting like the sexy, sometimes sweet, always exasperating guy I fell for.* "But Lois still needs help clearing herself from Earl's murder. If you didn't do it —"

He shook his head, as if outraged I'd harbor such an ugly suspicion. Well, hell, it was okay for him, but not for me?

"And I don't think Lois did, so I'm still going to follow my own leads and see if I can figure out who did do it. You can work with me, or stay out of my way."

"And you can stay out of mine," he said. "But you'd better watch your own back now. I'm not going to. Not until you turn the thumb drive over to me. My mind may have been messed up, but some things are still clear. See you around, Kendra." And then he stalked off, leaving me watching *his* back in bewilderment.

What the hell was on that thumb drive, and why did he think it was so important?

I headed back to Darryl's to pick up the dogs. Yes, I again kept an eye on my rear-view and side mirrors, but still saw no one following me.

Certainly not Jeff, in whatever guise.

But at least this afternoon's confrontation had taught me one thing. Jeff was alive and definitely kicking — against me. I'd seen on the Internet that ketamine could cause some of his symptoms: paranoia, amnesia, and all sorts of other stuff. But whether it was the drug Jeff had been administered and its lingering, scary effects, or simply his own pigheadedness, he now hated me. I didn't want to out him just yet to Ned Noralles or any authority, since he seemed to have some reason to stay undercover, logical or not. And he had, after all, ended up in the canal in his car, apparently as the result of Earl's attack on him.

If I found out who'd killed Earl, I should also be able to determine who'd conspired to harm Jeff. Would that encourage Jeff to get help? Bring back the Jeff I'd known and thought I loved? Who knew?

And that dumb thumb drive. I'd started pondering what might be on it. Did it matter? Probably — if it added to Jeff's lunacy.

But one thing I was sure of: All bets were off as far as following Jeff's rules. I wouldn't purposely divulge his secrets unless I became certain it was in his best interest — or mine. But I still intended to use whatever resources I could to achieve my own results.

What was all this about? Well, for the first time since I'd spoken to Jeff in the resurrected flesh, I called Althea and gave her a computer assignment.

"Have you heard anything about Jeff?" she of course asked as I explained only what I wanted, but not why.

"I'm still working on it, Althea," I told her. "I'm still hoping for a happy ending."

"But not expecting it anymore?" she asked sadly and almost resignedly.

I almost blurted the truth, but instead simply said, "Who knows?"

Back at my law office, the dogs lying on the

floor at my feet, I used another obvious resource. Only with this one, I had to be even more cautious about what I said and how I said it.

"Hi, Tom," I said to my formerly favorite vet when he answered the phone. Well, heck, he hadn't really done anything wrong. He'd been over his relationship with Debby Payne — even if she hadn't been over him — before he'd attempted to take up with me.

Hadn't he?

"Kendra, hi." His voice sounded exceedingly happy, as if he was glad to hear from me. Which made me feel somewhat guilty.

"Any chance of us getting together for dinner tonight?"

"For fun, or because you still have questions about The Clone Arranger?" He kept his tone light, yet there was an edge that said he'd seen through me. Not that it was especially difficult.

"A little of both," I admitted.

Which caused him to laugh. And agree. But with this disclaimer at the end: "I'll answer what questions I think are okay, Kendra. But even though I'm only a veterinarian and some of the Hippocratic and other oaths human doctors take don't apply, there are things I just won't talk about regarding my patients and their situations."

Like, is The Clone Arranger a huge fraud? I was almost certain now that it was, and this man could have the key.

I wasn't exactly certain how I'd ask those critical questions for which I needed answers, but I was sure as hell going to try.

We sat outside at a fast-food joint, of all places. Here, we could bring our dogs along. Tom hadn't schlepped all five of the rescue animals he now kept at his home, but he had brought one big galoot of a German shepherd–Rottweiler mix he called Big Boy. For protection? From me? It certainly wouldn't be from the leery Lexie. And even Odin appeared on his best, nonconfrontational behavior.

"It's good to see you, Kendra," Tom said as he handed me my hamburger from the bag of food he'd bought inside. Of course all three dogs sat at attention, enchanted by charbroiled beefy smells.

"Ditto." And I meant it. I still found Tom's looks charming, despite their not smacking of utter gorgeousness. Even more, I enjoyed his normally laid-back demeanor. Only now, I sensed a distance between us from both our perspectives. He knew I had ulterior motives for wanting to meet this evening. And I knew he knew more than he'd revealed so far about The Clone Arranger.

Ignoring comings and goings of other diners who occupied, then vacated, nearby tables, we chatted about all kinds of inconsequentials as I pondered how to lead into what I really wanted to discuss.

Eventually, I commenced with a kind of equivocation. "So how are things in the vet business?"

"Generally fine," he said.

"Save any lives lately?"

"Yeah." His features lit up as he recounted a tale of a cat hit by a car, and how he had helped to restore it so it could enjoy its remaining eight lives.

When he ended the story, I sat with moist eyes, enthralled and admiring. But I had to recall my purpose for seeing him this evening, keep it at the forefront of my unhappy mind.

"That's amazing," I said in all sincerity. I gave each pup a small piece of my hamburger bun, and they scarfed them up as if starved. And then I led into the topic I'd come to discuss. "What about at The Clone Arranger? What kinds of veterinary work have you done there lately?"

His half grin beneath that intriguing widow's peak was absolutely wry. "So here we are at last, the real reason you wanted to get together. But, Kendra, there's no more I'll say about my relationship with Debby or The Clone Arranger. Debby's part of my past. And as I said, I believe in veterinarian-patient confidentiality — to a point, at least. Here, it's with the company that wants me to make sure the animals it's about to clone are as healthy as possible. So, that's it. But if you want to talk about our getting together again for a romantic relationship . . . well, I'm available."

"And I might be, too, since my significant other has disappeared." And as far as the rest of the world knew, remained that way. Plus, I knew that the company to which Tom felt loyalty had been involved in what happened to Jeff. But I kept that to myself.

"I'm sorry in some respects, Kendra," Tom said. "I'm sure it's awful for you."

"Sure is," I said, and shoved another fry into my mouth as if to punctuate that I didn't want to discuss Jeff further. Then I said, somewhat offhandedly, "So, Tom, do you have any reason to think that The Clone Arranger did something that caused Lois Terrone's dog Flisa to die?"

"That's the kind of question I'd expect from a lawyer," he retorted, suddenly defensive. "Save it for when you've subpoenaed me to be a witness in whatever lawsuit your client Lois intends to bring against The Clone Arranger. Assuming she's cleared of Earl's murder."

Uh-oh. This pseudo date was suddenly deteriorating into something potentially ugly. But I really desired to dig out what, and how much, Tom actually knew.

I'd been continuously contemplating what could be on Jeff's purported thumb drive, assuming it even existed. Something that could exonerate Lois — despite its loss even before Earl Knox's demise? That demonstrated The Clone Arranger's foul misdeeds that resulted in Flisa's fatality? For Lois's sake, I hoped so. It would certainly explain Jeff's resolution to retrieve it — and his claim I knew what was on it, however untrue that might be, since I clearly was conducting my own investigation into Flisa's and Earl's deaths.

Plus, focusing on some of Jeff's flakiest comments, I was zeroing in on some additional suspicions — ones that could even mean Tom's involvement.

"I don't represent Lois in any civil action," I said, "and certainly not regarding any criminal charges that may be brought against her. But I feel sorry for her. You know my background in helping people who are falsely accused. And I've no reason to think she was the one who killed Earl."

"But she hated The Clone Arranger," countered Tom. "And she'd mostly had contact with Earl, so she's as likely a suspect as anyone."

I wasn't about to mention the little conversation Jeff had possibly overheard between that murder victim and his unidentified coconspirator. For one thing, it had occurred while Jeff was admittedly under the influence of a drug, so I still surmised it could have been at least partly his imagination.

And I still couldn't help a small misgiving that that discussion could have been intentionally manufactured by Jeff to divert suspicion away from himself.

Even so, after treating the dogs to a few leftover fries, I said, "Okay, Tom. We're obviously poles apart on this topic of conversation. Let's drop the whole suspicion thing, shall we?"

"Fine." He seemed visibly to relax, a good thing.

"But do you mind if I ask other questions about The Clone Arranger? Nothing controversial, honest. I'm just really curious about what they do."

Wariness returned to Tom's brown eyes, and rightly so, though I wasn't about to let on the rationale for my upcoming inquiries. If he understood them . . . well, he'd probably refuse to answer, on the grounds that it could incriminate his sometime employer.

"Ask away, but I won't necessarily answer."

I started off entirely innocently, asking about how Mason Payne had decided to get into the business. The answers sounded like the stock stuff on their website: A scientist by background, an animal lover by nature, he'd seen people's sadness after losing their beloved pets. And so forth.

"And the technology. I know they have expertise in analyzing DNA for people looking for answers to their dogs' true genetic backgrounds and the accuracy of their pedigrees." That was on a separate page on their website. "But the cloning part — is it anything like cloning of livestock? What's the science behind it?"

Tom shrugged beneath his snug blue T-shirt. "They've never shared the details with me. I gather they've developed their own means of doing things, maybe based on what else was out there and maybe not."

I wouldn't ask if the claims of Clark Weiss of CW Ultra Technologies that Earl Knox had stolen some secrets from him had any merit. Tom might not know, and could resent my asking.

Instead, I got to what I really wanted from Tom, as obliquely as I was able. "I know Beryl Leeds was thrilled about how her yellow Lab got cloned. And I saw some other successes on their website: standard poodles, Shih Tzus, pit bulls, and Chihuahuas. Even a Siamese cat, two Persians, a ferret, and a chinchilla. I found all that really exciting. Did you examine all the parents of those success stories? And were they healthier than Lois's dog Flisa — an Akita mix?"

Mix being the important word in that inquiry.

He looked at me closely for an instant, as if he knew exactly what I was asking. But I didn't press it any further.

And all he said was, "They promised not to try the procedure on any pet I determined had any ongoing genetic issue that could be passed along to any resulting puppies. And none of the successes did. Flisa? If I'd seen anything in her that indicated she wouldn't survive the cloning process — which I understand is fairly mild — I'd have told them. I care about my patients, Kendra. You know that. And I care about my own reputation. I wouldn't do anything to harm any animal. And I'd take whatever action I thought was called for if I believed someone was intentionally hurting any of my patients."

Including murder of a person? I wanted to inquire. But I didn't.

"What about the babies? Did you check them over after they were born?"

"Before they were handed off to their new owners, sure. But not while they were still subject to the cloning process."

Whatever that meant. Well, Tom hadn't directly given me what I'd wanted to know. He hadn't proclaimed that The Clone Arranger never harmed a hair on its subjects' furry heads. He also hadn't convinced me that their system was totally on the up-and-up.

But his response had boosted him, if only a little, toward the top of my suspect list.

CHAPTER
TWENTY-ONE

The pups and I headed to my home-sweet-garage after dinner with Tom. I felt exhausted after all our head games. Had I learned anything even an iota useful?

I hadn't wanted to maintain Tom as a major suspect, but before bed I revised my latest list on the Earl Knox murder. And hoped to hear from Jeff — er, Juan the scooper. But I didn't, not before or after my shower, or even when I got into bed.

I'd always felt a failure in the guy-choosing department. No more so than now. The fellow for whom I'd really fallen suspected me of being a thief and worse, for reasons I couldn't fathom in the least. And that same man, as sexually appealing as ever despite his disgusting disguise, hadn't trusted me enough to let me know he was alive after an astoundingly scary ordeal. All that hurt. A whole lot. Should I count him out?

Absolutely, at least till he regained some

of his senses. If ever.

And the other man was involved with an outfit where someone was killed. Might he be keeping some of their secrets that could point to their involvement in fraud, if not felony murder?

That was how my mind remained occupied as I lay there, long into the night, with both dogs snoring soundly at my sides.

By morning I'd hatched a plot, a way to follow up on my expanding suspicions about The Clone Arranger. But I had some phone calls to make first.

But not before I got the dogs eating and romping, then bundled them into the rental car and headed to Darryl's. I received his welcoming hug, then dropped the dogs with him. The pups seemed exceedingly happy with the setup. By the time I considered hitting the road, they'd already settled in their favorite Doggy Indulgence spots. Lexie leaped onto the sofa in the human furniture area, and Odin grabbed a large nylon bone and played keep away with a friendly pit bull. I almost felt lonesome, seeing them so happy to be away from me. But I had things to do, and they'd have more fun here.

"You okay, Kendra?" Darryl inquired as I said my goodbyes. He was always such a perceptive friend, and his caring nature brought tears once more to eyes that had become much too inclined to grow moist lately. *Make an appointment soon with a good ophthalmologist,* I noted in my melancholy mind.

"Hanging in," I assured him.

"Any word on that reality show idea?" He grinned in anticipation, and I wasn't about to puncture any hope — either for him or for my concerned clients.

"Not yet, but I'll follow up shortly. I'll let you know how things go."

Note to my legally inclined mind, I thought as I headed for the car. *Follow up, as promised, for everyone's benefit.*

Which I would, soon.

As I engaged in my pet-sitting exercises, I evaluated each of my charges. Of the cats I checked in on, Abra, the Siamese, was most likely a prime candidate for The Clone Arranger's slimy services. Her friend Cadabra, the equally arrogant tabby, might not be clonable, under that company's possibly stringent and slick standards.

Interesting, I considered as I eventually ended my rounds. If I was right, Stromboli, the shepherd mix, and his next-door neighbor Meph, a wiry terrier, would not be cloning material at all. Piglet the pug would be. So would Lexie and Odin, if either Jeff or I were so inclined — which I certainly wasn't now. So would Beggar, the Irish setter owned by my tenants and friends, the Preesingers. I'd no idea about Pansy, the potbellied pig.

Okay, I decided as I pulled my rental car into the law office lot.

Speaking of which car, I needed to figure out what next. My insurance funds for rental after an accident would run out soon. My Beamer was evidently a lost cause as far as repair and restoration.

I needed new wheels. What kind? I couldn't afford a new Beamer under my current circumstances, but how could I settle for a lesser automobile?

As I sat in the parking lot and pondered, I started a new list on the notepad I always kept in whatever car I drove. Things to do: Think about a new car. Follow up on the reality show resolution of the Hayhursts' lawsuit situation.

And what I intended to work on first thing this morning: Put together a party at The Clone Arranger's — a mixture of people, their pets, and The Clone Arranger staff to see what transpired. . . .

"You're looking good, Kendra." Mignon chirped today's assessment with a big smile as I entered the building.

"I'll say," our boss, Borden, echoed as he joined us in the lobby. "Have you resolved the Hayhursts' problem? I heard from Corbin and Shareen that you had one heck of a possible solution."

"Nothing's finalized yet," I disclaimed, as a decent lawyer should. "But I'm hopeful of the result."

"Good deal," Borden applauded. "Everything else okay?"

"Getting there," I said, perhaps a touch too optimistically. But at least I was working on it.

I waved greetings to some of the office staff as well as attorneys whom I'd come to really care about — Elaine Aames, the senior who often kept Gigi the macaw in her office, and some of the other old-timers.

And then I closed the door to my office.

First, I had to check on the status of a few things. I called Lois Terrone.

"How was your meeting with the Glendale cops yesterday?" I asked after assuring myself she was none the worse for her near fall in the police department's front yard. I pulled out pad and pen to take notes, in case I had suggestions about how to refute their allegations.

To my surprise, the interview had turned out to be almost a nonevent. "They leaned on me at first," Lois said, sounding somewhat scared. "But the things they asked seemed to rehash old ground: Why did I think The Clone Arranger had harmed my dog, and how had they done it? How well had I gotten to know Earl, and Mason, and the others? Did I have any impressions of Debby Payne, or the outside veterinarian, Dr. Venson?"

Interesting. Maybe my internal unwelcome suspicions about Tom were shared by the cops. I'd hoped I was way off base, but maybe, instead, I was hitting an unwanted home run.

Still, why would he have harmed Earl Knox?

Because the guy was hurting some of Tom's patients present at The Clone Arranger's premises? Or, even worse for the well-regarded vet, his reputation for stellar pet care?

Or maybe Earl had been hitting on Tom's local lady, Debby Payne . . . ?

Okay, that could just be my own cattiness — and insecurities — rising to the surface. I continued quizzing Lois, whom I still wanted to believe was absolutely innocent — not necessarily because of her relationship to Jeff, since my own relationship with him was so awful and incomprehensible now. But because she seemed like a nice, unjustly accused lady.

"Anything else?" I asked. "Did they say something that seemed to be edging in sideways, hoping that by asking you seemingly innocuous questions they would put you off guard, then hit you with a zinger?"

"Oh, Kendra, I didn't think of that." Lois's horror resounded through the phone. "But I don't believe there was anything too bad. And Esther seemed almost pleased afterward and said she thinks they're looking in other directions. I hope so. It sure feels good to be home right now, with my Ezekiel." Some muffled baby talk as she apparently spoke with her Akita. "But I don't know if this'll last. They ended up by telling me not to leave the area. And by saying there would be at least one more interrogation before they intended to make any arrests. The implication was that I'm still in the running."

"Well, you're still a free woman," I said. "Let's be grateful for that. Meantime, I'll conduct some further inquiries. What's your schedule for the rest of the week?"

I wrote down her responses. And then I called Althea.

"Interesting information," she told me. "I figured out what you're driving at. This says a lot about possible monkey business on the part of The Clone Arranger. Not that I'm aware that they've tried to duplicate any simians — actually or fraudulently." She gave me the info that she'd collected after my inquiry.

"This is really helpful," I told her. "It might lead to some real progress in putting them on the spot, if not out of business."

"Will it help to find Jeff?" she inquired hopefully.

"I have a feeling that once this is on the table, Jeff will make an appearance that none of them — or us — will forget."

I hoped I wasn't overly optimistic in any of this. What Althea had learned, I'd be able to use at least as ammunition. But there could be alternative explanations besides the one I felt almost certain of.

I'd be interested to hear The Clone Arrangers attempt to assert them with straight faces.

Next, I got the other information from Althea that I'd asked her to amass: some phone numbers, easy for someone with her hacker — er, computer — skills.

I thanked her, and started calling some of those numbers.

I'd hoped, after my good luck getting everyone together on a moment's notice on

the Show Biz Beasts matter, that this conclave I intended to call could be scheduled
equally easily. And quickly.

No such luck. But I was able to find a date
and time toward the end of the week that
appeared to suit everyone.

And I convinced them all, I hoped, that
the gathering was to be a surprise party, so
they shouldn't let the word get out.

It was, in fact, intended as a surprise
party. But the people to be surprised
wouldn't consider it a happy gathering — if
I had my facts correct.

Next, I called Jeff at What's the Scoop,
again playing our game that someone eavesdropped on everything. I equivocated yet
got across where I intended to be and when.
Jeff-Juan grumbled and growled and again
insinuated I'd stolen that stupid thumb
drive without answering a single query
about its alleged contents. He also indicated
that I'd better have someone watch my butt,
since he was no longer doing it. And I was
playing with fire by what I was doing.

Of course, he said, I undoubtedly knew
that. And I'd better hope that this whole
situation wasn't turned around to implicate
me, the way he believed I should be.

He couldn't see the way I rolled my eyes,
but he could hear how fast I hung up.

I only hoped I could wait as long as it took for that grand gathering to occur without having a conniption or a stroke or something terrible. Because if it went the way I wanted, at least part of the truth would come out. And that information would go a long way, I anticipated, in determining who had murdered Earl Knox — and, peripherally, who had co-connived with Earl in attempting to kill Jeff.

And, Jeff's ugly and utterly hurtful accusations notwithstanding, it wasn't me.

CHAPTER
TWENTY-TWO

"What is this really about, Ms. Ballantyne?" demanded Mason Payne, confronting me in a corner of the crowded Clone Arranger entry lounge. We were surrounded largely by former customers and their cloned pets — mostly animals I'd described to Tom Venson that I'd seen on the website, including three dogs and an equal number of cats. I hadn't tried to get the owners of the cloned ferret and chinchilla to come for the event. These more usual pets should be sufficient to make my very potent point — I hoped.

The noise was amazing. So were the scents, with all these animals about. But mostly it was the sight that made me sigh in anticipation. And at least so far no one had fled the compact room because of how over-stuffed it had become.

Even Beryl Leeds had come at my invitation with her two pale Labs, father and cloned son. Now, she sat on one of the lounge's uncomfortable yellow chairs, appearing utterly irritable.

Also present were a cloned standard poodle and her look-alike younger twin, plus similar sets of Shih Tzus, pit bulls, and Chihuahuas, and Siamese and Persian cats. And yes, they'd brought their human owners.

In addition, the room held several people who'd never previously come to The Clone Arranger. They brought not pets, but pedigrees and photos — plus their own experiences in selling their purebred animals' offspring. And those purebreds just happened to consist of poodles, Shih Tzus, pit bulls . . . well, you get it. I'd gotten them there on the falsest pretenses of all — maybe. But my intentions were entirely honorable.

"I think you know, Mason," I responded. Just then, the person I'd met in the parking lot, who'd sold a poodle only months ago to someone who looked exactly like Debby Payne, went dashing over to a pair of poodles in the lounge and exclaimed over the younger. How did I know this particular purchase had been made by Debby? Well, after checking out local breeders, Althea had e-mailed them photos of members of The Clone Arranger staff.

Other dog and cat breeders reacted similarly, reacquainting themselves with babies who were likely ones they'd sold recently as I continued talking to Mason. "Is it possible that The Clone Arranger keeps its costs as reasonable as they are to pet owners because they buy similar purebred animals from reputable breeders who don't know who the final owners will be?"

"How dare you make such allegations!" That wasn't Mason but Beryl Leeds, whose scowl obscured how attractive her TV star looks had once been. At the moment, she appeared every inch the arrogant former headliner she was. Maybe it was the red hue of her face that exaggerated how awfully she was aging. "Tell her, Mason. It doesn't matter that she's a lawyer. You'll sue her for defaming your wonderful organization. You can't let her harm The Clone Arranger — especially not before you've finished cloning my adorable Melville."

"That's right, Ms. Ballantyne. You can't just barge in here with all these people under false pretenses, then make claims with no proof."

Fortunately, that was when some other Clone Arrangers started to enter the lounge. Among them was Melba Slabach, the head so-called scientist of the group. She, if no one else, would pay attention to what I was about to allege. "I think proof will be readily available," I said. "I'm sure all purebreds of a particular breed share a lot of similar DNA, but it's not all identical, or every member of a breed would look and act exactly alike. In fact, that's a whole other aspect of the science you indulge in here — confirming DNA backgrounds for all kinds of animals. So maybe Melba, or better yet some independent lab, should run tests showing whether the so-called clones you've delivered to your clients have DNA closer to their purported papas and mamas, or to the animals owned by those breeders who sold similar puppies and kittens to people who appear astoundingly like members of your staff. Some of those sales occurred right around when you delivered supposed clones to your customers for exorbitant, but not outrageous, prices. Right, Melba?"

The tall scientist, whose dark hair was pulled starkly back from her face, grew pasty white, especially in comparison with Beryl's ruddiness. She made a sound that was absolutely noncommittal, but the infuriated glare she shot at me didn't amount to a denial, either.

Accompanying her were P.R. person Wally Yance, Mason's sister, Debby Payne — and

Dr. Tom Venson. Yes, I'd called Tom, too, and asked him to attend. Didn't describe what I was up to, but said he might be interested.

Was Tom's appearance here with his former girlfriend Debby his way of saying whose side he was on? Or was it for some other, even more nefarious, reason?

Even Earl Knox's former wife, Edwina Horton, and her husband, Marty, had come. I'd never made it to their store to meet Marty, but I'd invited them in order to have as full a complement of suspects as possible present when I dropped today's bomb. Unfortunately, Clark Weiss was out of town. Still, he wasn't my chief suspect.

I only hoped that the explosion resulted in the disclosure of who had actually perpetrated all the nasty stuff around here.

"Kendra, could you tell me what's really going on?" asked a small, plump woman who tapped my shoulder. She was the breeder of Chihuahuas who'd recently sold a puppy to someone who closely resembled Wally Yance, who, in a sport jacket and plaid pants, had shoehorned himself into the lounge and now stood near us. His normally military bearing had slumped as he obviously attempted not to be spotted by the Chihuahua lady beside me. Too late. "Oh, hi, Wally," she said. "I thought we were here for a seminar on how to choose the best sire and dam for our litters, genetically speaking." As I said, I'd fibbed to the breeders to bring them here today. "But I was really surprised to see the puppy you bought from me here, and the person who says she owns her now claims she's the clone of her own dog. Can you explain this to me?"

"That's what I'm asking them to do," I said.

Which was when I noticed, from the corner of my eye, two people enter the room almost simultaneously. One regarded the other with an apparent combination of amusement and suspicion. The other didn't spare his fellow enterer a single glance.

Oh, but he would.

I glanced at my watch. Yes, it was twenty minutes later than the time I'd asked the initial group, mostly here now, to arrive. And that meant . . .

Sure enough, the next two to squeeze through the door were Lois Terrone and her attorney, my dear friend Esther Ickes. And behind them was a suited guy I didn't recognize — a Glendale detective, I assumed. For once, I hadn't had direct contact with the cops who hovered around the friend I attempted to clear, so I left it to Esther to handle them.

This guy would need to meet one of the men who'd slipped in a few seconds earlier: Detective Ned Noralles, of the LAPD. He'd come because I'd aroused his curiosity about what would transpire. He was out of his jurisdiction, possibly not even on duty.

Which was probably best, considering what I was about to do.

And then — oh, yes! There she was, along with her cameraman — my media nemesis and primary contact, Corina Carey. As usual, she wore a brightly colored outfit — a lime green wrap dress — to set off the darkness of her stylishly shaggy hair. Yep, I'd turned this into one huge circus. Which meant I'd better be right.

And I was certain I was.

"Hey, everyone," I called out. I'm not the tallest person, but my voice projects pretty well. I've trained it to be heard in court, after all. Some courtrooms have microphones and adequate amplification systems, and others don't, so to impress judges and juries I've had to ensure I'd be heard. "May I have your attention, please?"

Corina sidled up to me and smiled in uncharacteristic silence, obeying my request to listen when she first arrived. But not everyone responded, so I shouted again, and this time the room quieted, except for the scrabbling of canines asserting their alphaness and the hisses of kitties in their crates.

"I'd like to explain why I've invited you all here." I could see Corina's cameraman focusing on me and was certain she'd soon start attempting to interview me, notwithstanding my instructions, but for now she simply let me speak. "At this time, I'm just telling a hypothetical tale, but I'm hoping it will help explain the motives for a couple of nasty situations. First, though, I want to try to ensure I'm correct. Is anyone here who's utilized The Clone Arranger, or knows people who have, aware of any successful cloning of a pet who's not a purebred of his or her breed?"

This caused a muted roar among attendees as they discussed this question among themselves. Not one raised a hand or otherwise indicated they knew of a mixed breed being cloned.

"Okay, then, Ms. Carey." I nodded toward Corina. "As an attorney I know I'm putting myself out on a limb here with hypothetical and unsubstantiated allegations, so I want to state for the record, and the camera, that this all is entirely speculation, still subject to being proven."

I launched into a brief but sincere assessment of my suspicions — on why Lois Terrone, whose Akita, Flisa, whom she'd wished to have cloned, was led on but eventually informed that the cloning could not be done successfully: Flisa wasn't a purebred, but an Akita mix. And then Flisa died, possibly as a result of mistreatment, or possibly just a result of old age. Of course Lois was distraught and made allegations that were sincere but unprovable. Since her primary contact was Earl Knox, he had been the object of most of her anger.

But Lois wasn't without resources of her own. She had hired her dear friend and almost-son Jeff Hubbard, a security expert and private investigator, to look into The Clone Arranger and its business practices, assuming that what he would find was mistreatment of its animal clients.

This mention caused Ned Noralles to stand up straighter in the crowd, his attention clearly captured.

I continued, "Jeff also happens to be a friend of mine." Yes, I spoke in present tense, which apparently wasn't lost on those who knew of his disappearance — Ned, Lois, and Corina — judging by their sudden smiles. That same surreptitious poop scooper who'd sneaked in at the same time as Ned now stood at one side of the room, his expression on the snide side. Well, we'd see what he thought as I finished my tentative tale. "I believe he found out what I suspect — that The Clone Arranger does in fact supply its clients with excellent pets that closely resemble those they want to duplicate, but instead of being clones, they're the closest purebred animals that they can find from alternative sources. They don't charge as much for their services as other cloners who truly duplicate livestock — for example, for owners that can recoup the expenses in future sales of prime cattle or horses or whatever. But they charge a whole lot more than their suppliers of wonderful purebred pups and kitties do."

The swell of voices convinced me that those suppliers who were here were fascinated by my ideas — and not pleased by the possibility. Probably the cloning customers weren't, either.

"Now, now, this is all nonsense," Mason Payne said, waving his arms in a manner suggesting he wanted to shove the furor to the floor. He seemed to try to draw himself up to his full, unimpressive height, but his usual silver tongue that complemented his silver hair appeared to fail him, since he offered no concrete rebuttal, only a denial.

"I absolutely hope so, Mason," I told him

in my raised voice. "Please give us facts to refute what I said. Have you ever cloned a mixed breed of any animal?"

He glanced toward Melba as if seeking assistance, but when she simply blinked, he said, "If not, it's because of the difficulty of dealing with their DNA. You must understand that the cloning process, although we have come a long way, has imperfections — not, of course, in the products of our cloning, but in how we must handle the animals being cloned, and —"

"*Allegedly* cloned. Am I accurate in assuming you haven't cloned *any* animal?" Of course I was, but would he confess? "That would explain why you prefer pretending with purebreds. With them, you can easily purchase pups that resemble the alleged parents you're claiming to copy."

"Why would you think such a thing?" He'd grown pale. "We take in all sorts of pets for cloning. Like your friend Lois's mixed-breed dog. We tried, we really tried, but we weren't successful."

"Are you admitting that you somehow harmed Flisa?" I demanded.

"No, no, not at all. That's not what I meant."

And then I was somewhat, but not entirely, surprised when a stooped, elderly-looking man in filthy clothing suddenly appeared at my side — then drew himself to his full hunky height and stared at the group, including Ned Noralles, who roared his immediate recognition. "Hubbard! Damn it, it's Hubbard. Why —"

My eyes hurriedly scanned the crowd, attempting to assess reactions as Jeff started to speak. Sure enough, I noticed one person who seemed especially upset by this revelation. Interesting . . .

"Although this should be handled by appropriate legal means, I wanted to add my comments here. Yes, I'm Jeff Hubbard, the friend Lois hired to help her learn the truth behind The Clone Arranger. And I did."

Lois screamed, squeezed her way through the crowd, and threw her arms around her almost-son. "You stinker! You didn't even tell me who you were at the police station. I wondered . . . but your disguise was so damn good — even to the smell, although it could have been worse."

The smile Jeff leveled at her made my heart sing. Yes, behind all that makeup and those facial enhancers that made him look so different, it was the same Jeff.

Who now hated me, without my really understanding why.

Only . . . I soon understood the why, even

though it was entirely erroneous.

"Anyway, I want to let people know that Ms. Ballantyne's speculations appear to be true, at least based on my initial investigation. I spoke secretly to as many employees of The Clone Arranger as I could. Most wanted nothing to do with me, but one was feeling guilty about what they did. What I didn't know was that guilt wasn't enough to keep him from trying to kill me later — in fear for his own life, I believe. That person was Earl Knox."

The name of the murdered man sent another wave of shocked comments through the crowded room.

Only then did I start wondering if I'd made a huge mistake in handling things as I had. I mean, in these close quarters with so many people, what if the true villain in this scenario had come here armed and dangerous and willing to do whatever was needed for self-protection — like taking hostages and killing others? Killing clearly was in the person's vocabulary.

Ah, but I wasn't the only one who'd been worried. Suddenly some uniformed cops shoved their way through the doors and into the crowd. Must have been called in by the detective who'd accompanied Esther and Lois.

Which made me feel a lot better.

Jeff didn't stop talking, and Corina never moved her eyes or microphone off him.

"Earl even provided me proof, in the form of a computer thumb drive with information about what animals were purchased from what breeder to appear to be clones, and how the selection procedure was handled."

So that *was* it! I'd suspected so. Made perfect sense — all except the part where Jeff refused to reveal to me what was on that damned thumb drive. Why hadn't he trusted me? I'd been traveling along the same speculations as he had. Maybe we could have arrived here faster if we'd worked together.

But no time to think about that now.

I watched the person I'd zeroed in on as the villain in this situation — whose face turned angry, then green.

"Okay, Hubbard, just where is this unequivocal proof now?" That was Ned Noralles, who, in his jurisdiction or not, had thrown himself into the situation and now stood beside us.

"It's in Ms. Ballanyne's care and custody," Jeff said. "I mailed it to her."

"And I told you I never received it." And neither had Rachel. She had looked, but she hadn't located it at the spot she sorted our mail. "In any event, you surely know that I didn't, and wouldn't, hide something like that from you, Jeff — even though you obviously were hiding a lot from me, like your survival."

"Which you figured out almost on your own, you bulldog of an attorney." Hey, that smile of his was leveled on me now. His old, somewhat familiar smile beneath his disguise. "And after all this — well, maybe I really was wrong, and you never did receive the thumb drive."

Well, duh. But at least that was a step toward an admission of error. Even so, I wasn't sure we were about to fully forgive one another, but at least the pressure between us was easing up — maybe.

But before I could follow up on anything in that direction, I had something else to do.

Put my foot in my mouth even deeper, perhaps. Or maybe solve this whole situation at last.

"So," I said, "it appears that Earl Knox was killed for revealing the truth to you, Jeff, and providing proof. Or maybe to shut him up after he'd tried to murder you on behalf of himself and a coconspirator." I swallowed, took a leap of faith based on my own observations. "So Beryl," I called, "it appears that your Cartwright may not be Churchill's clone after all. And Melville won't get cloned at all. Does that make you think twice about anything you've done lately? Although that all seems fairly flimsy as a motive for murder."

As if caught in the spotlight, Beryl Leeds froze. Then she rushed at me, her Labs at her sides and her fingernails extended. "You bitch! You're wrong about The Clone Arranger. I know you are, and you've ruined them, just like Earl intended to do. And we hadn't even begun filming those wonderful infomercials I promised to do for them. Only a week or two away now, and they were going to pay me so well and give me Melville's twin for free. I stopped Earl in time, or so I thought. But thanks to you, I killed him for nothing!"

CHAPTER
TWENTY-THREE

It was over.

Beryl Leeds was taken away in handcuffs, crying. Tom Venson took charge of her Labs, promising to care for them on her behalf.

Whatever else he might be, he was clearly a kind animal lover. But I felt certain that the afternoon's revelations about cloning, or lack thereof, were nothing new to him. He'd nearly admitted it — or at least not totally denied it — previously.

The cops started doing their things, asking questions, interviewing those present. This was again — still — a crime scene, the location of some underhanded activities as well as the murder of Earl Knox.

It was also the place where some cloning customers would seek restitution for the fraud perpetrated on them, even if they loved their noncloned children.

Would I, as a litigator, take any of their cases? Nope, I had a conflict of interest. But

I felt certain they had winnable positions.

Corina Carey thanked me prodigiously for the scoop I'd given her, then bustled around to partake in interviews.

"So, Ballantyne, you did it again," Ned Noralles said. Clad as always in the dark suit of a detective, he shook his head with its official close buzz cut, but his smile seemed anything but chastising. "You're one hell of an investigator. Like I told you before, the LAPD could use you."

"Like I told *you* before, Ned, I'm too busy with my pet-sitting and law careers to take on a third." But I smiled back. "At least this time it wasn't your case I tossed in the toilet."

"And you, Hubbard. What the hell was that all about? Your car was found in a canal and you lived to tell about it. What happened?"

"Best I can figure," Jeff responded, "I was drugged by Earl Knox when I was here investigating The Clone Arranger. I'd already left the facility and mailed that damned thumb drive to Kendra to ensure I didn't have it on me. But Earl called me back, claiming to have more evidence. I wasn't supposed to be conscious when he drove me up north to dump my Escalade and me into the aqueduct, but I was awake enough to hear snatches of his conversation with an unidentified accomplice — obviously this Beryl Leeds, of all people."

"And you didn't reveal your survival . . . why?" Ned peered at Jeff as if suspicious of his complicity in some unidentified infraction.

"Concern for my own life. And Kendra's. And Lois's. I wanted to protect us all and find the proof that Earl had given me." He looked at me. "And that ketamine he injected me with — it's available a lot of places, especially animal labs like The Clone Arranger's. It messed me up for a while. But I should be okay now."

Which sent another annoyed yet sorrowful shiver through me. What if I could never find that damned thumb drive? Would he still suspect me then? Would I care?

As soon as the Glendale cops were through with us, I headed my rental car toward Darryl's, followed by Jeff's beat-up What's the Scoop van. We picked up an enthusiastic Lexie and Odin, and I disclosed the day's revelations to Darryl, who welcomed Jeff back to the world of the living.

Then we headed to my home, where I quickly sought out Rachel.

"Believe it or not, your friendly poop scooper from What's the Scoop here" — I gestured toward my grungy male companion, and Rachel regarded him curiously — "that's Jeff Hubbard under that awful disguise."

"Jeff!" Rachel shrieked, her large brown eyes growing even bigger. "You're kidding! I had no idea. Why did you hide who you were? And who were those other guys you had working here?"

"I had an undercover assignment," he responded tersely, obviously preferring to keep the details to himself. "And they were former students of mine I hired to help out."

Rachel shook her head admiringly. "I had no idea."

"You weren't supposed to," I said dryly. "Oh, and by the way, that thumb drive I was asking about, the one that may have fallen out of that package — it was mailed here by Jeff. I don't suppose you —"

"Found it? Hell, yes. I got to thinking that my dad was home around then and asked him about it. He'd found it on the floor, thought it was his, and stuck it into a drawer in his office. Wait here."

"See!" I said in an I-told-you-so tone once she'd scooted from the room. "I never had it. I wasn't conspiring against you, you jerk."

"Hard to tell, the way you kept throwing yourself at that vet, Venson. All those visits to his clinic, and to The Clone Arranger while he was there. Romantic dinners, too. He was part of all this, and I figured that he'd convinced you to —"

Rachel reappeared then, before I could express my utter outrage to Jeff. She handed me a thumb drive, and I hung on to it while shooting daggers of antipathy at Jeff with my enraged gaze. The only way he could know when I'd seen Tom was if he'd followed me. And whether by ketamine-induced paranoia or pure miserable male jealousy, he'd elected to misinterpret it all.

When Jeff held out his hand, I managed to place the awful little object into it without throwing it — or shoving it up his tight and once beloved butt.

With a sense of relief, I soon sent a remorseful and definitely exhausted Jeff on his way back to his Sherman Oaks home. He took Odin, whom I'd absolutely miss. Lexie and I went upstairs to our garage apartment, where I got my act together, left Lexie there, and headed out for my evening pet-sitting. Unsurprisingly, it was uneventful.

The only phone call I got at home that night was from Lois, thanking me profusely. The cops were off her back, apparently forevermore. She'd spoken with Jeff, and he was coming out to see her over the weekend, to explain all that had happened to him, and why he'd hidden the way he had.

Too bad I wasn't invited to hear that revelation.

I watched Corina's astounding newscast on TV that night. She still seemed thrilled.

No word from Jeff, though. Our disagreements hadn't all been resolved with the restoration of the thumb drive into his possession.

And I still felt hurt.

Oddly, though, the last thing that crept into my mind as I crawled into bed with only my dear, snuggly Lexie for company was a really offbeat question.

Did Beryl Leeds own a silver hybrid car? Something showier seemed a lot more her type.

Well, what did I know? Although everyone I'd run into in this situation had been on my suspect list, she'd hardly been near the top. Not till I'd realized the truth that day at The Clone Arranger, and she'd confirmed it by shrieking out her admission.

At least I had only pet-sitting and legal cases to care about for now.

The next day, Saturday, I got good news about one of those. Charley Sherman called and said, "Kendra, can you get some of those unhappy pet students and their owners together tomorrow at Show Biz Beasts? I talked to a few of my old studio cronies about your reality show idea, and they're really interested."

"Hot dog!" I cried.

"Yep, lots of hot dogs. Or so we hope. I've already contacted your friend Charlotte La-Verne. She'll be there, too, with her staff that transforms reality show ideas into really cool TV, so I think we're all rarin' to go."

And so, on Sunday afternoon, the whole group from the other day was back in the Show Biz Beasts soundstage-like setup, with additions. They included half a dozen dubious-looking humans huddled along one wall with their amazingly well-trained dogs, courtesy of classes at Show Biz Beasts. Oh, yes, and their attorney, a guy I'd heard of but had never met, George Lanskie. He'd been a lawyer about the same ten-odd years as I, and had earned a reputation as a hot-shot plantiffs' counsel who always put on amazing courtroom performances, much too often swaying juries more with show-manship than good law.

A pitfall of our otherwise generally okay legal system.

I headed over to the group with my hand

outstretched, introducing myself to George. He was a chunky little guy, too dressed up for a doggy audition in a dark suit, white shirt, and red tie, with his thinning hair slicked back. Okay, I wasn't inclined to find him appealing; he seemed utter sleaze to me. Even so, I acted the polite and professional attorney, greeting him in an effusive and utterly friendly manner.

I'd decided to leave Lexie home alone, since as much fun as I thought she'd have here, she would only be a distraction for me, and I most certainly didn't want her showing up any of the other canines. That could utterly disrupt my proposed animal dispute resolution idea. Lexie could absolutely outsmart other trained animals if she was in the right mood.

But I had brought my pet-sitting assistant, Rachel. She had lots of experience with animals, staging them in settings like senior citizens' homes, and especially with showbiz auditions, since that was her absolute dream.

George introduced me to his clients, whose names I recalled from the complaint that had been served. The rabble-rouser, whom I'd been told owned Bichons, clearly stood out from the rest with her fuzzy white friends.

I politely greeted them all, then headed to where my clients, Corbin and Shareen Hayhurst, stood with Charlotte LaVerne, Charley Sherman, and other folks I didn't recognize but assumed were industry people. And then there were the camera operators circulating among all of us.

"Here we go," Charley said.

Charlotte LaVerne led Rachel to the center of the horde as her assistant.

"Hi, everyone," Charlotte cried, and the group grew quiet. "I'm Charlotte LaVerne —" As if most of them didn't know. "And I've brought some of my favorite reality show execs here. And cameramen, too. Here's what's going to happen today."

She proceeded to describe how this was going to go like a pilot for a new reality show that they would pitch to network and cable channels to see who would scarf it up. "That will determine what kind of prize will be offered to the winner, but everyone will get national television exposure. If someone buys it. In this business, there are never any guarantees."

She glared tellingly in the direction of George Lanskie and his horde of prima donna plaintiffs, including the Bichon bitch-owner. George looked straight back, as did the awful agitator, but some of his other clients were clearly embarrassed. Good!

"What we want to do is put together a scenario for each show during a season, and trained animals — which could include others besides dogs, by the way, though not today — will be put into groups to stage that scenario the best they can in a short time. The winners each week will come back at the end to compete for the grand prize. Again assuming someone buys the show so we have a grand prize to offer."

My turn to take this vast floor. "We've put this idea together to give you all a genuine shot at an on-screen role for your pets, courtesy of Show Biz Beasts. It's still our contention that the Hayhursts have no obligation to do any of this, but we want to settle your lawsuit against them. I hope that Mr. Lanskie has explained that to participate, you'll need to sign the settlement agreement he and I negotiated." Well, I negotiated it by drafting it and ramming it down Lanskie's tight throat and mentioning my media connection, Corina Carey, who owed me and would therefore be delighted, I was sure, to put something on air about this exciting new concept. If Lanskie decided not to tell his clients about this potentially perfect way of getting them what they wanted without his being awarded exorbitant legal fees, or to recommend this settlement, his public persona would suffer.

To my delight, all the plaintiffs stepped up to the designated tables with their dogs at their sides. Some read through the document. Others didn't bother, but asked what today's scenario would be.

"We can't tell you and give you an advantage over the others," Rachel said, obviously getting into the act. She was excited that she would be one of the hosts of today's filmed show, right at Charlotte's side. And she'd told me she had managed to mention this potentially exciting break to the casting guy she had met at Methuselah Manor, who'd seemed suitably impressed.

Then we were ready. The scenario? Each dog on a team would take on the role of a skilled cop K-9 who'd smelled contraband drugs in a car driven onto the set.

K-9 cops? A couple were yappy little Bichons, and others included lazy-looking midsize mutts — cute in their own ways, of course, but official-looking and professional-acting animals? But happily, all seemed to rise to the occasion under their owners' instructions.

And damned if the taping didn't exceed my expectations. Charlotte's and Charley's, too.

At the end, they came to me with shining eyes after conclaving with the industry reps who'd come with them.

"They're really happy with it," Charley said.

"I'm pretty sure we can sell it," Charlotte agreed.

Rachel, still at Charlotte's side, said nothing, but her grin told me she was one happy pet-sitting actress. I only hoped she would still be around to help me with my Critter TLC, LLC, obligations for a long time, despite today's potentially perfect outcome.

"Thank you so much, Kendra," Shareen Hayhurst said as the others started to file out of Show Biz Beasts. She looked a whole lot more relaxed now than when I'd first arrived. Her usual frumpiness had segued into squared-shoulder, queen-of-her-realm satisfaction. She smiled at me fondly.

Corbin, too, appeared more relaxed and happier than I'd ever seen him. "A wonderful result. A wonderful idea. I'll recommend you to all my friends if they ever have legal troubles, Kendra. Thanks so much."

I beamed as I retrieved Rachel and headed for my rental car. My legal fees for this case would end abruptly, but I figured that, with whatever proceeds I finally wrested out of the tightfisted insurance company, it would soon be time for me to forget renting and buy myself another vehicle. At least I could test-drive ones I could arguably afford.

Things were suddenly going well. No more murders at the moment for this magnet. No men, either, but maybe that was okay, at least for the moment.

Life was good.

Until almost one week later. That was when I heard, first, that Beryl Leeds had gotten out of jail on bail, despite the charges against her, including first-degree murder.

And second, that someone had attempted to murder Beryl.

CHAPTER
TWENTY-FOUR

The case wasn't my concern any longer. Was it?

I pondered this at home that Saturday night when I viewed the latest story on local TV news, Lexie sitting in my lap on my comfortably aging beige sofa.

"Did you see that?" I asked. She cocked her head in obvious interest but offered no other answer. I hugged her fuzzy body close.

Beryl Leeds. Not that I knew her well. And the news didn't explain what had happened to her. She'd been attacked and nearly killed. But she *was* someone else I knew.

Someone related to the situation I'd recently finished investigating. A coincidence?

Sure, coincidences too often appeared to exist, but I wasn't a huge believer.

Besides, as I'd thought about things over the past week, there had been a lot of loose threads that Beryl's confession hadn't completely cleared up.

Though I'd gotten only a hint of Beryl's unquenchable temper when she'd confessed, I could see her killing Earl for spoiling her plans for her beloved Lab, Melville. Even more, after asking Althea to perform a plethora of research on the once-admired, now has-been actress, we'd learned — and so, independently, had the media — that a lot of her blatant Beverly Hills lifestyle was financed on a very skinny shoestring. She needed money, a mound of it, and had been promised primo payments for The Clone Arranger's upcoming infomercials. Earl's threat to the company and its bottom line — and therefore Beryl's own extremely anticipated profits — seemed more than an adequate motive for murder to me. And to the screaming media.

But could I see her conniving with Earl to drug Jeff and drag him up to the aqueduct to drown him? Was she the one who'd been on the other end of the conversation Jeff asserted he'd heard?

Assuming, of course, that there had been such a discussion outside the realm of Jeff's continuing confused consciousness.

Without all the facts, I couldn't be sure of what Beryl had or hadn't done. But one fact

I now couldn't ignore was that someone had apparently tried to off her. If so, who else did I now know who might have attempted to do this? And why?

Because she truly had killed Earl? Sure, I hadn't discovered anyone who utterly adored the man before his untimely death, but that didn't mean there wasn't such a person around.

And if not a lover or friend, who else could it be?

Whoever had actually been speaking with Earl that night?

Well . . . I pondered for a while with the TV on mute and Lexie curled on my lap. For the past week I'd avoided taking calls from either Jeff or Tom. I'd also insisted to my psyche that I wasn't going to get in touch with men who clearly hadn't had my best interests in mind over the recent weeks. Jeff, especially, had hurt me badly.

I needed a break.

But I'd also previously suspected one or the other of these men could have had something to do with Earl Knox's death. Now we knew that Beryl Leeds had been guilty — didn't we?

Geez. My mind was spinning in eddies of confusion, and not just because of the awfully late hour.

But there was one person I could call, even though it was this late, who just might be available and have some information — though who knew if he'd share any with me? I gently lifted Lexie onto the couch cushions, where she immediately woke and leaped onto the floor, staying by my side as I went into the kitchen, where my cell phone was charging.

I called Detective Ned Noralles. After all, even though this was just an attempted homicide — at least so far — the news story had said that Beryl had been found slumped in her car somewhere in Studio City. Not only was it LAPD jurisdiction, but it was within Ned's North Hollywood district.

He had to know about it. Maybe even be involved. If so, he'd still be awake and on duty.

If not, I'd either awaken him or have to leave a message that might, if I was lucky, get returned tomorrow. And I'm not that patient a person.

"Hello, Kendra," he said nearly immediately in his smooth, wry voice. Was that a good thing — having an LAPD detective either recognize my number or have it programmed into his cell phone so caller ID would divulge who I was?

I didn't stop to worry about it. "I just

heard about Beryl Leeds, Ned. What happened?"

"Don't you ever stop?" He sounded more amused than exasperated for a change. Gee, were we becoming friends instead of always adversaries? Maybe he'd even like me to butt in and help figure out what had happened to Beryl.

"Only when I can't help it," I answered. "Is what happened to Beryl related to Earl Knox's murder? Something to do with The Clone Arranger?" And had he eventually interrogated Jeff to get the lowdown on his dunk in the aqueduct canal? Did he think that could relate to Beryl's awful attack?

Whatever it was. The news hadn't been overly specific.

"No comment," Ned said. My turn to get exasperated.

"But, Ned, you know I poked my nose in a lot in that situation. Maybe I can even help you solve this. You've said I should join the LAPD. How about if I become an unofficial and occasional consultant?" I swallowed. "For free — at least this time." Would he offer compensation? Maybe — when the California Aqueduct formed a waterfall into the sky.

"Back off, Ballanyne," he responded, less amused now. "I've got work to do. And if you do happen to know something useful, you'd better let me know, or I'll run you in for obstruction of justice. That won't help your resurrected law license, will it?"

"Hmmm, must be an interesting situation," I said, keeping my cool so well that I was sure it galled him. "Otherwise you wouldn't threaten me. Well, I don't actually know anything worthwhile to pass along . . . yet. But if I do, you'll be first to hear from me — after I look into Beryl's incident myself."

"Keep your — !" was all the roar I heard before I clicked my cell phone shut.

Tomorrow promised to be an interesting day, if I figured out the best way to dive into the attack on Beryl Leeds.

First things first. Lexie and I went pet-sitting, then I dropped her at Darryl's. The good and bad thing was that it was once again Sunday, which meant I didn't have to show up at my law office, but neither were many of my usual resources, like Althea, readily available.

Oh, I could always call Althea on her cell. But youthful grandma that she was, she had a family, and this was the weekend.

Besides, now that I was barely speaking to Jeff, I hadn't tested whether I still had

Althea as a resource for conducting computer searches, both legit and surreptitious.

So, how should I spend my snooping time?

Well, first, while sitting in Darryl's parking lot, I called Lois.

"Oh, Kendra, have you heard about what happened to Beryl Leeds?" she asked me immediately.

"Yes, I have," I said. "But we can't be sure it's a result of what happened before."

"Get real," she said. And then there was grumbling in the background that I couldn't quite decipher. In a moment, Lois said, "I'm trying hard not to pass the phone to Jeff, though he's grabbing for it. He wants to order you to butt out."

"He has nothing to say about what I do with my butt these days," I said primly, "and you can tell him so."

I heard her do so, laughingly, and in a moment I heard Jeff's voice. "Kendra, I really appreciate your helping Lois out before, when I felt I could only do it undercover. You did a great job getting Beryl to admit she was the one who killed Earl, and clearing Lois. I thank you. Lois thanks you. My mother thanks you. But there's obviously more to what happened than even you suspected, and considering the fact that Beryl was drugged like me, although actually more like Earl, and —"

"Is that what happened to her? How do you know?"

"Damn!" Jeff exploded. "You know I have resources, but that's beside the point. Stay out of it, Kendra. You're not helping to clear anyone unjustly accused now. It's not your concern. And it's obviously dangerous."

"I didn't know you cared," I said sweetly. " 'Bye, Jeff. Hugs to Lois and your mother." And then I hung up.

Hmmm. Interesting. I doubted Jeff had made this up. Why would he? To keep suspicion from settling on him in this latest attack? Beryl had apparently been set upon much as he had been. Only, his situation was unlikely to be proven, at least not easily. His car went into the canal. Presumably he did, too, then proceeded to disappear for a while, partly on purpose.

Or had he set it all up himself? And then killed Earl and gotten Beryl to confess and then shot her up with drugs, too? Yeah, right. But official eyes could settle on things that way.

I didn't. Even if Jeff had been a bit nuts lately — a bit nuts? Correction: *way,* distressingly deluded — I didn't see the scenario happening like that.

So . . . how did things really transpire? I

considered what to do next to figure it out as I watched owners bring animals into Darryl's while I sat in his parking lot.

And then, impulsively, I called Tom Venson's veterinary clinic — and was connected with the vet himself almost immediately. Sure, it was a Sunday, but he had afternoon hours. Had he told his staff to put me through *tout de suite* if I ever decided to return one of his calls? If so, why? To attempt to throw off my suspicions against him?

Did I really suspect him of complicity in all this cloning chaos? If it hadn't been for his hidden relationship with Debby Payne, probably not. But now . . .

"Have you heard the news about Beryl Leeds?" I asked after our hellos.

"Who hasn't?" he asked rhetorically and somewhat sadly. "Doesn't sound clear whether she'll survive, and I still have one of her dogs here. The two yellow Labs went to a family I know who'll take good care of them till Beryl can take them back — if ever, considering the circumstances. But I haven't found the right situation for Melville, temporary or otherwise."

That was the chocolate Lab with the protective streak. I had an idea. "I think I have a solution, but let me check."

A phone call to Tracy Owens, a delay of a few minutes while she checked with her client who'd recently lost his Lab, a return call to me, and I got back to Tom. "Let me come get him now," I said. I had one heck of an idea that could resolve the whole rest of this situation. Or not. But it wouldn't hurt to try.

It also gave me a few minutes alone with Tom in one of his exam rooms. Well, not exactly alone. Melville joined us, and the poor dog paced the entire time. "He's pretty high-strung for a Lab," Tom told me unnecessarily. "He seems to have taken a liking to one of our lady vets, and tried to attack her boyfriend when he took her into his arms for a kiss. I think it's a protective reaction, since when I told him to sit, he did."

"Beryl knew how to handle him," I said. I approached the uneasy pup, my hand extended so he could sniff and confirm who I was. "Friend, Melville." He sat and started panting. "Good boy." His long, silky tail swept the floor. "Okay, let's go." I looked first at Tom. "You knew that The Clone Arranger's purported cloning practices had problems, didn't you?"

He didn't dare deny it now. "I indicated to you before that I had suspicions. And before you ask, Debby had nothing to do with my decision not to try to stop them or turn them over to the authorities. I did as they asked, and checked animal health. Sure, they might have been fooling their customers, but people walked away happy, thinking they had reproductions of their favorite pets. I considered it kind of a win-win situation."

"Which could also give you legal liability, civil if not criminal. But I won't do anything against you," I interjected hurriedly when his expression soured and he took a step toward me. "As long as you didn't do anything to Earl or Beryl."

"Of course not," he said, sounding utterly disgusted that I would dare suggest such a thing.

"Good, then. I'm gone. And I'll let you know how things work out with Melville."

Melville's new home was in Hollywood, but I didn't head there. Not immediately. In all my musing about what had happened to Jeff, Earl, and Beryl, the common thread was, of course, The Clone Arranger. And at the moment, I had custody of one of their potential clonees. That, hopefully, would give me another entrée to the locale that was my current destination.

Yes, indeed, I headed for The Clone Arranger.

Why? Well, even though it was a weekend, they probably had some staff around, to care for the pets they were ostensibly preparing for their procedure.

Unless my little scene the other day had derailed their practices completely.

In any event, I hoped to see who was there. Perhaps get someone talking. Accusing me of defamation and preparing to prove me wrong.

As if they could.

Meantime, I'd ask subtle questions to see if I could figure out who had been on the phone with Earl while Jeff was under the influence. Beryl? I'd considered the possibility before. Didn't rule it out completely now.

But Jeff's story had been that he'd scared Earl into reluctant cooperation. Gotten him to hand over proof on that elusive thumb drive. Then been called back almost immediately for further information — allegedly. Instead, Earl had drugged and kidnapped him in his own car.

And spoken with whoever had convinced him to do that nearly the entire way — or at least as long as Jeff had been semiconscious.

To my way of thinking, that person had to

be someone Earl worked with who suspected what he'd turned over to Jeff, threatened him, gotten him to buckle under and bring Jeff back for ultimate disposal.

And then disposed of Earl. And later, when some shenanigans taking place at The Clone Arranger were outed by me, it was time for whoever it was to take further action. Place apparent blame elsewhere. Deal with Beryl, who'd claimed to have killed Earl.

Why had she confessed? Had she done it? To protect someone in the organization? Who would she care about enough to do that for?

The person who'd paid her back by attempting to kill her?

All these thoughts leaped through my stimulated mind as I aimed my overcrowded rented auto toward The Clone Arranger's facility. Poor Melville couldn't quite get comfortable in the car's passenger seat, but he'd whined and complained when I'd attempted to settle him in the back.

Fortunately, the freeway wasn't extremely crowded, so we made fast progress. Soon, I headed up the off-ramp toward The Clone Arranger.

And slowed down on a nearby surface street when I noticed a silver hybrid car parked there, not far from my destination.

Well, hell, there were thousands of those things on the road now, with people attempting to beat the price of gasoline that was especially outrageous in Southern California. And this one wasn't chasing me.

In fact, since my episode at The Clone Arranger and Beryl's confession, I hadn't seen my stalker anywhere, despite Jeff's direst warnings of danger — thank heavens.

This one was highly unlikely to belong to whoever had been stalking me. Even so, I slowed enough to jot a license number in my notebook full of lists.

I drove into The Clone Arranger's lot and easily found a spot to park. Hardly any cars were there. A couple of large vans, though. And a large door at the far end of the building appeared to be open.

Interesting. I grabbed Melville's leash and headed that way — which was when I noticed someone, off in the bushes, watching what was happening.

And suddenly I suspected I knew what really had happened with all the attacks and everything else, although I still couldn't quite imagine why.

Never a better time than now to find out. The open door and parked vans suggested I wouldn't be alone here, so I surely wasn't putting myself in danger.

Even so, in the interest of discretion, I placed phone calls to my usual backups.

I didn't reach Ned. And Jeff started his latest bout of angry badgering, so I hung up. And walked forward — but only after making yet another call.

With Melville, I sidled up to the guy at the edge of the bushes. "Hi, Clark," I said to the head of CW Ultra Technologies, who was obviously back in town. Assuming he had even left. "What brings you here? Have you come to see the possible demise of The Clone Arranger, thanks to my little game with them the other day?"

"Beryl Leeds told me about that," he said. "I saw it on the news, too." He stared at me through his geeky-looking black-rimmed glasses. Today, he was clad not in baggy blue pants but all in black. Which would have obscured him from visibility at night, but not on this nice sunny afternoon.

Still, when I glanced toward the building, I saw no activity. No one to see us out here talking.

Oops. Maybe I'd made an error in judgment. But one that was eminently curable, at least for now.

"Well, good seeing you again," I said. "Come on, Melville." The Lab had been tugging at the leash, as if eager to get into the building. He'd ignored Clark instead of confronting him the way I'd seen this dog do before. And this time, I couldn't assure him that the person I spoke with was a friend.

On the other hand, maybe he wasn't the fiend I'd suddenly considered him. Perhaps I had wronged him in my mind. Which meant I'd be better off inside, confronting The Clone Arranger people — as long as I had someone to watch my back.

Clark? Well, I'd feel a whole lot more comfortable with him if the men I'd already attempted to contact were around. Under the circumstances, hopefully one would be on his way. Maybe both.

"I wish you'd just left things alone, Kendra," Clark said with a nerdy smile, his tone utterly amiable despite a slight whine to his words. He stood with legs spread apart, hands behind his back, looking like some kind of naughty and repentant kid — maybe. "Like I told you before, my motive to kill Earl, at least the one everyone would have ascribed to me, was the theft of some pretty primitive technology. But one of my companies has gone a whole lot farther with it. We may be ready to start our own competing business any day."

"That's great," I attempted to interject, recalling that this man never let me get a word in edgewise or otherwise in our earlier conversation.

"But now, word will be out that there's something flawed about its basics. People around here knew that Earl walked away with some of my scientific discoveries. The other companies involved with cloning knew it, too."

"But if you went farther with the technology than what Earl stole, then everyone will applaud your ingenuity and your —"

"You don't get it. I thought that what this miserable place was selling was the real thing. I didn't let my people put aside what Earl stole and try a different direction. I had them start again with the same technology, and they're still fumbling with it. Now, we're going to lose millions. More. And now that your allegations are out there in public, our investors will dry up."

"But if you —"

He shook his head almost sadly. Was that a noise from the open door? No, it was simply Melville, sitting and panting and keeping an eye on the two of us. Clark continued, "See, that night when Earl panicked and gave a thumb drive to that damned investigator Hubbard, he called me.

Told me what was going on, apologized for double-crossing me in the first place, and told me he was making good on it now by letting the world know what he'd done — and how The Clone Arranger wasn't really using my technology but was scamming its customers. He thought I'd be pleased about it, stabbing his new employer in the back that way. But, hell, I was anything but. I told him so. His going along with their lies wound up hurting my business — keeping it set in the wrong direction. Plus, with word out there about the technology's failure, my reputation would suffer. I threatened not only to let the Paynes know what he'd done, but to blame everything on him. He'd never get another job. And if he didn't dispose of that interfering SOB Hubbard in exactly the way I told him, I'd dispose of *him* even more brutally." Clark's even huger smile made me shudder.

I considered inquiring why he was telling me all this, but I thought I knew.

"Well, I think he listened to you. Interesting stuff, Clark. But right now, we've got to —"

"There's a reason for my telling you everything, Kendra," he said, answering my unasked question as if I'd shouted it out. "You're a smart lady, and I figured you'd want to know why you're going to die. And you know the great part?"

He didn't stop to let me guess. Not that I necessarily would have gotten it. Not the way my mind was racing far, far away and my shuddering body intended to follow.

He whipped from behind his back an ugly and huge hypodermic needle held in hands swathed in slick vinyl gloves.

"This stuff comes from right inside there." He nodded toward The Clone Arranger.

Where the hell were the people who were apparently taking stuff out the open doors and loading those parked trucks?

Or had Clark been the one to gain entry to get that damned, scary needle?

Didn't matter. Not now.

"Let's get this over with, shall we?" he said, and sprang at me with his hand raised and the needle pointed square at my unprotected arm.

CHAPTER TWENTY-FIVE

I screamed. I aimed my best imitation of a kung fu kick right where it should hurt.

And best of all, Melville suddenly stood and seemed to understand that this man was not a friend. He lunged with teeth bared. "Kill, Melville," I shouted.

Just as I heard sirens approaching from not far away. And at long last people started pouring from the open Clone Arranger door.

Did this deter Clark Weiss? No way. Partly doubled over by the pain in his privates, and Melville's teeth clamped over his arm, he still came at me.

I suddenly feared for Melville. What if the idiot somehow shot the dog with a dose of whatever was designed to down a whole human being?

"Friend, Melville," I shouted, but the dog was too engrossed to hear or obey. So I did what I had to after seeing lots of martial arts videos: shrieked some unintelligible syllables and aimed my head right at Clark Weiss's unprotected side.

We went down in a tangle of legs — canine and human. I felt a needle prick in my thigh . . . and then nothing at all.

I woke up in an awful-odored hospital room. I mean, it was okay if you like sweet-smelling antiseptics and cleaners and all. I don't.

Well, hell. I wasn't alone. On one side sat Jeff Hubbard, leafing through a magazine.

On the other was Tom Venson, with a big veterinary-looking tome on his lap.

Help! my mind yelled. *Nurse! Anybody!*

But instead of crying out, I said very slowly, "Well, if either of you were paying attention to the guest of honor here, you'd know I was awake."

They both stood and crowded around me and made all sorts of excited noise. I tuned them out and fell back to sleep.

Next thing I knew, I awakened yet again — much more widely this time. When I glanced around half hopefully, and half dreading the possibility of facing both those men again, I was kinda pleased to see that the only person present besides me was Detective

Ned Noralles.

"What brings you here, Ned?" I asked after clearing my throat in a futile attempt to erase its hoarseness. "Isn't this St. Joe's?" Providence St. Joseph Medical Center was in Burbank, not within the official purview of the LAPD.

"Professional courtesy has been extended to me," he said with a sardonic smile. "Both the local PDs know I'm here and ready to question you about what happened. You're in Burbank, and your little altercation with Clark Weiss occurred in Glendale."

"Little altercation?" My voice rose in incredulous protest. "He attacked me. Tried to kill me."

"Could be. But the guy's not talking."

I eyed Ned wryly. "Did you meet him before? His silence is an obvious sign he's guilty. I couldn't get him to shut up any of the times I've spoken with him. He even confessed a whole lot to me before he came at me with that damned needle." I shuddered in my soft and too revealing hospital gown, which I quickly yanked back to a more modest level.

Ned looked awfully interested, or maybe he was just intending to make me feel uncomfortable. If so, he succeeded. So what if he was a nice-looking guy? I had had too many like that in my life — or I had before. Now, I wanted nothing to do with either of them.

Besides, where were they, now that I was awake enough to most likely stay that way?

"He's lawyered up, as they say," Ned informed me, peering at me in a pinched way that told me he was very much aware that I was one of those awful attorneys, too. "But only after claiming he came to talk to one of the Paynes that day about possibly joining their cloning technologies to fix their now-public problems and saw you stealing stuff from the building. When he confronted you, you confronted him right back with the ugly needle and the dog. Of course he had to defend himself."

"What!" I was becoming more and more enraged by the effrontery of that horrible Clark Weiss. "He tried to kill me! Look, Ned, let me tell you what happened. I brought Beryl Leeds's dog Melville to The Clone Arranger to try to use him to get my foot in the — Melville! Is he okay? Where is he?"

"You have a whole lot of friends worried about you," Ned said unresponsively, sitting on the edge of my high hospital bed. Only it wasn't actually unresponsive at all. Among those who'd come to visit and keep watch, he informed me, was Tracy Owens of the Pet-Sitters Club of Southern California, who knew where I'd intended to end up with Melville that day. "She took him to the foster home you'd discussed with her before, and said to tell you that once the guy there got across to the dog that he was friend, not enemy, they started getting along just fine."

"Oh," I said, suddenly exhausted once more. "That's a good thing."

"Sure is. Anyway, we'll take an official statement from you when you're feeling better, but you've already given several unofficial ones between bouts of unconsciousness."

"Really?" That unnerved me a whole lot. I didn't recall a single one. Which reminded me of Jeff and his assertions of what he did and did not recall at times.

Would I start obsessing about him as conspiring in all that had happened, the way he had done with me? Well, maybe *he* deserved it.

"So tell me what the cops think really happened in all this."

He wouldn't do it, since I was a percipient witness and he wouldn't want to taint any testimony I might give at the criminal trial of Clark Weiss that was apt to happen. So, instead, I asked if I could tell him what

I understood occurred, and he could either smile or frown in response. Which brought one of his usual sardonic grins, and he let me begin.

"I surmise that this whole thing was started by Lois's attempt to get her not-quite-Akita, Flisa, cloned. When Flisa died, Lois asked Jeff to surreptitiously check things out, so as not to make her look bad before her conservative church group. Jeff loves her like a mom, and did as she asked, somehow getting through to Earl and convincing him it was in his very best interest to save himself from a bad situation by giving Jeff proof — which he did. I gathered from Earl's ex-wife that he had stopped being enamored with The Clone Arranger. Maybe he felt guilty about its committing fraud on its customers. Now we'll never know. But that damned thumb drive he gave Jeff had evidence about what The Clone Arranger really did — and it wasn't genuine cloning."

I looked at Ned, who nodded ever so slightly, even as he lifted his quite nice butt, clad in one of his detective suits, off my bed and onto the nearby visitor's chair.

He crossed his arms and nodded yet again, encouraging me to continue.

I went over — again, according to Ned's

allegations — what I recalled Clark had confessed before attempting to inject me with that awful needle.

"Earl happily handed the thumb drive to Jeff, then called his old boss Clark to tell him what he'd done, thinking Clark would be pleased to learn that the people who'd allegedly stolen his scientific stuff were going to wind up potentially paying for fraud. Only Clark wasn't excited about it at all, and threatened Earl so he'd get the thumb drive back and get rid of Jeff. The first part turned out to be impossible, but he did attempt to dispose of Jeff, talking to Clark in the process. Jeff, while drugged, overheard parts of conversations. Has he told you that?"

"He sure has," Ned said. "Go on. This is good."

"Does it go along with official assumptions?"

"Close enough. So Earl kidnapped Jeff and dumped him into the canal, and damned if the guy didn't survive. I never considered him a lion in law enforcement, but he sure seems to have a cat's nine lives." Amazingly, though Ned and Jeff had long since ceased to be friends, Ned appeared to be impressed.

"Right. That deals with most of the Jeff

scenario, but not what happened to Beryl — at least not directly. Here's what I guess: Beryl had been very public in her adoration of The Clone Arranger, and she'd met Clark, who'd considered her a potential investor in his companies, which he claimed had even better technology. She found out, probably from Clark, that Earl was messing up her whole The Clone Arranger arrangement — including the infomercial they'd promised to hire her for at a lucrative and much needed price. That's why she went to confront Earl. Maybe she intended to kill him, but —"

Ned mumbled something I didn't quite catch.

"Pardon?"

"Slllldfffnn," he muttered again, staring at the ceiling.

I finally figured out what he wasn't exactly saying. "Er . . . oh, yeah, maybe she accosted Earl so angrily that he came at her with a hypodermic of ketamine stuff that sedated dogs and did wonders with Jeff, too. And now me." Ned sort of nodded, seeming encouraging. "So somehow she turned the tables on him and accidentally killed him in self-defense with that very same needle. Is that what her attorney's claiming?"

"Gee, Kendra, you're psychic!" Ned exclaimed. "That's exactly it."

I laughed.

"Okay, let's cut the rest of this long story short. Jeff's missing and presumed dead. Earl is dead and there's someone besides Clark to blame it on. Things suddenly look rosy yet again for The Clone Arranger and its flawed technology. Only there I am, butting in, snooping around. So Clark starts following me in a car owned by one of his subsidiaries, a nice but ordinary hybrid that he wouldn't otherwise be seen in. He parks one really nice auto outside his offices in his marked CEO's space. Did you run the plate number of the vehicle parked near The Clone Arranger the day I was attacked?"

"Yep. Registered to an outfit that's a subsidiary of a subsidiary of the big parent CW Ultra Technologies umbrella."

My turn to grin. Then frown. "He tried to run me over once, but Jeff, the super poop scooper, shoved me out of the way. And fortunately I was unstoppable. Showed how The Clone Arranger is a big fraud. Which upset Clark yet again about his potential investors. It may be a case of closing the barn door after the cloned cows have escaped, but he decided to get revenge against The Clone Arranger guys, which was why he happened to be there as they started attempting to remove any evidence of their fraud. I arrived as they were still packing up, and so did Clark. I was a bonus that day, although I was still high on his list for removal." I paused. "Oh, yeah, Beryl. Clark was pleased that she stepped up and confessed, but the idea of self-defense and their conversations coming up bothered him a bit. To ensure she couldn't testify, he contacted her the instant he found out she'd been released on bail — he'd been watching — and asked her to meet him to strategize about the whole cloning thing. He caught her in her car before she went into the restaurant where they were to meet." I looked at Ned. "Any word about whether she's going to survive?"

"Looking good," he said. "Though the dose she got was a lot more than yours, so she's still not out of the woods."

I grimaced, then made myself grin. "Okay. I'm through. Tell me if I got anything wrong."

"Well, like I said, I can't tell you even if you got it right, but looking at it all hypothetically — that's what you lawyers like to say — I'd say you've come up with a nice, tidy tale for several prosecutors in Glendale for Earl's murder, L.A. County for Jeff's abduction and attack, and good old L.A.

City for Beryl's attempted murder."

"Amazing," I said. "And complicated. Any chance Clark will get out of this?"

"Not if I have anything to say about it," Ned responded grimly. "But one never knows in our so-called justice system."

Which made me sink back into my pillows.

"Looks like you've exhausted yourself with your hypothetical," he surmised. "But thanks for your confirmation of where I figured we were going with all this. I'm sure we'll see more of each other as the official investigation continues."

"Good deal, Ned," I said. "And thanks — only next time I call for help, could you please answer your damned phone?"

"For you, Ballantyne, any time."

Which brought a bundle of tears to my eyes as he exited the hospital room. Damn, but that drug must have done something to my emotions.

But it still felt kinda good that the detective who'd once hated my guts had actually acted almost like a friend.

Rachel came to see me often in the next couple of days of my hospital recuperation. She was of course caring for Lexie.

"I wish you could bring her here," I

grumped one afternoon.

"They're letting you out of here tomorrow," Rachel responded. She'd jumped up to the plate and scored well with taking over my animal care chores during my inability.

Her dad, Russ, came with her once or twice. Others also visited me in the hospital — Althea and Buzz from Jeff's office. And Tracy Owens from PSCSC, who, like Ned, assured me that Melville was fine and enjoying his new home.

Even Jeff and Tom came again despite my previous rudeness in dropping off to sleep from boredom before in their combined presence. At least they arrived one at a time. Both acted caring and concerned. And I acted pleased to see them, but absolutely not bowled over by the appearance of either of them at my side.

Even so, I got teary-eyed when Jeff apologized for his suspicions. Sitting on the side of my hospital bed, he said, "You were absolutely right, Kendra. A lot of what I was saying was the result of a bad reaction to that drug. Ketamine can cause all kinds of awful results, like amnesia, flashbacks, and even delirium and paranoia." Not news to me, even if it was to him. I'd discovered all that from my own detailed research. "As far as I know now, no one was listening in on the phone conversations you and I had. And like you instructed me, I'm seeing a doctor now. Amanda recommended him, and —"

"Amanda? Your ex-wife?" I felt my eyes open wide in astonishment that was far from happy.

"She got in touch when she heard what happened on the news. Said she'd spoken with you to express how concerned she was. But don't worry. I thanked her and told her that things between her and me haven't changed." He leaned over and gave me a soft kiss. "I still want you in my life."

Really? Well, why wouldn't he? I'd helped to unravel the ugly situation in which he and his surrogate mom Lois had found themselves.

But he had the temerity to toss Amanda's name at me. Yet he hadn't trusted me partly because he'd seen me in entirely innocent situations with Tom.

Still, maybe he could explain enough to extract himself from the stinky dilemma of a doghouse that he'd crawled into in my mind.

"I still don't understand why you didn't tell me you were back in L.A. That was before you were drugged."

"I explained it was because I promised

Lois confidentiality." His sweetness had suddenly segued to defensiveness once more.

"Right," I said. "And Lois herself — how come you never mentioned her?"

"I thought I had." At my irritated expression he said, "Well, I wasn't going to introduce you to family till we were in some kind of committed relationship. I'd thought about getting you two together when you moved in with me."

I didn't consider that much of an explanation. But I had one more question. "Did you ever figure out who Earl was referring to when you were supposedly unconscious in the back of the Escalade and he talked to Clark on his cell phone and said he'd gotten to someone at your office — or your girlfriend?"

"It was a stretch, but apparently Clark had someone from one of his companies talk to Buzz Dulear about a security system for one of their facilities, and got him to quiz Buzz about me. And I still don't understand the reference to you, but maybe they were just acknowledging between them that I had someone who might worry about me when I disappeared."

It all sounded a stretch to me, too. But I was now exhausted. I pretended to fall back asleep a short time later.

Only to be awakened by a call from Tom.

Well, hell. I was still too irritated with them both to choose to see either one socially once I was feeling better. Even so, I let Tom relate what he professed to have called about. "I talked with Mason and Debby Payne, Kendra, and some of the others at The Clone Arranger. I can't speak to whether the allegations against them, and how they conducted their cloning, are true, but they all swore they didn't touch Lois Terrone's dog Flisa except in the most gentle way. They didn't even attempt to take any DNA samples from her."

Yeah, I'd figured, since she wasn't a purebred.

"Anyway," Tom continued, "I'd examined her as I did other animals brought in for cloning. Lois had told me about some of her existing symptoms, and I saw those but nothing more. My belief is that she died of natural causes."

Much as I hated to say so for Lois's sad sake, that had become my belief, and now I had a veterinary opinion to back me up. Too bad no one had convinced her of that concept before. It could have saved Earl's life, Jeff's Escalade and sanity, and The Clone Arranger's unearned, formerly non-

401

fraudulent reputation.

I thanked Tom for his opinion, then murmured a noncommittal non sequitur when he said he'd see me soon.

Eventually, it was time for me to leave the hospital. That was when Avvie Milton, an associate at my former law firm and owner of Pansy the pig, called me, crying. "Kendra, do you know what that louse Bill Sergement has done?" That same guy I'd called Drill Sergeant, who'd seduced me when I was in Avvie's position years ago at my old law firm.

"What's that?" I asked, although I suspected.

"He's called things off between us altogether. He's totally back with his wife, and they're having a baby."

Oops. It wasn't as if Bill had left his poor wife in the first place, but maybe this was a harbinger of a happy home life for him now. Or not. Who knew?

In any event, I told Avvie to meet me later at my home. Rachel brought me there, and Tracy Owens was present, too. We were joined by Maribelle Openheim, owner of Meph, the terrier mix who'd helped me start my clone investigation.

"Hey, Kendra," Tracy said as we five females sat in my small living room, a sweet and nuzzly Lexie happily ensconced on my lap. "Feel like a girls' night out to celebrate your homecoming?" I knew full well what had happened with the last man she'd let into her life, and she was well rid of him.

Same went for thirty-something Avvie, after her sordid situation with Bill Sergement. And for middle-aged Maribelle, who'd had the good sense to drop Judge Baird Roehmann, he of the roamin' hands, when they'd dated for a while after I'd introduced them. She had told me recently that she'd taken up with a new guy but now wasn't sure that one would stick, either.

"Great idea!" I said, sensing empathy emanating from this flock of caring females. "That damned drug's out of my system now." Or at least I hoped so, remembering Jeff's lingering effects. "So let's go somewhere I can get a glass of wine."

Just one, and I'd be careful. I felt great — well, I *would* feel great, once I got over the hypocrite who was Jeff. Sure, being drugged had been a bummer. But I couldn't buy into it as sufficient excuse to blame everything on me, including the case of the elusive thumb drive. Or to keep significant secrets from me, like when he happened to revisit my vicinity.

So now, I was without even a prospect of

a date with Tom, Jeff, or any old Harry who might be out there.

Who needed them? Not me.

Okay, so my old refrain was again reverberating in my mind: I had the world's worst taste in men.

So what? Although there were occasionally fish in the households in which I pet-sat for larger beloved animals, none had a bicycle awaiting them within their water-logged tanks.

What was that supposed to mean? Well, I had just recalled a quote from a woman much wiser than I: "A woman without a man is like a fish without a bicycle."

Who needed men?

I had no hint of what might transpire in the future between me and members of the incredibly unpredictable male gender. But for now, who cared?

Most likely, I'd swear off men forever.

But, hey, I reminded myself. Not if that meant swearing off good, old-fashioned, hot, and sweaty sex.

I'd just have to wait and see with whom I'd share it.

ABOUT THE AUTHOR

Linda O. Johnston is a lawyer and a writer of mysteries and romantic suspense. She lives in the hills overlooking the San Fernando Valley with her husband, Fred, and two Cavalier King Charles spaniels, Sparquie and Lexie. Her two young adult sons visit often.

You can visit Linda and *her* Lexie at Linda's website: www.LindaOJohnston .com.